THE LIGHT
IN US

—.—

EVELYN FLOOD

The Light in Us
Evelyn Flood
First published by Evelyn Flood in 2024

ISBN: 9798341498594
Imprint: Independently published

Copyright 2024 by Evelyn Flood

Cover by Temptation Creations

Content Overview

While all fictional, this book does contain some distressing scenes relating to coercive, financial, emotional, and physical abuse. This is not intended to be reflective of any single lived experience, and I respect that this may affect different readers in different ways. It also contains themes of grief, depression and parental death (off page, but grief is referenced throughout the book).

CONTENTS

ABOUT THIS BOOK

This book is an omegaverse.

That means that the characters have some of the characteristics often seen in wolves, but **they do not shift.**

— • —

This book is for you

Because they said you were being dramatic.

Because they don't hit you, so it's not abuse, right?

Because it's easier to wear what they want you to wear.

Because you didn't like that job anyway.

Because you wind them up.

Because your friends are a bad influence.

Because it's easier for them to manage your budget and give you an allowance.

Because you're scared to go home.

And because you are worth more.

1

FALLON – AGED SIX

I push my face into my knees, squeezing them tightly.

"Fallon?"

When I don't lift my head, my daddy sits next to me on my bed. He puts his hand on my back, rubbing it, and I sniff as I peek up at him. "Tough day, sweetheart?"

Nodding, I scramble into his lap when he holds out his arms. My daddy's hugs are much better than the ones I give myself. I curl myself into him, hiccupping through the tears that still sit on my face. "Lara told me my perfume smells like snot bubbles!"

"I see." It feels like he's shaking against my cheek, but my daddy is frowning when I glance up, the corners of his mouth turned down even though his eyes look bright. "That's not very nice. But you don't know what your perfume smells like yet, baby. It won't come in until you're older, so just ignore Lara."

"I know," I grumble. "But what if it does smell like snot?"

I don't want to be a walking snot bubble.

My daddy smiles. "I don't think snot has a scent, really. But even if it did, it won't matter. Remember why?"

I nod.

"Because I'll have a mate. Like you and mommy." I know *all* about mates. It means that somewhere out there, I have an alpha best friend. My daddy says they'll be the other half of my soul, like my mommy is to him.

Lara told me I'd have to kiss them, but my daddy got red in the face and shook his head really quickly when I asked him, so I know she's lying.

Good. Alphas are scary, except for my daddy.

But my mate won't be scary. He'll be my best friend. He'll look after me and keep me safe. I might even have more than one, like Kayla's mom. They have a whole *pack*.

I wouldn't mind a pack of best friends.

I hope they like reading.

"That's right." My dad gently presses his finger into my nose, booping it. "How's your light doing today?"

I wipe at my face, thinking about it. "S'okay."

My daddy rocks me. "How about pancakes and a movie night? Would that make it a bit brighter?"

Pursing my lips, I give him a narrow-eyed look, like the one my mom gives him when he eats all the leftovers. "*Things* don't help with the light. That's what you said."

My daddy told me that we could buy everything in the whole store, but it doesn't help the light fill up.

Only the things that make your heart happy can keep your light full, Fallon. And nothing you can buy can do that.

"You're right. I did say that." He stands, lifting me and settling me on his hip as he carries me out of the bedroom. I tuck my head into his neck as we head downstairs. "But spending time with people who love you – that will always help your light fill up. The pancakes and movie are just a bonus."

I turn my head to peek. My mom is setting down plates on the floor, blankets piled all over our living room like my little nest upstairs. She bends to press a button, and fairy lights come on all around us like twinkling stars.

My daddy squeezes me before he settles me between them. My mom leans in to kiss my forehead, her smile bright as she holds up pancakes with marshmallows and raspberry syrup – my *favorite*. She made a smiley face out of them, too.

And they picked my favorite film, the one with the fishies that my daddy grumbles about but still knows all the voices. I watch it and hum along to the songs tucked carefully between them, warm and comfortable and safe.

And I can feel my light filling up, just like my daddy promised. I try to stop the yawn that stretches my mouth open, but I can't stop it. "I feel better now."

"That's good, baby." My mommy strokes my hair.

My eyes start to close.

My light is full again. And my mommy and daddy carry me up to bed, tucking me in next to my favorite blue fluffy comforter and my turtle toy.

2

FALLON – AGED SIXTEEN

Groaning, I let my head thud against the scattered papers on my desk as I mutter to myself. "Man is not made for defeat. A man can be destroyed, but not defeated."

Although I'm feeling pretty defeated right now. Snowed under with essays and extra credit assignments.

A cough sounds behind me, and I jerk upright, flushing.

My dad steps into our home office. We share it, his large oak desk taking up one half, mine facing his and the rest of the room covered in shelves and shelves of books.

He's grinning as he places a steaming hot chocolate next to me. "Quoting Hemingway already? It can't be that bad. How's it going?"

I glower down at my essay. "It's going."

In the trash.

My dad only squeezes my shoulder. "You've got this. But maybe you should take a break, Fallon. You've been working on this for days."

When I fold my arms, mutiny on my face, my dad points his thumb over to his side of the room. "First copy arrived today."

I straighten at that. "It did?"

Nodding, my dad reaches for the book and hands it to me. I turn it over in my head, staring down. My chest warms, my smile tugging up my lips. "You changed the title!"

The Light in Us.

And beneath, my dad's name in block letters.

Rick Matthews.

"Open it." My dad settles into his battered leather chair.

I flick open the pages, indulging the freak inside me and taking a quick sniff. There's no better scent in the world to me than the pages of a book.

My eyes settle on the dedication.

For Fallon,
My unofficial editor and my brightest light.
This book is what it is because of you.
May you always shine.

I don't say anything. My throat is too tight, clogged up with sudden tears and words that don't feel right.

I don't hear my dad get up. But his hands curl over mine where they hold the first book I ever worked on – even if *unofficially*. "You put as much into the manuscript as I did, sweetheart. This one is yours. And the rest of it – it will work itself out. You were born to do this."

I clutch it tightly, soaking in his words. "Thank you."

He cups my cheek. "I meant every word."

My dad leaves me to work, and I place my first, precious copy of *The Light in Us* where I can see it as I work, my fingers running over the pages reverently.

The first book I ever worked on. But not the last.

And then I throw myself back into my assignments.

3

FALLON

"Oh, sweetheart. I'm so proud of you!"

"*Mom.*" Groaning, I fling my arm over my eyes dramatically, gesturing in the direction of my father as my mother's words ring down the hall. "Dad. *Please.*"

When she's excited, my mom can talk louder than a space shuttle launch. The Southern twang of her childhood still manages to break through even though we've lived on the East Coast for my entire life.

And she's *very* excited.

My father only laughs, the deep, bass tone such a familiar one that it curls around me like an embrace. "Give her this, Fallon. We only get to drop you off at college once."

My mom's eyes turn shiny as she approaches, and I don't pull away when she moves over to me and wraps her arms around me. "*So* proud of you, baby."

Her embrace is gentle but firm – steadying, and I breathe in her familiar scent, holding on to her almost as tightly as she holds me.

"My girls." My father's voice is full of affection as he wraps himself around both of us. Derrick Matthews is still an imposing alpha, even with his dark hair starting to gray around the edges. My mom says it makes him look distinguished. "I thought we'd caused a national tissue shortage in the car already."

His words are teasing, but there's sadness underneath too. He holds us both, and my mom and I stay where we are. My mom tries to hide the sniffling, but I let the tears fall. Neither of my parents have ever fallen for my brave face anyway. "I'm going to miss you both."

She shakes her head. "None of that. You're going to have an incredible time, and we'll pick you up for the Christmas break. December fourteenth."

"Already on the calendar." My dad murmurs the words with a smile. My mom leans into him as I step back, looking between them.

My chest suddenly feels tight. "I—,"

But he shakes his head. "Your mom is right. None of that, sweetheart. You earned your place here. You deserve to be here. And you're going to be an amazing editor. Hell, you already are."

My heart squeezes.

A book editor.

"Maybe I'll even work on your books. Properly, this time." I manage to smile, and it's genuine, even if it feels a little shaky on my face.

They're leaving any minute. I'll be alone.

No. Not alone.

You're in college, Fallon. It's not forever. It's going to be amazing.

"I would be very proud to have you as my editor."

My father's quiet words threaten to draw out more tears, and I throw myself into his arms, squeezing him tightly. "Drive safely, please."

"Always. I'm carrying precious cargo." His love for my mom shines as he releases me and takes her hand. "And we have a *lot* of plans for our empty house, kid. Don't worry about us. And if you come home early – which you can do at *any* time – just make sure you give us a heads up first."

Okay – *ew.*

I make a noise somewhere between a laugh and retching as my mom's face turns purple and she swats at his chest. "Damn it, Rick. You'll scar her."

But she's laughing, her eyes shining as she looks at him.

"I'm already scarred," I tease. "But at least I have high standards."

Growing up with two people who adore every part of each other will do that. I won't settle for anything less than my scent-matched mate. If it's one alpha or a pack, it doesn't matter.

I want what my parents have.

But... not *quite* yet.

"As you should." My father sounds outraged at even the thought of anything else. "You deserve the best, Fallon. But build your own life first."

Sound advice – advice he has never swayed from, even when the other omegas in my small friendship group started mating early and popping out babies, building homes instead of empires.

It's what worked for them. But not for me.

My father was always firm. I could do whatever I wanted to do, be whatever I wanted to be, as long as it gave me skills and something to call my own. Something nobody could ever take away from me.

And now I'm here. Separating from my parents for the first time and taking my own steps into the world. Moving out from their protection.

The thought feels... scary. But liberating, too.

I'm *ready* for this.

"Heads up!"

The panicked male shout makes me spin just in time to see the ball heading at full speed, directly for my head. My eyes barely have time to widen before my dad's hand shoots out and grabs it, narrowly rescuing me from a concussion.

"*Shi-* sorry!"

The male jogging down the hall has an apology on his face, but mischief in his eyes. He slides smoothly to a stop beside me, and the mischief is smothered by concern. "You okay?"

He's... *really* pretty. Blonde and green-eyed, *boy-next-door* vibes. A dimple flashes in his cheek as he grins at me. "It didn't get you, right? I'm Rory."

And I'm an alpha.

He doesn't need to say it. Rory's heavy scent, pine needles and winter air, washes over me. It reminds me a little of the forest behind our house at home as I force myself to smile awkwardly back at him. Heat rises on my face as I stretch my hand out for his. "No, all good. I'm Fallon."

"Fallon." He smiles at me as he takes my hand, holding it a little longer than is strictly necessary. "Nice to meet you."

"I forgot this was a *co-ed* dorm."

My father mutters the words to my mom, and my flush deepens. "Dad. Please."

Rory offers my parents a polite smile, holding his hand out, but his eyes slide back to my dad in recognition. "Wait – you're *Rick Matthews*?"

I watch in interest as he yanks his hand back hastily and wipes it before he offers it to my father again. "I queued for four hours to get my copy of *The Light in Us* signed. Totally worth it. Loved that book."

My father's expression doesn't soften as he takes Rory's hand. "Thank you."

Rory spins back to me. "You're Fallon? The Fallon from the book? You have to be studying English, right?"

When I nod, my cheeks flushing, he grins. "Sweet. Me too. And my packmates."

Two others slip into view behind him. The first, a dark-haired guy with cool blue eyes, nods at me in greeting. The other, red-haired with a steely gaze has a smirk on his face, but it wipes away as they both get a look at my dad and instantly start peppering him with questions, faces lighting up in genuine excitement.

My dad answers them patiently. Rory shakes his head and looks down at me with a smile. "Sorry. The three of us are big fans of his work."

I half-shrug, half-smile. "I'm used to it."

"I bet. How does it feel to be the chosen one?"

There's amusement in his face as I consider the question. "I love his writing. But he's my dad first."

My dad fends off the growing crowd with a few apologies. "Sorry, folks. I'm happy to sign anything, but it's my daughter's day right now, so you can catch me outside in a few if that works?"

The crowd slinks away with a few glances at me, leaving me with my parents, Rory and his roommates.

"This is Shaun." Rory points to the blue-eyed guy, who's watching me with a little more interest in his face before moving to the redhead. "And Ellis. Fallon is studying English too."

After we exchange greetings, my father draws me to his side. "We should get on the road, sweetheart."

They have a long drive back. "Of course."

But my mouth dries. This is it.

No going back now.

My mom has stopped crying, but her breathing hitches as she embraces me one last time. "Don't forget to have fun, Fallon."

"I have fun!" I defend myself weakly. "Books are fun."

She cups my cheek. "And so is having a social life. It's *good* to have friends, sweetheart."

Her eyes slide to the three alphas. "But always be careful."

Not many parents would support their daughter – an unmated omega, at that – moving into a co-ed dorm with alphas around. But we've never been that sort of family. If anything, my mother would love me to have a little *more* fun, and not just with the characters inside my books.

My father, on the other hand...

He mutters into my hair as he holds me. "Keep an eye on them, Fallon. Don't put yourself in any situations where you can be taken advantage of."

"*Dad*." But I grip him tightly.

"I mean it," he says quietly. "I know we're a long way away, but I'll be in that car the second you call. And I can get you help if you need it. I know you want to do this on your own, but I still have friends here."

I breathe him in before letting him go.

It's stupid. I'll see them again soon enough.

But as I follow them down to the exit, it feels as though this goodbye is more formal. As if I'm saying goodbye to my old life as I hug my dad, my mom, one last time.

My dad brushes his finger over my cheek. "Keep that light burning bright, Fallon. Don't ever let it go out."

He's had this saying since I was a kid. This *belief*, that everyone has a light inside them that burns brightly from the day we're born. And to keep it glowing, we have to feed it with what nourishes our soul. What makes us happy.

For him – it's always been us. My mom. Me. His writing, maybe. Long walks on crispy days, roasting chestnuts at Christmas.

I blink away the sheen of tears. "I won't. I promise."

And as they drive away, my mom stretching over the passenger seat to wave frantically through the back window, it feels like... an ending.

"Hey." Cold fingers brush my cheeks, a staunch opposite to my dad's familiar embrace.

I flinch back instinctively. Rory raises his hands in silent apology, one eyebrow lifting.

I take a breath. "God. Sorry. You – you scared me for a sec."

He looks repentant. "Didn't mean to. Just...you're crying, Fallon."

Rory looks concerned again, that expression drawing his brows down. His eyes are a pale shade of green, tight with worry. He takes a step closer to me, swallows. "And – your scent—,"

Shit.

Keep it together, Fallon.

I'm an omega on a college campus surrounded by alphas, and I'm leaking distress from every freaking pore like a homing beacon. Rory takes a step back, his jaw tightening.

I told my parents I could handle this.

I *can* handle this.

"Sorry," I force out. Wrapping my arms around myself, I try to duck past him, but his hand shoots out. He's shaking his head when I look up.

"Don't worry about it. We have more control than that. But... do you need a hug?"

The tightness in his jaw looks a little sharper now, as if he's physically holding himself back. Footsteps sound behind us, and Rory shoots a *look* over my shoulder at whoever is heading our way. "Turn around and take the other entrance. Now."

There's an edge of something in his voice that hovers dangerously close to a bark. I almost flinch, but I swallow it down.

He's just keeping the space clear. Keeping other alphas away so I can get myself under control.

The footsteps disappear, and my shoulders loosen slightly. "Thank you."

Maybe I should call my parents back. Maybe... maybe I'm not ready for this after all.

"You're welcome." His fingers brush my cheeks again, and I allow the contact. I let him step closer, my body tensing as he carefully wraps his arms around me. "We'll look after you, okay?"

It doesn't feel like my father's hug.

His arms are a little too tight, his scent a little *too* fresh, almost stinging my nose.

But I suddenly feel so damn alone that I take it, burying my face in his shirt. "I'm not – I'm not usually like this. Sorry."

I'm not generally whiny, or clingy. And yet I've apologized more to this alpha in the last few minutes than I have to anyone else in my entire life.

"Big day," he says casually. His hand runs up and down my back, over my soft brown leather jacket. "It's okay to need a minute."

So I take a minute.

My smile is wobbly, but it's there when I finally step back. Rory shifts as if he would follow, but my eyes drop to where his fists tighten as his side. They flex, straightening again.

"Your scent... it's nice." His voice sounds slightly strangled. "But like I said. You don't have to worry about anything from us."

Maybe I should change the subject, steer us away from scents. I'm here to study, not to tangle with alphas that aren't my scent-matches. I glance up to the doors of the dorm. "Are you on my floor?"

I'm suddenly grateful that my parents arranged for me to have my own room and bathroom.

Rory slips into place beside me as we walk back into the wide common space of the dorm. Cozy-looking armchairs and couches are scattered everywhere, students already sinking into them. But Rory leads me past them, blocking my view with his bulk. He's big – a sports player of some sort, if I had to guess.

His packmates are waiting up at the top of the stairs, their eyes on me. "Yeah. The three of us share. I think there's another two rooms on our floor, but you can give us a knock for anything you need."

"Thanks." I feel a little shaky. My arms are tight around me as we reach the stop of the stairs and Rory's packmates – *Ellis* and *Shaun*, I remind myself – continue to stare at me. Rory coughs.

"Hi," Ellis murmurs. "Did your folks get off okay?"

My throat tightens again, and Rory groans. "We're trying to distract her, idiots."

"Maybe a movie?" Shaun offers. He hasn't said much so far, and I look at him in surprise. His face still looks cold, but he smiles easily enough. "Plenty of time for unpacking. We have snacks."

My thoughts move to the blankets I unpacked first. I took them from my bedroom, sneaking one from my parents' room too. I was going to decorate the small nesting space attached to my room today. But my mom's words burrow in.

It's good to have friends.

I'm going to feel uncomfortable. This is so far out of my comfort zone I'm practically on Mars. But I glance over my shoulder, to the buzzing space downstairs. "Sure. I could do a movie."

"We'll leave the door open," Rory murmurs. "If you feel uncomfortable at any time, there'll be plenty of people around."

Oh. "I thought – maybe downstairs, with everyone else?"

But Ellis shakes his head, dismissing my words. "Too busy. Lots of scents floating around, and emotions are high."

He's probably right. Maybe I shouldn't push it on my first day.

"Come on then." Ellis smirks, tilting his head before he turns around. "I'm ready for popcorn."

Rory holds out his hand, and I stare down at it. He yanks it back, a dull flush curling over his face as he slaps his hand over his face. "Right. Sorry. We just met."

His awkwardness makes my own feel a little less out of place, and my smile feels more genuine. "Don't worry about it."

They wait by my door, respectfully staying out of my personal space despite their clear curiosity. I tug a blanket from one of my nesting boxes and move over to them. Shaun is studying the room behind me, taking in the double bed, the pretty rug my mom bought, the plants and piles of dog-eared, tabbed books already stacked on every available surface and the wooden floor as well. "You have your own bathroom?"

He sounds a little envious as my shoulders tip up. "My parents are worriers."

And no matter how relaxed my parents are, even they drew a hard line at me using a communal bathroom. If I have a heat spike, or – *god forbid* – start to perfume, I'll need a safe space to retreat to.

Shaun only nods. They lead me over to their room, Ellis and Shaun pushing two of the single beds together. I have to remind Rory to keep the door open when he forgets.

I wouldn't say it's *comfortable*. Not as they coax me down to sit beside them, their scents filling my nose. But then, I've never been in a space alone with so many alphas.

But I'm making friends. Part of choosing this college – as well as the fantastic English program – was so I could try to move outside of my own comfort zone, outside of the bubble created by my parents in the small town we lived in. And these three alphas are on the same course as me, and they're nice enough.

Rory is by far the friendliest, but Ellis and Shaun warm up as we watch the movie together and they start to pepper me with questions about my life.

So *many* questions.

I try to offer a few of my own, but they're so large around me that it's hard to even get the words out. "You're here on scholarships?"

"I'm not," Ellis wiggles his eyebrows. "I have student loans coming out of my ears. But these two got a full ride."

Rory offers me a small bow when I smile. "That's incredible. Congratulations."

I try not to flinch when he swings his arm around my shoulders, reaching in to snag some popcorn. "It was the only way we were gonna get here."

"Not everyone has a famous daddy in their corner."

Everyone around me tenses. And I flinch at Shaun's muttered words, my head rearing back. "My dad didn't get me in here."

My voice is sharp. I worked my ass off to get into this program. And my dad – he would *never* have pulled strings to get me in, not when he raised me to believe in hard work. "I think I should go."

Is that what they think? What they'll all think of me?

Fallon Matthews, riding on her daddy's success. A nepo baby.

My throat hurts.

"Fallon—,"

I slide out from under Rory's arms, iciness crawling up my chest. I don't look at Shaun at all, ignoring the hissed argument behind me as I head for the open door and slip through it. The hall outside is quiet, the only sound the murmurs of voices coming from the common area downstairs.

I should have stuck with the books.

Books are far, far easier than people.

Shaun catches up with me as I reach my own door. "Fallon – wait!"

Lifting my chin, I give him my best glare. It's a little weak – ruined by the shaking of my shoulders, but I refuse to look down, to back away. "Believe it or not, I came here on my own merit. And I don't appreciate your judgment when you don't know *me*, Shaun."

"I'm sorry." His hand shoots out, covering my door handle. And he looks sorry, his face pale and more emotion in his cold eyes than before as he stares down at me. He shakes his head. "I... look, I have a lot of hang ups. But I shouldn't have taken any of them out on you. Honestly, I'm just jealous. I'm such a big fan of your dad's writing, and... that's not who I am. I'm so sorry."

He sounds genuine enough. But the hurt doesn't fade. "Okay. Apology accepted."

But his hand doesn't move. I step back until I'm pressed against the wood, suddenly more aware of his bulk. He smells like asphalt. I've always found it pleasant, always lowering the car window to breathe in a freshly-paved road, but now it feels oily. A little slick, as though it's sticking to my skin. "Can you let go of my door, please?"

He drops his hand immediately. "Let me make it up to you. There's an orientation event tonight. Come with us."

I push my door open. "I think my social battery has well and truly emptied today."

"Please." He grabs my hand. "An hour. In and out. Just an hour to show you that I'm really not that much of a douchebag."

He gives me the worst puppy-dog expression I've ever seen. As if apologies don't quite fit his face.

But... I take a breath. I don't want my first experience of college to be a bad one. And I have to live across the hall from them for the rest of the year. "Okay."

His face lights up with a smile. "Great. Thank you. Pick you up in an hour?"

"Sure."

4

FALLON

I go with them to the mixer. They surround me at all times, giving me their full attention. I don't meet anyone else, but that's okay.

I'm tired. It's been a long day.

And when they're standing at my door to take me for breakfast the next day, I don't argue.

Nor when they walk me to my first class, Rory snagging my timetable as they match it up with theirs.

This is what having friends feels like, I remind myself.

And there aren't nearly as many omegas here as I'd hoped. Only one or two, and all of them already mated.

Rory, Shaun and Ellis are... nice. They take care of me. Make sure I'm not overwhelmed, make sure I'm fed as the first few weeks of college slip by in a haze of timetables and reading. Sometimes they even join me for my nightly call to my mom and dad, chatting with my mom about what we've been doing and how they're looking after me.

My mom is happy.

They're happy.

My dad... not so much.

"Fallon." His voice is cautious as I step away from Rory one night. I can feel his eyes on my back as I move across my room. They've made themselves comfortable here, often wandering in and out. Giving him a sheepish smile, I slip into my nest for some privacy. "You're spending a lot of time with that pack. What was their pack name again?"

"Smith." I settle down onto a nest of blankets. "It's fine, dad. They're... nice."

"Nothing else?"

Frowning, I answer his question. "No. It's not like that. We're just friends."

There's nothing else between the four of us. Sometimes, I think I catch Rory looking at me, but my stomach flips and churns, and I turn away. I don't have those sorts of feelings for them. And – I'd never tell them – but sometimes their scents feel... overwhelming. Almost sickly.

My father stays silent.

"Dad." I start to laugh. "I promise, I'm not going to be mated by the time you pick me up for Christmas."

He laughs too, but it's subdued. "Actually, we were thinking of driving up this weekend. There's an exhibition your mom would like to see in the city. Maybe we could take you out for dinner, just the three of us?"

My heart leaps inside my chest. "*Yes*. Yes please."

I miss my parents. More than I'll ever admit to them, after all of the support they gave to get me here.

"And you're enjoying the course still?"

This time, my smile is real, spreading across my face. "I *love* the course, dad."

I'm doing what I want to do. One day, I'm going to be a book editor. And if college isn't everything I expected it to be, it doesn't matter. "You didn't tell me that some of my tutors taught *you*."

My dad's laugh is more real this time. "You wanted to do it on your own, sweetheart. And you are. I'm so proud of you, you know. See you on Friday – we'll aim to be with you for around seven."

"Okay." My smile stretches across my face. "I can't wait to see you."

"Love you, kiddo."

"Love you too."

I end the call, jumping at the sound of Rory's voice. "Your dad is coming here?"

I glance up, startled. Rory has pushed the door open to my nest. He's looking in, his feet on the edge of the doorway, and I drag my blanket over to wrap around myself in a sudden burst of self-consciousness, tucking my hair behind my ear. "Uh. Yeah. Friday."

"Great." My throat tightens as he takes a step inside. Another. "Where are we eating?"

Flustered, I don't say anything as he toes off his shoes and walks straight over the mattress on the floor. His scent fills my nose, sharp and familiar as he settles beside me.

I've never had anyone else inside my nest before.

I'm not sure I like it.

"Oh. Actually... I think my dad wanted it to be just us. I won't be late, though."

I glance up at him sheepishly, my fingers gripping the blanket. "You don't mind, right?"

His face tightens for the barest instant. But then it relaxes into his familiar smile, and I feel like an idiot for being so... on edge. "Of course not. That'll be nice."

"Yeah," I admit. "I think they want to check in on me."

Rory flicks my nose. "That's because you need to be checked on. Good job you have us."

He flops onto his back, and I startle when he pulls me down beside him. But his hold is loose, his fingers soft as they run through my hair. "This is cozy. I like your nest, Fallon."

When I don't respond, his hold tightens. "You don't mind, right? I'm not invading?"

I wet my lips. "No. You're fine."

He was already upset that they weren't invited to dinner. I can give him this.

I'm *glad* that I have them.

Even navigating this single relationship takes up so much energy, I barely have time for anything else. Classwork and the Smith pack is about all I have the battery to maintain.

I never knew that it would be this exhausting.

But they do look after me.

I turn my head to look at Rory as his grip loosens, his fingers still tangled in my hair.

He's asleep, his arm still wrapped around me. We've all been working long hours this week, our professors putting on the pressure now that we've settled in. Ellis and Shaun are still buried in the library, even though it's getting late.

I lay beside him, trying to keep my breathing quiet as I stare at the ceiling.

This is *fine*.

It's not even my proper nest, not like at home. Just a resting space, really. And he would leave if I asked him to. But... I don't want to put that tension between us. I already asked them to leave, once, when it was getting late and Shaun and Ellis were sprawled across my bed, studying. And it hurt their feelings.

I haven't asked since. I don't mind sharing my space with them.

But the tension in my body doesn't ease, not for the hour that he sleeps beside me.

And not in the days that follow.

5

FALLON

"They're coming."

Rory's fingers tighten in mine. "Fallon, it's freezing out here. Come back inside."

But I shake my head. I'm sitting on the steps, staring out at the pitch-black sky. "They promised."

My parents don't break their promises.

A jacket settles around my shoulders. It smells citrusy, lemon and pine stinging my nose as Ellis settles beside me. "No sign of them? It's past ten."

Murmuring over my head.

I pull out my phone, checking the screen again.

Nothing. No response to the dozens of calls I've made to my mom and dad's cell. It just goes to voicemail.

Hi, you've reached Addison and Rick—

Hey there, this is Rick and his far better half, Addy—

Even their voicemails are a mixture of the two of them, laughing and joking together as they urge me to leave them another message.

Where are you?

Rory, Ellis and Shaun take up positions around me when I refuse to go back inside.

We wait. For a long time.

When my phone finally trills, my dad's name popping up on the screen, I seize it triumphantly. "See? They're just delayed—,"

My voice trails off as I raise the phone to my ear.

It's not my dad.

"Fallon?" There's a hand on my shoulder, but I can't speak.

Rory gently takes the phone from my hand, talking to the official-sounding person on the other end of the line as I sit there.

He has my dad's phone.

Why does he have his phone?

"Fallon." Gentle hands, shaking my shoulders. "We have to go to the hospital."

Shaun's eyes look cold again as he pulls me upright. But he holds my hand tightly on the way there. I don't let go, needing something to hold onto as a doctor leads us into a room—

"We're family," Rory interjects. "We're her pack."

I don't argue with him. I don't say anything at all, even as the kind doctor with the tired eyes tells me that my parents were traveling through an intersection when a truck ran a red light and plowed into the side of their car.

It was instant.

They wouldn't have been in any pain.

I'm sorry for your loss.

We need a formal identification.

Something inside me... splits. I watch as if I'm another person entirely, as Fallon Matthews walks into a room to identify her parent's bodies.

And she doesn't come back out.

I don't know who inhabits my body now. She's cold, and numb, and she can't do anything except cry.

I sit still, through all the movement that follows. I keep my battered copy of *The Light in Us* held tightly in my hands like a comfort blanket and I don't let it go, not even to sleep.

They take care of everything. Rory, Shaun, Ellis. It's easier to stay quiet, to ignore the sympathetic looks and the pity and hide behind them.

At the funeral, I put on the dress Ellis lays out, and I stand in the circle they create, offering a buffer between me and the hundreds of people who come to say their farewells.

I don't really know any of them, aside from some long-term work colleagues of my father's. We didn't have any family, lived in the middle of nowhere.

It was always the three of us.

People want to talk to me about my father, about his achievements, but I don't want to think about any of that at all. Certainly not the financials, as someone murmurs to me.

Shaun takes over the discussion with the older alpha, his hand on my arm.

It's easier to let the Smith pack take care of that, too.

To take care of *me*.

Because they're the only thing keeping me together at all.

6

FALLON

"Fallon?"

I turn. Rory is in my room again. We came back to the dorms after the funeral, my body and my heart too tired for anything else.

I glance down. I'm only in my underwear, the black dress discarded on the floor behind me. I've lost weight in the last two weeks. A lot of weight. "I'm not dressed."

My voice sounds empty.

"I know." His words are soft as he crosses the room toward me. "Doesn't bother me. You don't mind, right?"

I shake my head. I don't particularly care about anything. Rory cups my cheek, his grip tight as he angles my head.

"Talk to us," he breathes. "You're so quiet, baby."

He hasn't called me that before.

I try. I try to find words as he stares down at me. But there's nothing *there*.

"I feel so empty, Rory," I whisper finally.

My mom is gone. So is my dad. And all that's left behind is me, and I feel as if I'm unraveling.

My fault.

They came for me.

Soon, there will be nothing left of me at all.

I'm alone.

I don't realize I've said the words aloud, but Rory's eyes darken as he scans my face. "You're not on your own. You have a pack now, Fallon. We're going to take care of everything, okay?"

I startle, a small spark of... *something*, flickering to life inside me when his lips press against mine. They feel... wet, papery. Rory pushes his tongue between my lips before he pulls away.

His arms are tight around me as he moves to my neck. "You're ours, Fallon. We're going to take care of you. Give you everything you need. Let us fill up those empty spaces inside you."

For the first time in days, I can *feel*.

And it doesn't feel right.

They don't feel right.

But at least I can feel something.

And feeling something is better than feeling nothing at all.

Isn't it?

When I tilt my head back in silent acceptance, Rory groans, deep in his throat. I feel lips press against my shoulder, turn my head to see Ellis and Shaun behind me.

My pulse begins to pound beneath Rory's tongue.

Not right.

Not right.

But I force the thoughts away, embrace the feel of something – anything – as they step up to surround me. The whine that slips out holds more emotion that I've managed for the past fortnight.

Fear is better than nothing.

None of them mention the cloying scent that fills the air around us. If anything, they push closer.

I press my lips into theirs with increasing desperation. "I need—,"

I need to feel.

I need to not feel like *this*.

Need something else. And it's easier to let them take over, to be what *they* need instead of looking inside, at the pain and the grief.

They've been good to me. I can give them this, whatever part of me is left.

Let them have it.

Let them have *me*.

Hands on my skin. Shaun's voice in my ear. "You're sure?"

"She's sure." Rory answers for me, his hands buried in my hair. "You want us to take care of you, Fallon?"

I nod.

And later, when I'm lying between them, our bodies tangled together and sweat cooling on our skin, I don't flinch when Ellis cups me, his hands tightening over the bruises of their fingerprints. "No going back now, Fallon."

My body aches. I stare up at the ceiling.

"Part of the Smith pack." Shaun's lips feel as cold as his eyes. But I don't mind that. It matches the ice inside my own heart.

"Sleep now." Rory's voice sounds sharp, and my body tenses. He strokes a hand down my back. "I don't want to use my bark, but you need rest, Fallon. Close your eyes."

When I do as he says, I feel a rumble of approval from the three of them, and the tension loosens.

Easier to do what they say.

Easier to not think at all.

My dad would be so—

I cut that thought off.

He's not here anymore.

And I can't do this by myself.

So I curl into Rory's embrace, and both of us ignore the tears that soak his skin as I do as I'm told.

And my light – the little piece of my soul, the light that my parents cherished and guarded and fought for…it flickers inside my chest.

And goes out.

7

FALLON – SEVEN YEARS LATER

I count the packages lining the counter again, my lips moving. Count the coins on the counter.

Not right.

Then I look down at the receipt in my hand, as if it will have somehow changed in the ten seconds since I last checked.

Cold hands curl around my throat in a phantom grip, and I swallow hard.

It'll be fine.

Slowly, I pack the shopping away, making sure everything is at least in the right place, before I clean around the kitchen again.

There's not much to clean. The white marble around me is sharp and cold and smells like bleach. Shaun prefers it that way.

He doesn't like clutter.

I head upstairs to shower and wash my hair. I take a few minutes extra to curl it, to apply my make-up like I'm heading into battle and slip into a tea dress, before I move back down the stairs and into the kitchen.

I glance at the clock, the phone. Waiting, but it doesn't ring.

They're coming home, then.

When the door finally opens a few hours later, the candles have burned down to almost stumps. Almost as much as my own nerves, as I sat here and waited.

I stand up, my hands brushing over my dress.

Shaun walks in first. His eyes, icy blue and so familiar, scan me and then the table, curving up. "You look lovely this evening, Fallon. Dinner, not so much."

Smiling, I force down the lump in my throat. "I can reheat dinner. It was fresh an hour ago. I... I wasn't sure what time you'd be home."

He only raises an eyebrow, setting his briefcase down on the side as the others follow him in. Ellis already looks irritated, and my stomach curls in on itself as he shakes raindrops from his hair. "Forgot my umbrella this morning. You should have reminded me."

"Sorry." Rushing around the table, I help him out of his jacket and duck around Rory to hang it up in the hall. He doesn't look at me at all, engrossed in his emails. "Are you hungry?"

"Not for *that*." Ellis scowls, ignoring the food set out in favor of sticking his head into the fridge instead. "I thought you went shopping today."

My anxiety explodes into a waterfall of butterflies. "I – I did."

Shaun rounds the table. He doesn't say anything. Just holds out his hand. Slowly, I turn behind me and grab the receipt, handing it over to him.

He checks it carefully, as he always does, moving over to the dish where I place the change. I move to the table to clear the space in front of Ellis as he sits, shoving the steak away with a grimace. My heart thumps almost painfully inside my chest.

Today will not be a good day.

"It's not all here." At Shaun's terse words, Rory looks up from his phone. He smiles, but his brows knot.

"Fallon?"

He sounds so reasonable. As if there's a simple explanation for my fuck-up.

I half-raise my shoulders, half shake my head. My words are small when I force them out. "I... I think I might have dropped some money at the store. I'm really sorry—."

The queue was too long, the rush to put the groceries through and get home on time a frantic one.

I flinch back as Shaun raises his hand. But he only gives me an exasperated look, crumpling the receipt as he runs his other hand through his hair. "Honestly, Fallon, you act like I'm going to *hit* you."

My legs begin to shake. "No – it's just... I'm sorry, Shaun."

Shaun nods after a moment. And hope – such a dangerous emotion – makes me brave. I offer him a smile, hiding the twisting of my fingers in my dress. "I can... make you something else for dinner?"

He glances down at the table. "I think we've wasted quite enough today, don't you?"

"Of course." I rush to the table as they take their seats. Ellis ignores the cold food in favor of slapping together a sandwich, ripping into the leftovers of the chicken I cooked yesterday as Rory and Shaun dig into the food I made tonight.

It's silent. I settle down between them, staring down at my own food. "How was work today?"

"Busy," Rory says. "It would have been nice to come home to a hot meal."

My eyes start to burn. I don't touch my plate. "Sorry."

Shaun's fingers are cool as he tangles them with mine. A small pulse of pain echoes in my stomach at the contact. I peer up at him as he lifts my hand, presses his lips to the back of my hand. "No, *I'm* sorry."

I... blink.

He's never apologized to me. Not once. Not since that first day we met.

"We're not doing a good job, are we?" He turns to the others. "We need to work harder, it seems. Particularly if our omega is going to spend money as if it's water – even throwing it away."

There it is.

"It was an accident." I keep my head low. "I'd be happy to replace it."

Laughter, from Shaun. Ellis joins in, his chuckles mocking and cruel. "With what, exactly?"

Breathe.

I hold his gaze. "I was actually thinking... I could get a job."

The laughter cuts off abruptly. Rory is well and truly paying attention now. "What?"

They're all staring at me as if I've announced I want to go to the moon.

"A job." Shaun still has my hand in his. It feels as if he's holding me hostage. "Just for some... some extra money for the house. Then I could replace anything I lost, and... and I wouldn't be such a burden to you."

"You're not a burden." Shaun's eyes are burning now. He tugs my hand, pulls me into his lap. His hold is a little too tight as he grips my chin. "But we work hard to support you, Fallon. We work our asses off to give you a home. Everything you need. We take care of you. And in return, you take care of us. That goes both ways. It's how a relationship works. That's your role as our mate."

But I'm not your mate.

I don't wear their bites on my skin - although I wear plenty of them elsewhere, savage and deep tears that barely ever have a chance to heal before the next ones sink in.

In my self-confidence.

In my independence.

In my damn *soul*.

But not in my skin. Something I started to be grateful for a long time ago. Even though it hurts – a physical pain that never truly goes away.

Manageable, though. For the most part.

Something must flash across my face, then, because his grip tightens. Not quite pain, but not pleasant, either. "Say whatever it is that's in that empty little head of yours."

I don't want to stray down the path of mating bites.

"I want to work," I whisper. I lift my hand, wrap it around his as I hold his gaze. "*Please*, Shaun. Just a few hours each week. You wouldn't even notice. I'll make sure it doesn't interfere with the house."

"You want a little more independence, Fallon?" I break our stare, twist to Ellis. He's smiling, but there's nothing pleasant in it. "You got it."

Shaun stiffens beneath me, a look passing between them as Ellis holds out his hand. "Come here, baby."

Slowly, I take it, letting him pull me off Shaun's lap. "Where are we going?"

His hand slips up to my wrist, tugging me down the hall. We walk into my bedroom as he drops his hold, moving to my small wooden wardrobe tucked away in the corner. "Ellis?"

Shaun and Rory fill the doorway behind me.

Ellis yanks the doors open, glancing at me over his shoulder. "If what we're providing you isn't good enough, then clearly we should take it *away*."

He reaches in, ripping out a rail of the dresses they prefer me to wear.

The butterflies in my stomach turn to lead. "That's not what I meant."

Behind me, Rory sighs heavily, but he doesn't say anything.

"How else are we supposed to take it?" Shaun's hands land on my shoulders, holding me in place as Ellis tears one dress down the middle. "Clearly, these things aren't good enough. So you can go and get a job by all means, and buy your own from now on. Don't forget about the make-up, Ellis."

His fingers massage into my skin as Ellis works his way through my clothes. Nothing is left untouched, the pile of ripped material on my bed growing. And all the while, Shaun keeps me in my place.

"I'm sorry," I whisper finally. "I didn't mean to hurt you."

Lips on my neck, stabbing pain. "Well, you did. And there are consequences to that."

Ellis moves to my dressing table next, tugging over the trash can and emptying my make-up into it.

"Don't cry," Shaun murmurs. "I never realized you were so... *avaricious*, Fallon. Such a greedy little omega. I'm disappointed in you."

I shake my head, tears dripping from my chin. "I'm not. I promise. *Please* don't."

But they don't listen. Shaun holds me in place, making me watch as Ellis rips through everything else. He yanks out my drawers, emptying the meager contents. Even my underwear is torn.

My fingers grip the dress I'm wearing. Ellis shoots me a considering glance, but he props the trash under his arm. "I think the lesson's been learned."

His eyes slide toward my bedside table, and I freeze, terror suddenly tightening my throat.

No—

But he only smiles at me. As if he's reminding me what else he could take. "See? I'm not *cruel*, Fallon. I'd never hurt you like that. Not unless you deserved it."

Ice in my blood, crystallizing in my veins as he waits and I force my lips to form the words he's waiting for. "I know. Thank you, Ellis."

The lesson was learned a long time ago.

"Get a job by all means," Shaun murmurs into my ear. He presses a kiss to my cheek, lingering as if he's tasting my pain. "We're not stopping you, Fallon. I don't know what kind of work an omega with no skills or degree can get, though. Do you, Ellis?"

"I have a few ideas." He smirks at me. "But she's pretty useless at that, too."

My whole body flushes in humiliation. The pain in my stomach peaks.

"Enough," Rory murmurs from the doorway. He's frowning, as he hasn't stood there and watched the whole thing. And pathetically, I'm grateful for it. "Leave her alone now. You're upsetting her."

Shaun turns me to face him. He cups my cheek, studying me. "She's not upset. Are you, baby?"

Slowly, my head twists as he watches me expectantly. "You're... you're right. I don't need to work."

"That's right." He pulls me closer, cold lips brushing mine. "And if you're a good girl, we'll buy you some new things to replace these old ones. Something that doesn't make you look like you stepped out of the fifties."

His tone is accusatory, even though he picked out my now-ruined clothes himself. "Thank you."

Shaun raises an eyebrow. My skin crawls as I choke the words out. "Thank you, *alpha*."

"There." He turns to leave. "All we ask for is a little gratitude, Fallon. But you have to throw it back in our faces all the damn time."

Ellis follows him, whistling, a trash can stuffed with the few things I have, broken and ripped beneath his arm.

And Rory – Rory stays where he is.

I hug myself as tight as I can, blinking away the mist that covers my eyes.

I'm tired. So fucking tired. "I'm sorry, Rory."

"I know." His voice is soft. "It's been a long day."

I swallow. Hating myself for asking. "Will you... can I stay with you tonight?"

He shakes his head, and I hate myself even more. "I don't think that's a good idea."

"Please." My voice drops to the barest whisper. "It's been... a long time."

Weeks.

And for an omega surrounded by her pack, even if we're not formally mated... that long without physical contact *hurts*. Even Shaun's grip on my shoulders sent a pulse of pain through my abdomen.

I *need* them. My body has been conditioned to think of them as my pack.

I need them almost as much as I fucking despise them.

Rory keeps me waiting for another minute.

Pathetic, Fallon.

I can see it on his face, even as he watches me.

"Why do you keep me here?" I say finally. "If you don't *want* me?"

I could leave. I don't think they would bother to stop me. I could walk out the door, but I have *nothing*.

No bank account. No phone. No identity documentation.

They have it all. Everything that made me Fallon Matthews. The Smith pack stole my entire life from me. They stole it with lies disguised as kindness, and I was too numb to see it.

Not until it was too late.

And now, my life is carefully segmented into the boxes they choose for me.

I didn't want to be alone, so I chose them. And now... now I'm more alone than I ever could have realized.

Rory's face softens into something that almost borders regret, and he holds out his hand to me. "Don't say that. You're ours, Fallon. Come on, then."

I go to him. Pathetically grateful for the skin contact as he palms my neck, pulls me closer. And then he digs into his pocket, pulling out a few crumpled dollar bills. Five of them.

I stare down as he presses them into my hands before his lips press to my skin, trailing down my throat. "Get yourself a coffee from that little place by the grocery store tomorrow. You deserve a treat. Just between us, okay? I don't need a receipt."

I clutch the money in my trembling fingers as his fingers slip beneath my dress. "Thank you."

And at this moment, I hate him. Hate all of them.

Almost as much as I hate myself.

8

TEDDY

"*Family meeting!*"

I bellow the words down the thickly carpeted corridor, ignoring the curious faces that pop out of the meeting rooms scattered down the hall as I pivot back to Emily.

It's mainly for effect, to be honest. I'm not sure my pack is even on this floor right now.

I'm pouting. Full-blown, pushing my lip out pouting in the way only an omega can do. "You're breaking my heart, Em."

She clucks at me, a warm smile spreading across the older woman's face. "You'll be just fine without me, Theodore Quill."

"I won't." It sounds suspiciously close to a petulant whine. "I need you. You're my right hand. *Better* than my right hand."

My secretary puffs up a little behind her little wire glasses. In her early sixties with a neat gray bob, Emily McMahon is a fiery ball of productivity tucked away behind the façade of a kindly-looking grandmother.

I've seen her beat off alphas several feet taller than her with a baseball bat.

Several times, in fact. I even bought her an engraved one as a joke last year that she keeps behind her desk – for *Teddy-related-emergencies*, as she calls them.

"Is it the money?" I ask. Possibly even beg. "Do you need fewer hours? Less stress? Better healthcare? A bigger office? You can redesign your whole package, Em. Whatever you want. I just can't lose you."

It took me months of searching to find her five years ago. Months of wading through applications from hundreds of people desperate to work with me. A little *too* desperate.

I can't go through that again.

My scent actually thickens with my distress, and Emily gets up from her chair. Desolate, I follow her as she gently takes my arm and leads me into the meeting room we use for family meetings. Nobody but pack and Em is allowed in here. "Sit, Teddy. Before you pass out."

I sit. My chin slumps into my hands as I watch her glumly. "You make the best coffee I've ever tasted. I can feel the dehydration setting in already. You've ruined me for anyone else, Emily."

She laughs from where she's handling the fancy coffee machine Wilder is addicted to like the absolute pro she is. "I'll leave instructions behind, don't worry."

Because Emily McMahon is abandoning me in my time of need to waltz off on her undoubtedly well-earned - but highly inconvenient - retirement.

I glower down at the rich heaven she slides in front of me. Emily tuts. "Four sugars. How the hell you still have such pretty teeth, I don't know."

I flash them at her, offering my sweetest look. "I'll quadruple your salary?"

"You already pay me more than I ever needed, Teddy Quill. There's not a single benefit I don't have. Now stop pouting. You have a busy day ahead."

Sighing, I sit silently and stew in my devastation as she bustles around me, reading out my appointments. I can't concentrate on any of them, but I force myself to take notes.

When the door finally opens, I'm on my feet before the scent even registers, diving toward my alpha.

"Teddy. You know I could feel you through the bond? I was in a meeting with an author. An *omega* author." To anyone else, Fox would look as sleek and sophisticated as he always does, perfectly dressed in his tailored suits. But I can see the way he's run his fingers through his hair, the tightness in his jaw as he scans me. "I had to open a damn window. And then Emily messaged too, said you needed me. I nearly bowled the poor omega over as I ran out."

I bite down savagely on my lip at that. And my perfume floods out in a waterfall of melted chocolate, yanking Fox closer to me like an invisible leash. His face softens, arms opening.

Em slips out behind him, winking over her shoulder.

See? She knows exactly what I need.

I sink into him, my head nestled perfectly beneath his chin. Fox towers over me, always has, even though I'm not on the short side. His arms wrap around me as I breathe him in. "Emily is *leaving* me."

He rubs his chin across my hair, absent-mindedly scent-marking as his hand smooths down my back in soothing strokes. "Leaving *us*. Yes. She's retiring. We've known about this for three months, Teddy."

Traitor.

"But I didn't think she'd actually go through with it." I tip my head up to pout at him. "I thought I could talk her out of it. But tomorrow is her last day!"

Fox studies me, his brows drawing down. "I thought you were reviewing the applications for a replacement?"

My eyes slide away guiltily. "I *looked* at them."

Looked at them once, hid from them, buried them under paperwork on my desk - even though they kept annoyingly reappearing, thanks to the magical Emily fairy.

Who's abandoning me. Tomorrow. And with it, leaving our pack without someone to keep our heads screwed on straight.

Mainly mine, if we're all being honest.

Fox grips my chin, turning me back to face him. "*Theodore.*"

My whole body shivers at his tone, a little burst of heat flickering to life in my stomach that is highly inconvenient. "Not *now*, Fox, I'm panicking."

He sighs. "You're incorrigible. I should put you on your knees and fuck that pout off your face. I thought you had this sorted."

I swat at his shoulder before brushing my lips against his and pulling away. "Don't threaten me with a good time. I'm trying to *mope*."

Fox stalks after me as I settle back into my chair. Emily sweeps in with a tray of pastries, setting them down in the middle of the large wooden table. I glare down as she drops papers beside me and hands another set to Fox. "What's this?"

"Applications," she says crisply. "I dug your copies out of the trash, Teddy. For the third time. Stop wasting paper."

The flush curls up the back of my neck as Fox swings his gaze to me, raising an eyebrow. *Damn it.* "*Et tu*, brute?"

She only pats my shoulder as she walks past, dropping additional packs onto the table as Fox's look heats my skin.

Oh, he's *definitely* going to bend me over the desk later.

And I'm definitely going to let him.

But not, apparently, until I find a replacement for the sole female in my life. A female who is, quite frankly, irreplaceable. I grumble over my coffee as Wilder sweeps in through the door.

Emily called in the cavalry. I feel slightly guilty. Everyone is so busy at the moment. But I'm stressed, and I *need* my pack.

Wilder swaggers past me, his hand brushing my shoulder before he chokes. "Jesus. It smells like someone farted hot chocolate and s'mores in here. Who upset you, Teddy bear?"

I sniff. "Emily has broken my heart."

She rolls her eyes as she offers Wilder a coffee. Even Emily blushes, though, when he presses a kiss to her cheek, his smile soft and genuine. "Only one more day until you're free of our chaos. What are we gonna do without you, Em?"

He winks at her, but I can see the tightness on his face.

Emily is *safe*.

Emily doesn't trigger anything in him.

Shit. My eyes slide back to the applications. Now I feel really fucking guilty for not thinking of that sooner.

It's not all about you, Theodore.

A hand lands on my nape, massaging it, and I shoot Fox a miserable glance. He sighs, holding up his pack of paperwork. "That's why we're all in the building, Teddy. To go through the applications, and to pick a few to interview."

I straighten. "Even—,"

"Even me." Rowan sinks his hands into my shoulders from behind, and I lean back into my beta, breathing him in. Cherry gum, the faintest traces of ink and general yumminess. "If we're replacing the irreplaceable Emily, do you think we'd leave you to it alone?"

"I thought—,"

"We were just giving you a head start." Rowan drops into the seat on my other side, pushing his glasses up his face as he pulls the paperwork toward him. "Fox figured it might take you a while to adjust to Emily leaving."

My alpha at least *tries* not to look too smug when I glance at him.

"And I knew you wouldn't want anyone new coming in while Em was still here." Fox's voice rumbles beside me, low and soothing as my pulse finally begins to settle. "So we're going to find some possibilities together, and you can interview them tomorrow. We'll be happy with whoever you pick, as long as the scent works for Wilder."

"It's been in your diary for a month," Emily observes drily from where she's picking over the pastry selection. She cheerfully selects a flaky *pain au chocolat* and picks up her own coffee.

"Oh." I'm not the *best* at checking my calendar. I stare down at the set of applications.

I should have been more prepared for this. I'm the damn CEO.

My scent turns heavier, rich chocolate and marshmallow entwining with the warm scent of the pastries in front of us.

"It doesn't matter." Wilder murmurs the words from across the table. "You're a phenomenal CEO, Teddy."

Something in my chest loosens at that, at the way that he reads me so easily. "I am? Really?"

He rips off a piece of his croissant and throws it at my head, and I break into a smirk as he rolls his eyes. "Fuck off, Theodore. You *know* you are. Don't let it go to your head."

I can feel my chest puffing up.

Hell yeah, I am.

Ink & Quill is the largest romance publisher on this side of the Atlantic. Our revenue dwarfs our nearest competitor by close to forty percent.

We're both grinning when Wilder leans back in his chair. He rips off another piece of croissant and tosses it into his mouth. "Where's Zeke, anyway?"

"Here. Sorry. I got caught up - issue with one of the accountants on my team."

I turn in my seat. Zeke ducks his head and twists to get through the door, his heavily muscled body broad enough that he struggles with anything less than custom-made. Our quietest pack member is by *far* the largest.

Frowning, I tilt my head, momentarily distracted from my pain. "We need to get that door replaced. I've said it before."

He shrugs, offering me a small smile as he collects his own coffee from Em with a murmured thanks and sits beside Wilder. "Doesn't bother me. Most doors are the same outside of home."

But it bothers me. This space – more than any other space in this building we own – is just for *us*. It doesn't sit right with me that one of our pack struggles to even get inside. My lips draw down - and Rowan runs his hand over my knee, soothing and calm in the barrage of scents that fill the room now that we're all here. "I'll arrange it."

I tangle our fingers together. With my beta on one side and my alpha on the other, my packmates opposite me, I take a calming breath. "Thank you."

I don't have meltdowns often – although they might disagree – but when I do, they have a tendency to reach truly epic omega strop levels.

Emily leaves us, waving off my offer to stay. "I have a lot to get done before I go, so I'll leave you be."

My mouth snaps shut at her words. Rowan has a small smile on his face when I glance at him. "I've never known anyone so bad at handling change."

"I'm not bad," I mutter. Just *traumatized*. "You remember what happened last time, Ro."

His smile vanishes, eyes flickering past me to Fox. The tension in the room ratchets up. "That's not going to happen again."

"No." Fox's words are icy. Rage swirls beneath them, and I push my chair closer to his, leaning into him until he settles. "One of us will be with you for every interview."

I nod. We learned the hard way to screen every applicant carefully. Especially the alphas. "No arguments from me."

Wilder is flicking through some of the applications, his forehead worried in a deep frown. "Can we still ask for a scent test? It's not too intrusive, right?"

"I put it in the application," Rowan murmurs, and Wilder nods, gratitude flickering over his face. "We'll find the right person. And if it takes a little time, we can manage."

"I can help," Rowan offers, but I shake my head.

"You're way too busy for that."

Smiling, he brushes his fingers over my cheek. "Never too busy for you."

Awh. My cheeks crease.

Blowing him a kiss, I sigh and pull the application forms toward me. Resigning myself to my fate. A future without heavenly coffee and goddess-level organization skills.

We will find the right person for our pack.

But they won't be *Emily*.

9

Fox

Teddy sighs as he tosses the last of the applications onto the table. He blows out a breath. "That's it, then. Four to interview."

None of them really stood out.

I stop fighting the urge and tug him into my lap. My omega settles back against me as I breathe him in. "I'll do the interviews with you."

Teddy twists, his lips brushing my cheek as they twitch into a teasing smile. "*Not* a good idea, Fox."

Murmurs of agreement from the rest of our pack. Rowan tilts so I can see his face, his eyebrows raised. His eyes glitter with a mixture of amusement and fury at the memory. "Last time, you threw someone through a *window*."

I have no regrets. "He was pretending to be a beta to get close to Teddy. And we were on the ground floor."

Although I wouldn't have stopped if we'd been on the roof of the damn building.

If I hadn't caught Teddy's distress through the bond, I might not have gotten there in time to pull him off. Just the memory of it, of the panic soaking the room, makes my scent thicken, and Teddy starts running his fingers through my hair, calming me as my hands tighten on him.

"I thought *I* was bad," Wilder mutters. "It took weeks to keep that shit out of the press, you know."

"I'll do it. I'll do the interviews with Teddy," Rowan offers, and my body tightens further. Something which *might* be a growl rumbles in my throat.

"*No*. Absolutely not."

Teddy sighs. "Fox will genuinely have a meltdown if we're both in there. Zeke, you're it, my lamb. If you don't mind staying with me?"

"Of course not." Zeke nods. "You know I won't let anyone get close, Fox."

My eyes close as I rest my forehead against Teddy's arm. "Good choice."

"I make *excellent* decisions," Teddy says smartly. He wriggles on my lap. "That's why I'm the boss."

Something thuds against his head, and he twists to glare at Wilder. "Throw another damn croissant at my head, Wilder Quill, and I'll perfume on your pillow. *Ass first*. Right after I fire you."

Wilder pales. "You *wouldn't*."

Amusement fills my chest.

Teddy angles his head, his voice angelic. "Wouldn't I what? Fire you, or rub my ass on your pillow? Sleep with one eye open, *sweetpea*."

He wouldn't do either. We all know it, even Wilder. But he drops the croissant in his hand to the plate anyway, flicking his fingers free of crumbs to get rid of the evidence. "Yes, boss. You need me for anything else before I go? I've got an advertising meeting with the social team to get to."

Teddy leans forward. Completely comfortable on my lap, he snags a folder from beneath the application pile and pulls it toward him, switching into focused work-mode as effortlessly as breathing. "We've got the quarterly acquisitions meeting on Monday, so we can go through most things then. Fox, you wanted to talk about Wordsmith, right? Now, or Monday?"

The mention of our biggest adversaries – and all-around assholes – makes my teeth snap together. "Monday is fine to go over the details. I asked Em to put it on the agenda. But just so you know, they tried to poach another one of ours. Adelaide Fedor. Made her feel damn uncomfortable, too."

Teddy stiffens on my lap. "*Bastards*. I'll call Addy today. Is she okay?"

Slowly, I nod. "Apparently, Shaun Smith went to her office, got a little too close. Nothing technically reportable, but enough that she wanted us to know. That's the third one of ours Wordsmith has targeted in the last month."

Teddy is frowning. "Can we get legal on it?"

Zeke stirs, the irritation in his voice bleeding out in a sudden spike of spiced cardamom. "I called them this morning. They're looking into what we can do – and Addy is happy to talk to them – but it doesn't look likely that we'll be able to take any direct action against them. They're snakes, never do enough to make anything stick. And it's not illegal for them to approach authors working with us."

I tap my finger on the table, directing my question to Teddy. "But they're targeting the omegas, trying to intimidate them. Is anyone showing signs of refusing to resign their contract with us?"

He and some of his beta acquisition editors manage the omega authors under our imprint for exactly this reason. I can feel the tension in his body, my hand rising to massage his neck. "Nobody yet, but a couple *have* gone quiet. I'll check in with them. Fuck, I hate those assholes."

"We all hate those assholes." Wilder downs the rest of his coffee. "They're hemorrhaging their own authors, by all accounts. Nobody wants to work with them."

"Their last quarterly profit was down thirty per cent." Teddy nods. "They're going to crash and burn."

"Unless they can force omegas to work with them, lock them into contracts." And then threaten them with legal action if they try to leave. Wordsmith represents the worst of the publishing business.

But Teddy shakes his head. "I'll make some calls today. I'll speak to anyone they might approach – see who's already been spoken to. Our authors trust me. If I tell them to be careful, they will be."

For many of them, having an omega at the helm is why they chose to sign with Ink & Quill in the first place. There aren't many omega CEO's around. It's a sign they can trust us not to take advantage of them.

Teddy sighs, pinching the bridge of his nose. "I'm not worried about Wordsmith coming close to catching up with us financially. But I *am* worried about the people they've trapped into working with them."

I rub at his back. "We'll help anyone who comes to us."

"Damned straight we will." He flows off my lap in favor of pacing, his hands behind his back. Agitation makes his scent deepen, a knife edge from perfuming. "Any signs of them trying to sabotage us directly?"

My hand tightens on my chair. "Not yet. But we need to double-check those interview names before they get anywhere near you, and I'm going to tighten measures at Reception for walk-ins. Just in case they try the same thing again."

"That, I can do." Rowan's voice is hard, but his eyes are soft as he watches Teddy.

Who waves a hand, distracted with his own thoughts. "We don't know that Wordsmith was definitely behind what happened before."

"It was them." Zeke's voice rumbles, anger underscoring his words. "I have no doubts."

I nod in agreement. They saw a small pack attempting to build a rival publishing company and tried to destroy us by sending in an alpha to attack our damn *omega*.

They wanted to hit us where it would hurt the most.

They're lucky all I did was throw him through a window.

And now... my gut tightens. We've outgrown them tenfold since then.

My voice raises just enough that my pack all straighten in their seats, even Zeke and Wilder. "I want you all to be careful. Flag anything suspicious. Wordsmith felt threatened before, when we were only a start-up. And now they're drowning. That makes them potentially dangerous, if they have nothing to lose."

Teddy taps his lips, his eyes narrowing at the command in my voice. "They have bigger problems in their own company to fix before they bother with ours. They're trying to fill the gap with more authors, and they're targeting the ones who won't argue with their shitty demands."

The ones they can bully.

I hold his gaze. "My order stands. You'll be careful."

The dominance rings out in my voice, and his golden cheeks darken, a mixture of irritation and desire. "*Fox.*"

"No." My voice stays hard. "This isn't an Ink & Quill issue, Teddy."

And therefore, not something he has the authority to make the call on. "This is a pack issue, and therefore it's on me. *They're* making this personal. I'm not risking you."

Our gazes lock for a moment, before he drops his eyes. His neck tilts to the side, gifting me with an irresistible stretch of flawless golden skin. "Fine. Damn it, you sexy asshole. Hitting me with all your *bend-over* vibes."

My eyes don't move from his neck. Around me, the others shift. Wilder and Zeke murmur to themselves, their amusement filling the air. Wilder fiddles with the coffee machine, taking his damn time as I hold my omega still through sheer will alone, barely breathing.

When Rowan shifts, I twist. "*Stay.*"

The tension in the room skyrockets into the stratosphere.

"Jesus," Wilder mutters. When I glance at him, a clear directive in my eyes, he fans himself. "I'm ready to bend over myself."

"*Wilder.*"

"Going." He smartly slips through the door, Zeke following him with a silent wave. I wait, and the audible sound of the lock clicking into place echoes behind them.

Leaving me alone with my beta and my omega. Teddy is almost vibrating, his perfume pulsing from him in waves that fill my nose. "Fox...,"

The longing in his voice... my knot thickens just hearing it. "You don't get to put yourself in danger."

He's almost panting, his need clear, glazing his bronze eyes. "I'm not in danger here."

"You could be." I turn, pinning my gaze on Rowan. "And you. You're not a *substitute*, Ro. What the hell makes you think I'd be any happier with you in that room? Both of you, *unprotected*?"

I growl the last word, and Rowan shifts from his seat. He makes sure I can still see Teddy, can see both of them as he kneels down in front of my chair. His hands grip my thighs, steadying me. Soothing me.

My muscles are quivering beneath his touch. I didn't realize how much the thought of them being in danger affected me.

"Fox," Rowan's voice is steady as he leans forward. His hand spreads across my chest, feeling the thump of my heartbeat. "We're fine. Teddy is fine. Nothing is going to get to us, okay? The Wordsmith pack are just a bunch of assholes burning through their daddy's money. Stop worrying."

Slowly, I nod. Rowan's fingers spread, tangling into my shirt, twisting the material as my muscles coil.

And I lunge from my seat.

I crowd Rowan back against the table. My hand is already tearing through his shirt, spreading over his olive skin, tracing the intricate black ink of his tattoos as he pants, his toned stomach flexing beneath my hands. I reach out, beckoning. "*Teddy*."

But Teddy is already there, his mouth nuzzling against my back as he presses heated kisses that burn through my shirt.

My bark rings out. "Clothes off."

My eyes latch on the clock above our heads. It's not even nine on *Monday fucking morning.*

No wonder Wilder looked so smug. I owe the fucker fifty bucks. He bet me that I couldn't last until Wednesday.

Something in my chest loosens as they obey. Rowan snags Teddy, drawing him around until I can cage them both. I don't give them any space, watching as Teddy yanks Rowan's shirt open. Rowan's fingers are nimble on Teddy's tie, their eyes flickering between me and each other. Teddy's scent, melted chocolate, sticky marshmallow, bursts on my tongue, underscored by the sweet cherry of the gum Rowan is addicted to, and that smoky, almost leather-like scent of ink that follows him everywhere.

They smell like home.

They both pause when I reach out and grip their necks. "Mine."

Gods. This feeling – this need for them – it never gets any easier to manage, even after years of learning every part of them. Of learning to be what they need.

But it goes both ways. And they know me, both of them. Know when I need them, when I need to lean on them... and when I need them to lean on me.

And when I need to work off this punishing *need* for them that hounds my every damn step.

Teddy's hands move to his trousers, unbuckling his belt. His lips quirk up. "I have a meeting in twenty minutes. And I'm stealing Rowan to take with me. *Alpha*."

His breath catches as the purr ripples in my throat. "Then I'd better make it quick, *boss*. No knotting today."

He pouts, plump lips begging for a kiss. "But—,"

"No buts," Rowan interjects. "Fox is right. You don't have time."

Not when Teddy's reaction to being knotted is so... *interesting*.

My eyes flit between them. Rowan's pants are already open, but he casually leans back against the table, his legs spread and his hands slid into his pockets as if I can't see his cock stiffening, begging for my attention since he didn't bother with underwear under his dark jeans. It jumps when I lick my lips.

Rowan wraps his elegant fingers around it, tugging. His thumb swipes through a bead of pre-cum, and Teddy moans, desperation lacing his words. "Oh, I volunteer as tribute. *Please*."

But he stays still. They both stay still, waiting.

For me.

I drag it out for a few seconds longer, aware of our time ticking away, before I nod in permission. "On the table, then."

Rowan pulls himself up and over the wood until he's lying on his back. I press Teddy over him, watching as their lips connect, licking and nipping at each other's mouths until I can't watch anymore.

My own cock is rock-hard, swollen and thick, my knot already growing as I reach for Teddy's hips and drag him back. "Suck his cock, Teddy. And I want to hear you enjoying it."

"Fuck." Rowan throws his head back, banging against the table as Teddy's mouth seals around his cock and draws on it. The sound is wet, almost obscene, as Teddy moans around him, pushing his hips back in silent request.

My fingers find him first. Testing, just to make sure. But he's slick and hot against my hand. "Oh, Theodore. Your ass is begging for a knot. Begging for *my* fucking knot."

A choked plea. Teddy pulls up on his tiptoes. I'm swimming in his scent now, drowning in chocolate as I slide my cock through the slick already building. "Needy little omega, wanting his alpha's knot, sucking at me so desperately."

Teddy tears his mouth away from a gasping Rowan. "I swear to God, Fox—,"

I drag my nails down his back as he cries out, drinking in his voice before I notch the head of my cock to his tight, yet soft opening and *thrust.*

He takes me, takes every fucking inch of me as I fill him to the hilt, teasing him with my knot before I pull back and slam into him again.

Rowan's gasps, Teddy's moans, they fill my ears like a beautiful symphony as I fuck my omega and he sucks off our beta, the three of us moving in harmony that can only be learned through familiarity until the tendons in Rowan's neck tighten and he presses Teddy's head down with a bellow, his hips lifting as he fucks his mouth through his release and Teddy takes every drop with audible swallows that push me to fuck him harder.

Teddy's ass squeezes and grips me, pulling on my cock, seeking my knot.

"Please." Teddy tears his mouth from Rowan, who takes us both in with glazed eyes. He licks his lips as he stares over his shoulder. "Fox. I *need* it."

I yank my cock free, watching his ass flutter. "You need my knot? You know what'll happen."

He whines for me then, lifting himself up. He's dripping for me, almost presenting as he drops his forehead to Rowan's thigh and Ro runs his fingers through his hair in a gentle caress. "I don't care. I need it more than I need *coffee*."

The half-laugh catches in my throat. "You're going to be late for your meeting."

"Don't care," he snaps petulantly. "The whole damn office knows we're in here fucking anyway."

Not since I soundproofed the walls last month, but he doesn't know that. I enjoy the way he struts about the office too much afterward to ruin the fun.

My hand reaches out, tangling with Rowan's as I slam forward, burying myself inside my omega with a roar as my other hand grips Teddy's hips, shooting ropes of thick cum into him. "Take it all, then, Theodore. You can carry my scent on you for the rest of the day. Walk around smelling like your alpha so everyone here knows exactly who you fucking belong to."

He almost screams, writhing against my cock as I pin him down for my knot, heavy and aching. "You wanted it. *Take it*."

Biology takes over, Teddy going limp beneath me as I push my knot into him with a deep grunt, feeling it twist and thicken as it seals into place. My hands stroke over his sweat-slicked back, steadying him as low whimpers fall from his lips. "Hush, now."

He told me once that to be knotted was a combination of sheer pleasure and exquisite pain. That it felt like ownership, like a branding. I stay still as Rowan shifts down until Teddy's head is pillowed on his stomach, our legs brushing together as he scrapes bronze strands from Teddy's face affectionately. I stay where I am, pressing into my omega. Holding his legs in place, to stop them collapsing.

"Oh, you gave him the good stuff." Rowan's green eyes are dancing, satisfaction and heat running through them. "He's out like a light, Fox."

Frowning, I lean forward, cupping his cheek. "Shit."

Because our omega is softly *snoring*, a contented smile on his face... and my knot buried inside his ass. Rowan starts to shake with his laughter as he keeps stroking Teddy's forehead.

"Don't laugh." But my own amusement lightens my chest, along with affection. "I did warn him."

The shaking grows harder, a muffled snort slipping out. "Every time, he thinks he can handle it."

I glance down at where our bodies are connected, satisfaction thrumming through me as my eyes trace up, landing on Teddy's bite mark. My bonding mark is barely visible from this angle, a silvery circle of scars that glint at me as they disappear over the junction of his neck.

Mine.

Rowan is already twisting his neck to show me what he knows I want to see. His own bonding mark shines back at me, the sight of the tattooed stars that line it settling something in my chest.

"Better?" he asks lightly. His own satisfaction, his calmness, washes through me, a fainter echo than what I get from Teddy, but more than enough.

I nod.

"Good." Perfectly at ease, he settles back, still cradling Teddy's head as he naps between us. "This Wordsmith thing... they're going down, Fox. It's only a matter of time. Teddy is right. They won't be looking at us when their own house is burning."

My chest feels tight as I take them both in.

I hope he's right.

Between us, Teddy starts to stir. His eyes blink open as he yawns. A grin pulls at his mouth as he shifts, feeling my knot nestled inside him. It's showing no sign of deflating just yet – especially as I watch him cuddle shamelessly into Rowan, their lips brushing.

He grins at me over his shoulder, more than aware of what watching the two of them together does to me. "I hate audit meetings anyway. This is a *much* better use of my Monday morning. Excellent work."

I glance at Rowan, my lips quirking. Teddy swallows as I press into him, my hips rotating as my knot starts to soften. "What time does the audit meeting finish?"

Rowan barely hides his laughter. "Ten."

I flash a smile at them both. "Then we've got another forty-five minutes. Swap places."

And Wilder can shove his fifty bucks up his ass. Worth it.

10

FALLON

I slip out of bed early, gingerly avoiding Rory's grip as he turns over in his sleep with a muttered grumble.

After grabbing one of his shirts from his closet, I shrug it on and tiptoe through the silent house with my dress and underwear from yesterday in my arms.

I have one dress, and one set of underwear to work with.

Sighing, I close the door on the washer and hit the button to turn it on.

"Fallon."

My gasp catches in my throat as I spin, my hand flying to my throat. "Good – good morning."

I dart past Shaun where he stands in the doorway. He's already dressed, his hair damp around the edges and impeccably dressed in a dark navy suit. "I haven't gotten breakfast ready yet—,"

"Hey." He catches my hand, drawing me back. "Calm down. It's fine. I can grab food on the way."

His voice is softer this morning. I don't look at him, fixing my gaze on his pale gray tie instead. "I don't mind."

I can feel him watching me, my body tensing up. He lifts a hand, his fingers curling into my hair. "You have such beautiful hair, you know. Like liquid onyx."

A lump appears in my throat. "Thank you."

Cold fingers lift up my chin. He searches my face as if he's looking for something. "Are you still in pain? Do you need me?"

He looks genuinely concerned. Swallowing, I shake my head slightly. "No. I... I stayed with Rory last night."

My skin still itches, my body still aches, but it's not the sharp pains I've experienced over the last week or so.

Shaun nods, still watching me. "Stay with me tonight. I don't want you to be in pain."

My gut clenches as his fingers trail across my cheek.

But you still walked away from me last night. You still left me, even knowing I was hurting.

Shaun exhales. And I stiffen as he draws me to him, his arms wrapping around me as he cups my head. His scent, oily and cloying, fills my nose. "Why don't I take you shopping this weekend? We could have lunch somewhere."

It's not an apology. But it's close.

Slowly, my arms raise to wrap around his stomach, my cheek pressed to his chest. "That sounds nice."

I can't remember the last time they took me anywhere.

"Good." Shaun's breath is hot as he tilts my neck to the side.

I barely breathe as his teeth graze my skin. "W-what are you doing?"

The teeth disappear, replaced by his tongue. But my stiffness doesn't ease. His voice is gruff, deep with *need*. "Your heat is coming in soon. Your scent is a little richer than usual."

Oh, *god*. "I didn't realize."

But it explains his unusual softness. I stay quiet as Shaun explores my neck. When he finally pulls back, his face is flushed. "I'll... pick up a prescription."

What he really means is that he'll source under the counter illegal heat suppressants from who the hell knows where. But I'd choose that a hundred times over a bonding mark, over that final tie to them.

Over going through my heat, my most vulnerable time, with *them* watching over me.

The only boundary I've ever managed to successfully set. And only because, by all accounts, I lost my mind going into my first heat with them.

I *fought* them, until they left me alone. Rory still has a scar on his chest from my nails.

I wonder where that Fallon has gone. Where that *fight* went.

I doubt I'd even have the energy to fight them off now. Not when I've spent the last seven years sharing their beds, begging for scraps of attention. But I stay silent as Shaun slides away from me, clearing his throat. He tosses some cash down onto the side. "For the groceries. Get a receipt. And don't *lose* any."

The tension begins to drain away. This, at least, is familiar ground. "I won't."

He's leaving much earlier than usual, not waiting for the others. After he's gone, I start on a full breakfast spread, working on their preferred choices. Ellis prefers an omelet with crispy bacon on the side, Rory usually opting for eggs benedict.

He appears thirty minutes later, burying his face in my neck as his food is cooking and inhaling deeply. "Fuck, you smell good."

I slide out from beneath him as Ellis strolls in. He stiffens, nostrils flaring as he sits at the table. "You're going into heat?"

I lift one shoulder. Rory tracks the movement as his shirt drops, and I tug it back into place. "Shaun thinks so. He's going to get the suppressants today."

Rory's brows crease. "You don't need those anymore, Fallon. We're your pack. I don't like you taking them."

I force myself to breathe, to shift around him and take his food off the burner. And I direct my words to Ellis. "It's such a disruption. Much easier with the suppressants."

But there's a gleam in Ellis's eyes. "Maybe Rory is right. Maybe it's time we give you a bonding mark, too."

No.

The refusal rises on my tongue, but I swallow it down. Ellis would pin me down and bite me as a punishment. "Maybe you're right. But you have a lot on at work at the moment. Is this the right time?"

That takes the wind out of his sails. Even Rory starts to look uncertain, his eyes sliding to Ellis.

Not that I have any idea of the details. They keep their work at the publishing house well away from me, never even talking about it. I used to think it was a way of looking after me - them trying not to hurt me anymore, trying not to rub it in.

But then I realized it was just another punishment for a crime I don't remember committing. "Is there anything I can help you with? For work?"

Ellis's face twists, his words dripping with disdain. "You? How the hell could *you* help us?"

He buries himself in his breakfast, muttering to Rory about some deal they're working on, and I back away from them.

Out of sight, out of mind.

And well away from any talk of heats or bonding marks.

I hide out in the utility room until they leave, taking my clothes out and putting them into the dryer before darting into Rory's bedroom. My shoulders sag in relief as I grasp the five dollars he left me from the bedside table.

My dress is still slightly damp when I shrug it on, too impatient to wait. I run a brush through my hair, going without make-up since Ellis left me nothing to work with.

The coffee shop is on the way to the grocery store. It's a ten-minute walk. If I time it right, I can spend an hour there and still do the groceries before Shaun calls to check on me at midday.

He always calls.

And even if Rory gave me the money, Shaun still wouldn't be happy about me going to the coffee place on my own. I don't even want to think about what he'd do, or Ellis.

It's colder today, that tentative time where autumn takes a step back and winter takes its place. The wind nips at my bare lower arms, goose pimples rising as I hurry through our neighborhood. We're fairly central to the city; Rory, Shaun and Ellis wanting to be close to their office, and it's already busy out. My footsteps swallow the distance with my eagerness, my copy of *The Light in Us* tucked under my arm.

Moving out of the way of an overzealous mom brandishing a huge double buggy with determination, I step up to the window. I've never been inside here – never had any spare money to go in. But the small, handwritten sign they keep in the window draws my attention, trepidation warring with a hint of excitement as I duck past it and push the door open.

Jobs board inside.

11

TEDDY

I breeze past Emily, whistling.

"Teddy."

Pausing in the doorway that leads out to the rest of the meeting rooms on this floor, I swivel and bat my eyelashes. "Emily."

She folds her arms, unimpressed. "Where are you off to?"

I wince. She catches it and raises one gray eyebrow. "I'm just heading out to grab a coffee. Stretch my legs a bit."

She regards me silently, and I try not to squirm. "Didn't Fox tell you to stay here?"

I bite down on my lip. "Maybe."

"*Teddy.*"

Throwing up my hands, I give her a pleading look. "Just ten minutes, Em. He won't even know. I need some air. My head is pounding."

I'm not lying. After a delicious morning spent with Fox and Rowan, I buried myself in paperwork and phone calls, contacting every omega under our imprint to check in on them.

All of them have been contacted by Wordsmith. Every single one.

"Fox and Rowan rearranged all of the security for the building, as of thirty minutes ago." Emily gives me a dry look. "He's worried about you. Have pity on him."

I nod, but my feet are already turning. "You know I think better when I'm walking, Em. If I'm not back in thirty minutes, call the cavalry. I'm only going to that place down the road and back."

Which takes me directly past the Wordsmith building, but I'm not going to mention that. My fabulous secretary sighs. "If Fox asks, I didn't see you leave."

I blow her a kiss, bouncing on my feet before I dart out of the door, calling over my shoulder. "I adore you, Emily McMahon. Even if you are abandoning me."

I can hear her eyes rolling as I stab the button for the elevator.

Humming, I stroll up the street, pausing to retie my shoe and ignoring the looks I get from people passing by.

Yes, I'm aware that I smell like a warm chocolate muffin drizzled with melted marshmallows.

No, you can't lick me.

I'm very aware of the effect my scent has on people. Thankfully, for most people it's a similar reaction to passing a delicious-smelling bakery. They pause, breathe in, and then they move on.

My phone vibrates in my pocket, and I wince, not bothering to pull it out. It stops for barely a second before it starts again.

God, that was quick.

I can only imagine Fox's reaction. And his punishment.

My scent deepens, my core squeezing at the thought of *exactly* what that could be, and I offer a small, apologetic smile to a beta woman who slows, her eyes glazing before she shakes her head and scurries away.

Getting punished by my alpha always feels like the *best* kind of present.

Standing, I lean against a railing, my eyes traveling over to the building on the other side of the busy road.

The Wordsmith building is nothing short of... gaudy. No wonder they're pissing money when they've clearly thrown it around like it's nothing, splashing out on an expensive exterior. My eyes latch onto what looks like a damn gold statue, of a woman holding an open book and fanning herself.

Honestly. *So fucking cliché.*

They have no idea what romance readers want. Hence their business swirling away down the pan after just a few years.

I watch the building for a few moments longer before I pull my eyes away with a frown. Fox will actually spank me if he finds out I'm lingering, and I did want a walk.

I stroll to the café. A small bundle of female is hovering in the doorway, her hand gripping the heavy door as she stays inside. As I pull it open for her, she spins, a dark curtain of hair trailing across my chest.

I breathe in as deep amber eyes lock with mine.

They skitter away quickly, the omega ducking inside the café with her head bowed, but I stay where I am. Her scent – something about it hits me hard. Sledgehammer-hard.

Orange blossom and nutmeg. Deep, spicy, and absolutely freaking *delicious.*

I blink.

I don't really notice omega scents, as a rule. But this one... it winds around me, strange but familiar at the same time.

And my cock... stiffens.

What the *fuck*?

Dazed, I step through the doorway, my eyes latched onto her back. Her shoulders are hunched as she murmurs to the beta behind the counter. The pretty blue tea-dress sweeps her knees, and I frown as I take in her bare legs, the lack of a coat.

It's cold out today. Too cold to be out without any sort of jacket.

I finally start paying attention as she mumbles an apology. Darting forward, I smile over her shoulder at the frowning barista. "I'll take a black americano, as well as what she's having. To sit in."

To hell with my plan to get back quickly. I'm invested.

She stiffens as my coat brushes against her back. "It's fine, honestly. I'm just going to go and get my purse—,"

"Wait." She pauses, hugging her elbows. I sweep my eyes over her, taking in the deep flush on her cheeks.

Embarrassment.

"Hey," I say more gently. "It's all good. Just a coffee."

Although the prices here are extortionate. The beta blinks at me, her eyes softening as I reach forward and add a bag of mini muffins to the tray she sets out. "Those too."

The omega waits, her muscles locked as if she'll burst into a run at any moment. I busy myself by adding sugars to the tray, my eyes flicking to her and away before I drop a large tip into the jar and tap her elbow, pointing to an empty table by the window.

She jerks away from me. My muscles still. "Sorry."

Hastily, she pushes her hair back. "No. I'm just...,"

"Long day?" I offer.

"Kind of." White teeth drop down to nibble at plump pale pink lips. "I can give you the money for the coffee."

She twists a few dollar bills in her hands, and something in my chest constricts. "You seem like the type of person I'd enjoy having a coffee with. Indulge me."

Her mouth opens and closes. Flushing, she glances up at the clock and back to me. A tiny crease appears between her eyes. "Okay."

She doesn't flinch this time, but I'm careful not to touch her. Instead, my arm hovers behind her as I steer her over to a table in the corner. I take the chair between the table and window, pinning myself in and leaving her with a clear route to the door.

Her shoulders relax slightly as she sinks down. "I didn't even thank you, did I? Thank you."

Grinning, I wave a hand. "No need. My pleasure. I'm Teddy."

She graces me with a small, self-conscious smile. "Fallon."

Fallon.

She's tall for an omega. I'm over six foot, but still lagging well behind the rest of my pack. Fallon's head came up to my shoulder, but she shrinks into her seat as if trying to make herself smaller. We wait quietly as the beta barista brings our drinks over and I thank her, taking the tray and setting it down.

The barista hovers, breathing in. Her eyes dart between me and Fallon.

"Thank you." I say it again, my smile flashing easily. But a dismissal all the same. She shakes her head and heads back to the counter.

"Does that... happen to you a lot?" Her shy question makes me frown. Because her scent is just as rich as mine – if not a little spicier, a little more unusual.

Alphas would queue up just to take a sniff. "Sometimes. You don't get that when you're out?"

She shakes her head. "I... I don't get out much, really."

I get it. Many omegas tend to avoid public places. Fox used to loudly complain that I couldn't do the same, even as he went everywhere I wanted to go, buying tickets for places I'd only mentioned in passing and then following me around like a shield from any overly-curious alphas.

My phone buzzes again. I bite down on my lip, but I don't want to spook Fallon by taking a call. Something tells me she'd spook easily.

We settle back in our chairs, and my eyes lower to the book Fallon sets out on the table. Her fingers trace the title as if it's a familiar movement. "I love that book."

She clears her throat. "You've read it?"

Many times. A thought occurs to me, but I don't let it show on my face. "I have. It was *incredible*. The prose... I've never found anything that quite lives up to it. And I read a lot. You like books?"

Fallon half-nods, half-shakes her head, and then blushes. A spark of something I recognise all too well enters her gaze. "Of course. Who wouldn't?"

"Many people," I declare. "Idiots, mostly."

She grins, then. It's small but there, and it feels like a victory.

Fallon twists slightly in her chair, her eyes jumping to the jobs board. "You're looking for a job?"

The color in her cheeks deepens, dark pink spreading down her neck in a flush. "Maybe. I just wanted to have a look. I doubt they'd have anything I can do."

My head tilts. "Why not?"

She shrugs. Looks away from me, her fingers fiddling with the edge of her dress. It's a little bit adorable, but her words make me stiffen.

"I'm not very good at anything, really."

And her voice... it's so *sad*.

But it echoes, too. As if she's repeating the words that someone else has told her.

And my own voice hardens. "Who made you feel like that?"

12

FALLON

I can barely breathe because of the delicious scent swimming in my nose.

Rich, melting chocolate. It suits the omega in front of me, because he's *flawless*.

His skin shimmers like molten gold, his eyes a deep shade of whiskey that I could drown in as he leans across the table, fury flashing across his face. He rakes one hand back through thick, almost bronze curls that spring back into place, one curling over his eye that he shoves back impatiently.

Who made you feel like that?

His words are like a shock of ice-cold water. I shouldn't have said anything. Should have just kept my mouth shut and enjoyed this time with him. I've never met anyone like Teddy before, even if he makes me feel like a limp rag in comparison to his perfection.

"Fallon." He reaches for my hand, squeezes it. The furrow between his eyes deepens. "Are you okay?"

And he sees too much.

Forcing a smile, I reluctantly pull my hand free, away from his warmth. "Of course. Why wouldn't I be? I should get going, though."

"Wait." He stands with me, grabbing his coat as I turn to leave. "I'm sorry. I don't really have an off switch. My pack is always telling me I'm a nosy little shit."

There's nothing but fondness in his tone. Adoration, and a hint of sheepishness.

My eyes suddenly feel damp, and I don't know why.

Except I do.

An omega I've never met before asked me if I was okay, and he *meant* it.

An omega who is now chasing me out of the café as I snag my copy of *The Light in Us* and almost run for the exit. I turn to him on the street, wrapping my arms around myself to ward off the cold. "I need to get going. Thank you so much for the coffee."

But Teddy is shrugging out of his coat, wrapping it around me. It settles around my shoulders, heavy warmth laced with that delicious chocolate scent. And *marshmallows*. "Take this. It's too cold not to have a coat."

"What?" I protest, my throat tightening. "I can't take your coat!"

"Sure you can." His fingers are already doing up the buttons, brisk and efficient as my head swims from the heady combination of our scents. "You can give it back to me tomorrow, at your job interview. Or keep it."

"I – wait. *What?*"

But he's digging into the pocket of his suit trousers, nudging a business card into my hands. Thick, black card with beautiful calligraphy spells out his name.

Teddy Quill
CEO
Ink & Quill Publishers Inc.

Teddy's cheeks flush too as he closes my fingers over it. But he keeps hold of my hands. "I have an opening. For an assistant. No experience needed, just a good work ethic. We're interviewing tomorrow."

I blink. "I – I can't."

And even saying the words hurts. Teddy's brow knots. "Why not? You want a job, and we're hiring. Plenty of books at Ink and Quill. I promise I'm not *that* bad to work with."

I'm shaking my head. "It wouldn't work. I need certain hours. To work around – appointments. And—,"

"Done," he says promptly. "We're a flexible employer, Fallon. We can make it work. Part-time, or job share."

I fall silent, staring down at the card as my fingers rub over the gold writing.

Ink & Quill.

A publishing company. Like Wordsmith.

I look up at Teddy. We're pressed together, close enough that anyone watching might see another scene entirely. His nose is slightly pink from the cold, flecks of gold visible in his eyes.

His smile is crooked, and all the more devastating for it. It softens into something more understanding as we stare at each other.

"I'm not a violent omega," he says finally. "But I would very much like to hurt whoever it was that made you feel that you are anything less than perfect, Fallon."

My breathing stutters. But Teddy takes a step back, slipping his hands into his pockets as he backs away. His cheeks are flushed with gold, as if he's a little embarrassed.

"Tomorrow," he calls to me, nodding down at my hands. "Come anytime before six, and ask for me at Reception. *Please* come."

Sometimes the world offers us chances in ways we never expected.

I breathe in his scent, this omega with the perfect features and kinder heart... and I nod.

Teddy grins at me, as if we're conspiring. An answering smile tugs at my own lips.

And then he's gone, swallowed up by the busy street.

And I'm left alone again. But this time, I'm surrounded by a warm coat that smells like chocolate and marshmallows, with my battered copy of *The Light in Us* in one hand and Teddy's card in the other.

Not feeling quite so alone as I did this morning.

13

WILDER

Fox snarls at me from his position beside the window. "Do not tell me to *calm down*."

Holding back my smile, I raise my hands in silent apology and stay where I am, leaning against the door. "Sorry."

Although it's nice to see someone other than me losing my mind for a change.

Rowan burrows beneath his arm, and I watch as Fox wraps his arm around him, dragging him in until his face is buried in Rowan's shoulder. Scent-marking, his teeth closing over Rowan's bonding mark as if it can calm the panic inside him that fills the room. "He's just gone for a walk, Fox. He'll be back soon."

Rowan's calm, gentle words pull an answering growl from deep in Fox's throat. "Then why isn't he answering his damn *phone*?"

"Because he's a little git?" Fox glares at me over Rowan's shoulder.

Rowan twists his head to offer me a matching look. He rolls his eyes. "Not helping, Wild."

Crossing my arms, I wait. Barely a few seconds pass before Fox is spinning back to the window, almost pressing his face against the glass. "I'm going after him."

He's not paying attention to the door. But a finger pokes me in the ribs, nudging me out of the way. "After who? And – uh, *woah*. Smells a bit like overkill in here."

Teddy looks sheepish – and cold – as he slips into the room beside me. "Sorry. Long story, but I mislaid my phone on the way back. But I met someone—,"

Fox is there within a second, dragging Teddy to him. He takes a deep, shuddering breath. "What do you mean, you *mislaid your phone*? I swear to god, Teddy, I'm going to put a damn tag on your ass—,"

His voice cuts off.

Everyone stops.

"Uh. Yeah." Teddy rubs his neck. He eyes me carefully. Then he steps a little closer. "Like I said. I met someone, and I needed to check if I was right."

My snort is amused. If he thinks I'll be able to protect him from Fox, he's wrong.

And he loves it anyway, so I'm not sure why he's watching me like that, his brows lowered.

Like I said. *Little git*. I take a breath, teasing words on the tip of my tongue.

"About what?" Rowan asks.

I have no idea what Teddy says in response to that.

Because the familiar haze sweeps over me in a sudden *rush*, dragging down over my vision and tinting it with a deep, blushing red. I feel my teeth draw back into a snarl, the part of me that's Wilder disappearing beneath a wave of sudden, crushing *need*.

I try to fight it. The same as I always do, try desperately to shove that door closed. But there's no stopping *this*.

A roar rings out. A body slams into mine, throwing me off as I launch myself at the omega in front of me, shoving me sideways.

Hands – yelling – pinning me down as I struggle against the hands holding me.

"*Wilder!*"

I roar, bucking beneath their grip. They can't hold me.

Because that scent – delicate, floral, underpinned with a spiciness that goes directly to my rapidly stiffening cock - is digging deep into my lungs, gripping onto my heart and squeezing it – a torturous, clawing desperation that has me bucking them off and barrelling toward it.

Nothing keeps an alpha from their scent-match.

Nothing will keep me from mine.

Mate.

But... it's wrong.

I bury my face into the neck of the omega, drawing their scent into my lungs. My teeth graze his neck, and he whines beneath me as he softens, his body bending for mine. Hands grip my shoulders, words babbling into my ear. Soothing. Placating.

Pack.

Not my mate.

Teddy. Pack.

The haze is slow to pull away. I stay where I am, sucking in deep lungfuls of that scent even as it begins to fade beneath me.

No. I push into it, my nose seeking it out as my hands tighten.

"Wilder – it's not him!"

"Get the hell off him *right fucking now—*,"

"Stop it!" The voice comes from close to my ear, breathless and pleading. "Get back. I'm fine. Wilder – god, I'm sorry. I thought – I didn't realize you'd think it was me. She's perfect. She's so fucking perfect, you're going to love her, but it's not me. It's Fallon. *Fallon*. That's your mate. She's your scent-match. Not me."

Fallon.

My arms loosen slightly. The omega buries his hands in my hair, running through it with gentle touches. "That's it. She's beautiful, Wild. Tall, with these wide amber eyes. And she's coming back here, so we need to make sure you're ready. Okay? Deep breath. You can come out of this, for her. Right?"

His touch is familiar. Grounding.

Pack.

Fallon.

My voice is a rasp, rusty speech dragged over razor blades from deep in my chest. "*Mate.*"

Tension ratchets up in the air around me, but the hands on my face are soft. "Yes. She's your mate. But she needs you to be *Wilder*. You don't want to scare her, right?"

No. I don't want to scare her.

But that need – it physically hurts. "*Scent.*"

"Yep," Teddy murmurs. *Teddy*. He keeps touching me, grounding me with pack as the red tinge in my vision slowly rolls back. "She smells really good, huh? And she loves books, too."

"Teddy." A choking sound from behind me. "How did you know?"

"The bond," he breathes beneath me. "It feels like... like an *echo*. Weird feeling."

I become more aware of my surroundings. The room around me is silent, all attention on us. My arms are banded around Teddy, his back against the wall and my hand in his hair, tugging his neck to the side.

My nose is buried in his skin.

Chocolate and marshmallows.

And beneath that... *heaven*.

I rip myself away, stumbling back as Fox body checks me out of the way and dives for Teddy. "You okay?"

But Teddy doesn't say anything. He grabs Fox by the back of the neck and drags him down, to the place where I scented her.

Fallon.

My breathing shudders, and I scoot across the floor to put space between us as I watch our pack leader bend to breathe Teddy in.

It's a position I've seen them in hundreds of times. Thousands.

Fox stiffens, his face in the crook of Teddy's neck.

I'm not sure he's even breathing.

Hell, I'm not sure *I'm* breathing. Probably for the best, in case I attack our omega again.

But Fox... he drops, his knees hitting the floor with a solid thump. His shoulders seem to widen, a low growl rumbling through the room as he stares up at Teddy with a dazed expression. And his voice... it's half ecstasy, half *pain*.

"*Mate*."

14

— · —

TEDDY

*Y*ou've really fucked up this time, Theodore.

Fox doesn't look away from my face. I can read every expression there, the flickering between need and panic as he reaches for me. "*Teddy.*"

I drop down, too, throwing my words at Rowan where he stands stock-still by the door. Beside him, Wild is slumped against the wall, his gaze still clouded with the battle he's fighting internally. "Get Zeke. *Quickly,* before it fades. We need to know if it's all of them, Ro."

The scent on my skin won't last forever. That they even picked it up is only because my suspicions were right.

Fallon is their *mate.* Their scent-match.

All three of our pack alphas, with the same damn scent-match.

My smile begins to grow, but Fox makes an anguished sound. His hands come up to cup my face. "I—,"

"No." I lean in until our foreheads press together. "This is a good thing, Fox. She's your scent-match. Your *mate.*"

I can see it already. See Fallon, tucked into our pack. Safe, and loved.

A missing piece we didn't even know we needed.

Happiness bubbles through our pack bond, finally breaking through the petrified expression on Fox's face. He swallows, his fingers gentle on my skin.

This changes things. I can see the worry in his face.

"Not between us," he says, his voice gravelly. "I love you."

My smile turns to a beam. "I know. But you're gonna love her, too."

He blinks at that. "*Two* omegas."

I give a little, happy wriggle. "Double the trouble."

This is going to be amazing. They're going to lose their minds.

"*Teddy*." He groans it, but there's something else in his eyes, too. Something that grows as I watch him. Slowly, he leans forward to take another breath, his eyes closing. "What... what's she like?"

I peek over his shoulder. Wilder has his knees up, a pained expression on his face. "I feel like this is a nest conversation? Maybe."

Wild doesn't look at me, his fists tightening.

Guilt swoops, low and tight in my stomach. I brush a kiss across Fox's lips, and he reluctantly releases me as I crawl over to my packmate. "*Wilder*. I shouldn't have ambushed you like that."

I may have gotten a little overexcited. And a little dramatic.

But it's not every day I stumble on my pack's scent-matched *mate*.

Wilder sighs. And then lifts up his arm. I immediately curl myself underneath it, my eyes wide in silent apology. He stiffens. "I can still smell her."

Oh. *Whoops*. I pat his chest as his face flickers again. "No more feral today. Fox will have a coronary."

Both alphas look as though someone has clubbed them over the head.

A small omega with a spicy scent and sadness in her soul.

Chewing my lip, I wonder when to broach that.

Something isn't right with Fallon.

But if I voice it now, Wilder will definitely go full-on feral. So I make a call to keep it to myself. When I glance at Fox, his eyes are narrowed.

Rowan pushes the door open before he can call me out. Relief fills his face as he scans us, sprawled across the floor. "Zeke's behind me. He didn't want to walk in... just in case."

"Can't be any worse than my reaction," Wilder rasps.

I grin up at Rowan. "Send him in. I feel like a perfume sample in a store."

Zeke ducks inside, his gaze landing on me immediately. I wait as he inhales the air, his brows knotting. He doesn't spring himself on me, though.

Instead, he settles himself next to Fox on the floor before he opens his arms in silent request.

My heart smooshes. "You're such a softy, Zeke Quill."

"I heard you had a run-in with the Wild Side." Wilder rolls his eyes at the nickname for his *other half*, as we call it. "Figured I'd take it easy. I can wait if it's easier."

Wait?

My ass is already shimmying across the floor to him. "You kidding? We need to test it before it fades. Besides, I'm *desperate* to see if I'm right. *Three for three.*"

"Try not to sound too victorious," Rowan says drily. He crosses paths with me, settling into Fox's lap and murmuring something to him as I reach Zeke.

At first glance, he looks stoic. Almost scary. With his size, his beard, his shaved head – hell, his dominance, just a hair beneath Fox's ridiculous levels - I've seen others judge him on their first meeting too many times to count.

But then I look down. His fingers are trembling, the giant alpha avoiding my gaze as a blush curls over his cheeks. He clears his throat.

"It would be unusual, wouldn't it?" He murmurs. His eyes land on my face, skate away. "For all three of us."

He doesn't want to hope. Not when he might be disappointed.

I think Fallon could use an alpha like Zeke. And I think Zeke would adore an omega like Fallon.

Oh, god. Let me be right.

Slowly, I lean forward and wait.

Zeke inhales. And then I feel his nose brush my neck, respectful and brief.

He's frowning when I pull back. Disappointment shines on his face. "I... I can't smell anything."

Everyone pauses.

"*What*?" Wilder shoves himself away from the wall. I lock eyes with Fox, see the worry there as Wilder comes down beside me. But he waits as Wilder buries his face in my neck.

He relaxes. "It's not that, Zeke. Her scent has faded. I can't smell it either."

Damn. If I'd stayed with her longer...

Zeke half-shrugs, his disappointment easing a little. "So... a maybe, then. That's okay."

"Awh." My heart squeezes, my face falling. "Sorry, Zeke. I should have been faster."

Smiling, he cups my cheek and I lean into the touch. "Don't worry about it. The anticipation might kill me, though."

"So," Rowan says slowly. "You gonna give us the details, Teddy?"

I jump to my feet. "At home. With snacks."

Everyone groans.

"Don't make us wait that long." Wilder's voice still holds an edge of roughness, and he grimaces as I ruffle his hair.

"Come on, my little feral one. I'm not feeding you the deets until you feed me."

I skitter over Fox, avoiding eye contact as I turn for the door. But his voice rumbles through me, dragging me to a stop.

"Don't think I've forgotten your little escapade." He sounds a smidgeon more relaxed than he did earlier. I followed his shouting all the way from the elevator.

The grin I shoot at him over my shoulder is more of a taunt. I raise my voice as I sweep through the door, winking at a wide-eyed Emily. "Please. I brought back your scent-matched *mate*. That spanking better be a good one. Also, I left my phone in my coat pocket... which I gave to Fallon. So if you're *very* nice to me, I'll call her, and you can hear her actual voice."

Silence.

I press the button for the elevator with a satisfied hum. "We'll be back tomorrow morning, Em. Breakfast is on me for your last day."

And then there's a stampede behind me, as my entire pack jams into the meeting room door at the same time.

15

FALLON

I skid through the front door just as the phone begins to ring.

Breathless, I snatch it from the cradle. "Sorry. I'm here."

Shaun pauses. "Fallon. Why do you sound out of breath?"

I force myself to take a breath. Teddy's scent washes over me, something settling in my chest. "I was grocery shopping. Just got home."

Silence.

I glance down at the warm wool coat. It's too big for me, but I couldn't bear to take it off. Quietly, I tug the lapel to my nose and breathe in as Shaun's words filter through.

"I picked up your medication. How is your scent?"

Ah. Yes. My heat suppressants.

I push my tongue into the side of my mouth as I consider his question. "Fine, I think. I don't need them yet."

"We'll talk about it later." And the abrupt words sound like a threat, the single small bubble of happiness draining from me. "We won't be home for dinner."

"That's—,"

The low droning of the line is the only thing I hear as he hangs up.

Slowly, I place the phone back in the cradle.

Teddy's face flashes into my mind. The playful way he referenced his pack, so *easily*. With so much love in his voice.

I take off the thick, warm coat he gave me, my fingers sinking into the fabric. I'll need to hide it, to wrap it up as soon as possible so the scent doesn't linger. Beneath it, I'm left in my pathetic blue dress. It's unraveling at the hem after being washed one too many times, the fabric fading in patchy spots.

My vision blurs. And sudden, blinding anger sears my throat, *burns* it as I spin back to that damn phone that dictates my days.

And I rip it off the wall, flinging it to the floor.

It smashes, pieces of plastic flying everywhere as I stagger back, my breathing heavy.

Euphoria wars with dawning horror that grips my throat.

What have I done—

I step back, digging into Teddy's pocket for the glittering card.

Ink & Quill.

An interview, tomorrow.

Swallowing, I press my icy hands against my flaming cheeks, the card still between my fingers. I grip it like a lifeline as I sink down on a chair at the table and stare at it.

Think, Fallon.

One month of income. That's all I'd need.

One month, to earn enough to buy a bus ticket and have a few dollars left over. It wouldn't be much, but I don't need much.

I could run away.

I could go somewhere they'd never find me. If they even bothered coming after me.

I would be free of this. Of *them*.

But to do that, I need to get this job. And get through an entire month without Rory, Shaun or Ellis finding out.

It's impossible.

Dropping my head into my hands, I consider it. Teddy said they could be flexible. If I can get the right hours... I could leave and be home before they ever realized.

My eyes slide to the broken phone. There'll be a price to pay for that tonight.

But... Ellis hates that phone. My breathing speeds up.

Maybe I could make this work.

With a wish and a prayer. I'd only need to last long enough to get my first paycheck.

A twinge of guilt hits me then, for Teddy.

But... I wonder if he'd understand.

Not that I plan on telling him anything. He's done more than he ever realizes, just by giving me an interview.

"Okay," I whisper to myself. "I can do this."

First, I take Teddy's coat. My brows draw together as I hear a buzzing sound, and I slide my hand into the other pocket.

The phone vibrates in my hand. "Hello?"

Silence, for a second.

"Fallon!" The warmth of Teddy's voice fills me up. "I'm *so* sorry. Totally forgot that I left my phone in my coat. But you're coming tomorrow, right?"

"I... yes." I swallow. "I'll be there."

"Great." There's genuine relief in his voice. "I'm really looking forward to seeing you again. I think you'll like it here, you know?"

I bite down on my lip.

He's so... *nice.* "I hope I don't disappoint you."

"Oh, sweetheart. You couldn't disappoint me if you tried. We'll work it out, okay?"

"Okay," I whisper. "Thank you, Teddy."

"Don't thank me yet." I can hear the smile in his voice. "Actually, you never need to thank me for anything. Especially not before you've seen me in action. I'm a chaos cannon – I need all the help I can get."

He waits for me to say goodbye before he ends the call. I brush my fingers over my lips as I carefully turn the phone off and place it back in his coat.

I'm smiling.

I carefully wrap the coat in cellophane, spritzing the plastic with some de-scenter we keep in the utility room before I carry it to my bedroom. Wincing, I send Teddy a mental apology as I yank my bed forward and jam it down the back, mentally praying that it doesn't damage the material as I shove the bed frame back into place.

I head back into the kitchen and tidy up the broken pieces of the phone, placing them into a small pile that I put on the table. I won't be able to hide it. Better to admit it up front than try to lie.

My stomach churns as I pick up a shattered piece of black plastic.

But I can't exactly go to work if Shaun is checking in on me several times a day.

Which was the whole point, Fallon.

Which *also* means I'll have to play this exactly right. Chewing my lip, I glance at the time. Shaun said they'd be late home. And they'll be expecting their food to be ready and waiting on the table, even though they haven't given me a time.

Anxiety fills my chest as I back out of the kitchen. But there's determination, too, my chest fluttering as I disappear back to my bedroom. Grabbing my duvet off my bed, I drag it into the closet, arranging it until I can crawl inside it with *The Light in Us* clutched tightly in my hand.

I pull the door closed, flicking on a flashlight.

Time to put your game face on, Fallon.

Go big or go home.

16

FALLON

"**F**allon!"

The roar of my name wakes me. The flashlight in my lax grip clatters against the side of the closet as I jerk, my head banging against the wall. My heartbeat thumps heavily against my ribcage as I jerk to full, petrified wakefulness in an instant.

They're back.

And they're furious.

I can hear them tearing the house apart, searching for me.

Oh, god.

I stay where I am, curled up inside the comforter of my tiny makeshift nest. I don't have to feign the moisture that gathers in my eyes as I bury my face into the cotton, breathing in deeply.

Footsteps.

I jolt back, a low whine slipping out involuntarily as Shaun rips the door of my closet open. His scent bursts over me like an oil slick as I shrink back against the wall, tilting my neck to the side. "I'm sorry."

My blurted, panicked apology; the tears that flood my face, the shaking of my hands as I lift them – none of it is fake. Nor is the fear that permeates the small space, flowing out and hitting Shaun *hard*.

But the *timing*—

Shaun pauses. I keep my neck bared, my panting breaths the only sound.

"What happened?"

His voice is harsh... but not as harsh as it could be. Instead, it's wary.

I keep my hands up, a barrier between the two of us that he doesn't miss. "I don't know. I got really hot, and everything was too much, and the phone was ringing and *ringing* and it made my head hurt—,"

Shaun swears over my babbling, low and vicious as he reaches in and hauls me out, his hand wrapped around my arm. "Jesus, you're burning up."

Wrapping myself in a comforter for six hours will do that.

I blink, forcing haziness to my face as I sway. "*Hurts.*"

"Okay." His grip isn't tight, but it's not exactly gentle, either. "Rory!"

Ellis appears instead. He doesn't look concerned as he lounges in the doorway, cold eyes sweeping me. "She's here, then. What happened to dinner?"

"She's not well," Shaun grounds out. "Burning up. Could be a heat spike."

Ellis rolls his eyes. "We'd smell it. And feel it. I don't feel anything apart from hungry."

I clutch my stomach, turning to cling to Shaun. "*Hurts.*"

"Honestly." Cold hands grab me and pull me back. I sag against Ellis, my perfume flooding out in unfeigned fear as he drags me away from Shaun. My stomach flips.

"Where are we going?"

"To cool you down."

He pulls me into the bathroom and thrusts me into the shower. My hands slap against the cold tiles. "*Stay.*"

He doesn't say it. He barks it at me, and I lock into place as he reaches in to turn the shower on.

Water pours over me, drenching me within seconds. My hair, my dress, everything is soaked. And... it's *cold*.

My teeth start to chatter. "Ellis...,"

He watches me, his head tilted to the side. "Feeling better?"

My nod is rapid. My body begins to shake as more water pelts down over my head. "B-better now."

"Good." His smile is nothing short of sadistic. "You can stay there for a little while."

He turns... and he walks away, closing the door behind him.

I stay where I am as the water keeps going. And going.

And going.

I don't know how long passes before the door opens again. "Fallon?"

I stare at Rory, trying to form the words. But my lips feel numb. He darts into the shower, slapping his hand to turn the water off. "What the hell?"

I can't stop the shaking. It takes over, every part of me vibrating with cold and fear as he reaches for a towel and wraps it around me. "E-Ellis left me."

Even my blinking feels slow, my words slurring. Rory pauses to look at my face. Something flits across his expression too quickly to see. "He didn't mean to leave you. He... he forgot, Fallon. That's all."

But we both know he didn't forget about me. Rory steps closer, and I flinch.

"I'm not going to hurt you." A devastated look fills his eyes. "I would *never* hurt you, Fallon."

The shaking is getting worse. And the pain – pins and needles ripple through my legs, my arms, my teeth chattering so loudly it becomes audible.

It shifts from a dulled pain to searing agony, and I whimper into Rory as he steps closer, his hands rubbing at my arms. I can taste my own distress in the air as he lifts me.

"I've got you." He carries me into the bedroom. "You'll be fine in a minute. You just need to warm up."

He undresses me silently, getting another towel for my hair before he settles me back in the bed and drags his quilted coverlet over me. The shivering grows worse as he leans over to feel my forehead. "You might need a doctor."

I shake my head, fighting off the ache that appears. I don't want a doctor. I just need to get *warm*.

Rory scans me and sighs. The bed beside me dips as he sinks into it, his hand tracing over my face and into my damp hair. "Always getting yourself into trouble, aren't you?"

The lump that appears in my throat grows. And grows, until I couldn't say anything in response, even if I wanted to.

Because there is nothing I can say that Rory would want to hear. He has no interest in the truth. He only sees what he wants to see.

His lips press to my forehead. "Get some sleep. Let the others sort their own dinner tonight."

It's almost teasing. I don't respond, my eyes closing.

One month.

I'll go to Ink & Quill tomorrow, and in a month – hopefully – I'll have enough to run.

And I won't look back.

17

ROWAN

Teddy throws out his arms dramatically. "I'm *stuffed*. Great food, Wilder."

I bury my smile under another mouthful of *chicken arrabbiata*, reaching for my wine. The five of us are gathered in our kitchen, dishes sprawled across our well-used table. Candles flicker, casting shadows across our faces as music plays softly in the background.

Across from me, Wilder's hands are braced against the table, his knuckles white. "Teddy."

My omega's arms drop to the floor. "Okay, okay. I've been appropriately fed, and my mouth is now available for other things."

I watch as the three alphas in our pack all lean forward. Even Fox, his thumb still tracing a circle over my knee. Even Zeke is starting to look a little frayed as they wait for an update.

On their scent-matched omega. Their *mate*.

Their scents swirl heavily in the air, the three of them mixing together in a way that I haven't smelled before. It's surprisingly heady, even for me.

Stay grounded, Ro. One of us has to.

Even Teddy is clearly a little in love with this omega already. So much so that he's reluctant to share, an omega trait to the core.

Omegas can be far more possessive than even an alpha.

"So." Teddy looks a little nervous as he glances around. "Her name is Fallon."

We wait.

"*And*...," I prompt finally, taking pity on the three of them.

"Uh." Teddy rubs at his neck. "She smells *phenomenal* – orange blossoms and nutmeg, all spicy and sweet. Like Christmas."

Fox's voice is dry, but I can sense the longing underneath. "Trust me, we *know*."

"*Some* of us know," Zeke mutters. He looks a little gutted still.

"Right, right." Teddy clears his throat. "She has long dark hair – *really* dark, like midnight – down to her waist. These really pretty amber eyes that take up half of her face. Kinda pale. Came up to my shoulder."

Silence again. "Didn't you take a creative writing class at college? Is she an omega or a frog?"

He cackles at that, but he throws his napkin at me. "Shut up. You're all *staring* at me. I have stage fright."

"You do *not*." He's loving every second of this.

Teddy narrows his eyes at me. "Stop calling me out, RoRo. Emily is leaving, and I got mauled by Wilder. It's been a chaotic day. Let me have my moment."

But then he sighs, his eyes dropping. "I... don't know much more than that. She likes books. Loves them, I think. She had a really old copy of *The Light in Us* with her. Well-thumbed."

Murmurs of approval. We all love that book.

"Excellent taste," Fox murmurs next to me. He looks proud, a small smile tugging at his lips. "That's good."

"Yeah." Teddy reaches for his wine glass, takes a large swig. "That's it, really."

"Teddy," I say softly. He doesn't look at me. "What else?"

The others flick their eyes between us.

"Teddy?" Wilder leans forward. "If there's something else, tell us. Please."

The strain on his face is obvious, Teddy sees it too, and he sighs. "It's not... it's nothing concrete. But I get the feeling that she's not... her home life isn't *great*. Maybe?"

Oh, shit.

The three of them burst into questions at the same time. Wilder and Fox actually jump to their feet, their questions mingling together as Teddy shrivels.

And their scents increase tenfold. Teddy whines at the heavy distress that thickens the air around us. For him, it must feel like being smothered. Even I fight to take a breath.

"Okay – woah – *woah*!" I round the table, my hands gripping Teddy's shoulder. "*Enough*."

"Sorry," Teddy says quietly as they all shut up. His face is darkening. "I mean, I don't know that for *sure*. But she had this blue floral dress on that looked really old, and she didn't have a coat – so I gave her mine. That's how she has my phone."

I glance down at that. "You gave her your coat? Your wool one?"

Teddy *loves* that coat. It was one of the first things he bought when we finally started making money at Ink & Quill. He half-shrugs. "So?"

Fox's face softens as we exchange glances. "Teddy."

"I liked her," he whispers. He cranes his head to look up at me. "I *really* liked her. She'll fit with us, Ro. But she's so *sad*."

The tension creeps up again at that. Wilder pushes back his seat abruptly. "I need—,"

"Go," Fox says firmly. "Work it off in the gym, Wild."

Wilder is already heading out the door, his fists clenched, but Teddy suddenly flings himself forward. "I could *call* her. See if she answers?"

Everyone pauses. Wilder turns, slowly, but the haze is clearing from his eyes. "Yes. Please."

His expression says it all. He won't be able to sleep otherwise, not after what Teddy confessed.

My chest constricts, wondering what her life looks like.

I wonder if she has any idea how much it's about to change.

Fox hands over his phone and Teddy pulls up his number on the screen, putting it on speakerphone. We all crowd around him, our faces pressed together and Teddy almost buried beneath the four of us. Wilder's scent is still heavy, and I rub absently at his shoulder as the phone rings. "Maybe she's—,"

"Hello?"

My throat locks up at the sound of the husky, sweet voice that comes out of the phone. And she's not even *my* damned mate.

We all stare at it like idiots, until Teddy clears his throat. Beside me, Wilder is barely breathing, his hands gripping the back of Teddy's chair. Zeke is frozen, his jaw tight as if he can sense their connection through the small device on the table.

"Fallon!" Teddy jerks into action when I flick his ear. "I'm *so* sorry. Totally forgot that I left my phone in my coat. But you're coming tomorrow, right?"

"I... yes." Her voice drops to nearly a whisper. "I'll be there."

God. Fox lurches forward, his brows creasing as if he's in pain.

I suddenly realize exactly what Teddy means.

Fallon seems... *sad*. So sad that it drips from her voice as if she doesn't even notice. Like she's used to it.

"Great." Teddy closes his eyes, relief leaking from him like rain over my senses. "I'm really looking forward to seeing you again. I think you'll like it here, you know?"

We all wait.

Silence. And then a small voice. "I hope I don't disappoint you."

Fuck.

The bang is almost audible.

That's the sound of three alphas metaphorically falling to their knees for an omega they haven't even *met* yet.

"Oh, sweetheart." Teddy's voice wavers. "You couldn't disappoint me if you tried. We'll work it out, okay?"

"Okay." A pause. "Thank you, Teddy."

"Don't thank me yet." He forces a smile into his voice, but his eyes are glittering. I drop my fingers to his neck, squeezing gently, and he grabs for my hand. "Actually, you never need to thank me for anything. Especially not before you've seen me in action. I'm a chaos cannon – I need all the help I can get."

They murmur a goodbye before he silently ends the call.

None of us move.

"You were right." Fox's words are hoarse as he leans against Teddy. Teddy buries his face in his shoulder. "She's...,"

"Hurt," I say bleakly. "She's hurting."

Their mate is *bleeding* with it, her emotions sinking us even through the phone.

Shit. "Wilder—,"

But he's already gone, the door swinging closed behind him.

Teddy squares his shoulders. "It's a day. We're seeing her tomorrow. We can last until then, right?"

Slowly, I slide my own phone out of my pocket, and flick through the passcode, swiping until I reach the family app I built last year.

I don't use it to track the others unless there's an emergency. I wouldn't even let Fox use it earlier, not when Teddy was only out for a walk.

This feels like it could be an emergency.

My throat tightens.

"Well?" Teddy demands.

They're all staring at me when I look up.

"She turned the phone off," I say heavily. The tracker we use doesn't show Teddy's phone at all, only a small cluster showing the rest of us here, at home.

I can't track her. Can't *find* her.

Zeke stirs, running a hand over his face. "Then we have to hope she shows up."

18

FALLON

I trudge along, my feet heavy on the sidewalk.

At my hacking cough, an older male skitters away, giving me a dirty look. My cheeks flush. "Sorry."

It comes out as a rasp, and I wince.

My throat hurts. My whole *body* hurts.

The house was empty when I got up this morning. They'd already left, several bills left on the side with a scrawled note to remind me to get a receipt.

As if I could ever forget.

Just like I won't forget the look in Ellis's eyes when he switched the shower on. There was *glee* there as he watched the cold water hit me.

He's never done anything like that before.

They've never... *hurt* me. But last night felt close to it.

Too close.

I have to get out. And to get out, I need this job.

I just hope Teddy can overlook the mess I'm in. My hair is clean and tidy, but my dress is the same one I was wearing yesterday.

Ellis picked the wrong week to ruin my entire wardrobe.

I reach a busy intersection and glance down to double-check the address in my hand. As I look up, a building opposite catches my eye.

The statue raised outside, gaudy and huge and gold, would be enough, but it's the tall, gilded letters across the front of the gothic architecture that make me stop, my brows drawing together in consternation.

Wordsmith.

I stare at it for several long seconds, until somebody bumps into me, their irritation clear as I block the crossing. Quickly, I dart across, shooting small glances over the road as if the words will change.

It looks... huge. Successful.

Far more successful than I realized.

Just a start-up, Rory had told me with an apologetic wince. *Not much money in it.*

I've never seen their building before. But it doesn't *look* like a start-up.

My hand drops down to my small, slightly battered bag, where my grocery money is kept.

I have to count every damn penny, and they own this?

I swallow the hurt down, force the unwelcome thoughts away. I have no space for them in my head today. And if my growing suspicions are right, then it's even more of a reason to get away from them.

I stay on the other side of the road until I'm well past their building before I cross over.

The Ink & Quill building is on the same street. It's quiet, understated, sheets of darkened glass behind a small, calligraphic sign.

Taking a breath, I pause.

I can do this.

Teddy invited me here. They're not exactly going to throw me out.

I take another breath before I step into the revolving doors.

The lobby on the other side is a hive of activity. Several large groups are clustered around a flustered-looking receptionist seated at a long oak counter, each of them clamoring for attention. People of all designations move across through the security area, swiping their badges and heading toward the large elevator.

My feet tap against the marble floor as I hoist Teddy's coat into my arms and stride forward.

You can do this.

I wait for the two groups to get their security badges, overhearing enough to learn they're students from local colleges touring the publishing house. Their excitement fills my ears, and I shrink back.

Maybe—

No.

By the time I reach the receptionist, my throat is burning. She flicks her eyes over me, and her painted lips tighten a fraction. "Can I help you?"

I clear my throat. "Yes. Ah – I'm here to see Teddy... Quill."

Her lips purse a little more, her eyes tightening at the edges. "Do you have an appointment? What's your name?"

I nod. Then I shrug. "He... ah, told me to come anytime before six? It's Fallon. He's expecting me."

The lips stretch into an insincere smile. "Can I see some identification, Fallon?"

My face falls.

You fucking idiot, Fallon. "I don't have any."

She blinks. "I can't let you in without an ID, I'm afraid. We implemented new rules just yesterday, and Fox is very particular about safety."

I grip the side of the counter, and her eyes slide down. "But... he's expecting me. We made the appointment yesterday."

Slowly, her eyebrows raise. Her tone isn't cruel, but it's clear she doesn't believe me. "Teddy has a lot of people asking for him. None of them ever have appointments. I'm truly sorry."

"But I do," I insist. My throat grows tight, my eyes prickling. "*Please*. Look - I even have his coat."

I hold it up like evidence, and hesitation flickers on her face. Then she holds out a hand. "I'll take that for him. If you take a seat, I'll try to get hold of someone for you to check. That's the best I can do. But I'd recommend calling him yourself and asking him to come down."

I stare at her outstretched hand. Slowly, I hand the coat over, hugging my arms around myself as she glances around me for the next person. The cough rattles my throat, burns my lungs. "Sorry. Could I – can I possibly have a glass of water?"

She points silently behind me, already greeting the next person in line as I turn and see a water cooler.

It whirrs when I press the button, but no water comes out.

Empty.

I cough again, and a security guard on the other side of the lobby glances at me, his gaze sweeping my dress. Backing away, I take a seat as close as I can to the counter, tucked away in the corner.

I can wait for her to make the call.

I have all day.

19

ZEKE

I cast another glance at the clock on the wall. Then I check my phone.

Again.

Hushed whispers around me. "Zeke?"

I look up. My entire senior team is watching me, waiting on a response to a question I didn't hear. "Sorry. Run that by me again."

I *like* numbers. Usually. Numbers have order. You move them around knowing that eventually, you'll find the logic in them. There's always an answer to be found.

But I'm not feeling overly logical today. My stomach is churning, my palms beginning to sweat as I glance at my phone again. Rising to my feet, I interrupt my audit manager as he launches into a discussion on quarterly profits. "Sorry. I... I have an appointment. Let's reschedule."

They trail out with a few curious looks in my direction. Since Teddy canceled the planned assistant interviews for today, my calendar is pretty clear. I head up to the top floor, pausing to greet Emily. She's tapping away as if she'll still be here tomorrow. "We're going to miss you, you know."

"Oh, you." She waves a dismissive hand at me, but her cheeks pink. She reaches out to adjust the obscene bouquet of flowers on her desk from all of us. "You'll be just fine, Zeke Quill. The rest of them, I'm not so sure about."

I'd laugh, if my chest didn't feel so tight. I head past her, into Teddy's official office. It's an interesting mix of comfort and functionality. His huge walnut desk takes up most of the back wall in front of a huge sheet of tinted glass facing out into the city. It's piled high with various pieces of paperwork and the many submissions from potential authors he refuses to give up, even though he barely has time to breathe most of the time. The rest of the room is a mixture of soft, comfortable chairs and low tables with shelves of books lining every wall.

Teddy is pacing a hole in the carpet, twisting his neck to the side. Fox meets me eyes, his jaw tight. "No sign of her yet."

Teddy sighs, spinning on his heel as he tugs at his pale gold tie. He's dressed up for her today in his favorite navy silk shirt. I resist the urge to glance down at my own choice of deep green cotton and a black tie. "I left notes for Lauren to call as *soon* as she arrived. Several notes."

"Then she will." Rowan pushes up his glasses as he hands me a coffee I desperately need. "She'll be here, Teddy."

I hold onto that calmness as I take a sip.

"Where's Wilder?" I ask, noticing the empty space where he normally lounges.

Fox crosses his arms. "He's staying away for now. Just in case."

Just in case he loses control. Fuck. I can't even imagine how he's feeling. My dominance is strong, but I've never had a single feral experience. Fox has his moments – mainly when he falls into rut, but not often. And it's not quite the same, a focused attention rather than a frantic burst of dominance that steals his personality away and replaces it with something more... animalistic. Wilder battles with it on the daily. None of us – including him – ever truly know what might set him off, although we've worked out the big triggers so he can avoid them.

But he can't avoid his *mate*.

"He'll be fine," Teddy says, throwing up his hands. He sounds exasperated. "He'd never hurt her."

"But he might scare her. At least at first." Rowan's voice is reasonable. "It makes sense for her to meet the rest of you, get a sense for the pack first. He'll feel more settled that way too."

"For her to meet *all* of us," Fox says firmly. He reaches out and draws Rowan to him, setting him between his hips as he leans back. "That includes you too."

Rowan's lips twitch. "Maybe. But I'll wait until the pheromones clear to introduce myself."

Teddy half-laughs, half-scoffs. "You wait. You'll be head over heels before the day is out."

As long as she shows up.

"We'll take it slowly." Fox drops his head, resting it on Rowan's shoulder. "Remember, she may not realize we're her scent-matches. Not straight away, at least. And we don't know her circumstances. So we'll need to tread carefully – Teddy, that includes you too."

Something else to consider. Nobody truly knows how scent-matching works, the process boggling the minds of scientists for centuries. It looks different for everyone – the alphas always know first, a biological advantage to help us woo our mates. But every omega is different. For some omegas, it's an immediate awareness that slams into their minds. For others, it grows over time. And I've heard of some scent-matches that snap into place after *years*.

Most agree that it somehow comes down to the omega, but nobody can explain *why*.

Teddy throws himself into a chair with a huff. "I can do slow. I'm sure."

We wait until the silence begins to itch at my skin.

"I'm going down there." Teddy jumps to his feet, but Fox pins him with a look.

"No. We don't know who's around. Everyone on this side of security has been cleared."

Teddy pouts. "You can come with me."

"And ambush her?" Rowan glances at me. "Zeke should go. It'll give him a chance to scent her without the rest of us overwhelming things."

I still at the thought.

Fallon might be my mate. My scent-match.

I don't know what's more frightening.

The thought that she is, and I'm about to meet the omega that will reshape my whole world.

Or that she *won't* be, and my mate will be someone else.

My mouth dries, but Rowan's face is understanding. "You can stay on the edges, Zeke. Just take a little look. It might... help."

I follow his gaze, to where my knee is jiggling. I slap my hand down on it. "Fine."

I'm almost at the elevator when I hear Teddy's outraged squawk. "Stay on the *edges*? He's *seven-feet freaking tall* and the width of a football field. At least I can blend in!"

"You smell like a hot chocolate muffin at twenty paces. You couldn't blend in if you tried," Rowan retorts. "Not unless you were in a damn bakery. And he can *hear* you."

I can almost hear the wince. Teddy's voice carries through the open doorway. "Sorry. You've got this, Zeke!"

At her desk, Emily rolls her eyes affectionately. The silent message is obvious.

See what I mean?

I'm glad that the elevator is empty as I travel down from the top floor to the lobby. My fingers pluck at my tie before I fiddle with my sleeves. I've pushed them up over my elbows as I always do, but now I wonder if Fallon would prefer me to look smarter. More put together than a beast of an alpha playing at wearing office clothes when I look like a damn lumberjack.

It's almost a relief when the doors open, saving me from my own chaotic thoughts. I step out into the lobby, my eyes traveling over the jam-packed area. We have several college groups in today. There must be over fifty people in front of me, talking, laughing, pointing up at the artwork Wilder chose for the walls. Scenes from all of our favorite books form a complex and beautiful mural that carries around the room.

I crane my head, but I can't see any sign of an omega waiting. The room is filled with the scent of everyone lingering and passing through, making it impossible to pick a single thread. A weight settles inside my chest as I pull out my phone.

No sign of her. I'll wait.

I can't think of a single thing more important right now than watching those doors. I lean against a pillar and settle in as the minutes tick by, watching the hustle and bustle around me and nodding to a few curious colleagues who pass by.

The college groups ebb and flow, some passing through into the building as more arrive. It's coming up to the opening of our paid internship programme. We have spots available for everything from marketing to finance, editing and acquisitions to business management. Competition is fierce, given we pay an excellent wage and offer real experience.

Too many others rely on their interns for unpaid administrative labor.

An hour passes, then another. The churning in my stomach only grows as every minute ticks by and there's no sign of Fallon.

When the lobby eventually begins to clear, I take a breath and make my way over to the counter. There's no sign of Lauren, our usual beta receptionist. Instead, an unfamiliar beta with painted red lips and heavily lacquered blond hair stands in her place.

She turns to me, her face flickering in recognition. "Mr Quill?"

I offer her an apologetic smile. "You have me at a disadvantage. I was expecting Lauren."

"Oh." The beta nods. "She's not well this week. But I've covered her before, so I'm well-versed in how things work around here. I'm Caroline."

A smile grows on her lips, stretching out as she leans forward. Her eyes flicker over my chest. "Maybe I can be of assistance?"

I take a small step back. "A message was left for Lauren that we were expecting an omega to come in for an interview. Fallon. Has she arrived?"

Caroline's lips part, her eyes widening. "Uh – well. We've had a few walk-ins without set appointments. The security arrangements changed yesterday, so we had to turn them away – the instructions were very clear."

I stare at her. My heart thuds, the beat growing faster. "What? Was she *here*?"

Caroline swallows. She reaches down and pulls out a familiar coat. "She left this behind. I'm so sorry, Mr Quill. It's been a very busy morning. I was going to call up for her, but she had no identification on her either, so I assumed she didn't actually have an appointment."

It's not an unfair assumption. We get a lot of people trying their luck to get to Teddy, thinking they can influence him into publishing their manuscript because he's an omega.

My heart wrenches as I take the coat from her. And as I pull it into my arms, a small whisper of scent trickles into the air and directly into my nose.

Sweet and spicy. Mouth-watering, fresh orange blossoms underpinned by the musky spice of nutmeg.

I stagger back, gripping the coat tightly as the blood rushes from my face.

Mate.

Caroline's mouth is moving, babbling, apologizing, but I'm not paying her any attention. Instead, I bring Teddy's coat up to my nose and breathe in deeply. His scent is the deepest, layered in familiarity and years of wear, but my mate's scent is a thin layer over the top. Delicate and feminine, but with a surprising strength that sends my head spinning.

Mine.

My mate.

Slowly, I lift my head. "*Where is she?*"

"She was here," Caroline is clearly petrified that she's fucked up. She jabs her finger toward the corner. "She was waiting – but I don't remember seeing her leave."

My mate was here. Turned away at the entrance, but she still waited.

How the fuck did I miss her? "Where was she sitting?"

Caroline points behind her with shaking fingers, to the very corner of the lobby. The *one* seat hidden from my line of sight, blocked by the counter. "There."

Keeping hold of the coat with shaking fingers, I stalk around the counter and stare down at the empty seat.

"Mr Quill," Caroline is nearly whimpering now, and I belatedly realize that my own scent is blasting out of me, soaking the air. "I'm really sorry."

I try to breathe, to think. My phone starts to buzz, Fox undoubtedly picking up on the emotions blasting through the pack bond, but I can't answer it.

I lost her.

And her scent is even stronger here, curling around me and threatening to pull a roar from my throat. It feels like it's growing, *deepening*.

"Um. Excuse me?"

I jolt at the quiet voice that comes from behind me. And slowly, I turn.

Her fingers tangled in a faded blue tea dress, my *mate* stares at me. Beautiful amber eyes widen. She breathes in, sways slightly. "Sorry. I was... in the bathroom."

Her voice is hoarse as she pushes a long, thick strand of dark hair back over her shoulder. And her hand... it's shaking. "Am I too late? For the interviews?"

"*Fallon,*" I finally find my voice somewhere along with my lost brain, her name a rasp on my lips. "You're Fallon?"

She shifts on her feet, her hands gripping her upper arms like she's building armor. "Yes?"

Fallon offers me a soft, uncertain smile. And then she does something that has my lungs emptying of oxygen, my chest threatening to rumble with the beginnings of a damn purr.

Because my mate shows me her *throat*.

Fallon tilts her neck in a gentle, unconscious act of submission that nearly takes me to my knees, wiping out the tension gripping my spine in one fell swoop.

I don't know if she's aware that she's doing it at all, giving me a good look at the pale column of unmarked skin as my fingers twist and clench into fists.

There's no bonding mark, no bite. Just a perfect, empty space begging for my teeth to gently grip, to mark, to brand her as *mine*.

She's unclaimed.

And she's exactly what I need.

The heaviness of my scent, the panic soaking into my bones... it shifts into something *else*. Something infinitely more tender, but with a fire underneath that threatens to burn my soul.

In a single moment, my heart ceases to belong inside my body. It's *hers* now, this omega who barely reaches my upper chest, even though she's taller than most.

My mate is perfect.

And she clearly has no idea that I'm her scent-match. I try not to swallow my tongue, force a nod. "I'm so sorry we kept you waiting. I'm here to... take you up. To Teddy. For the... for the interview."

Smooth. Real smooth, Zeke.

Briefly, Fallon closes her eyes. Something that looks an awful lot like relief flits over her face before she opens them again. Her smile deepens. "That sounds perfect. Thank you."

I don't move, though. I don't think I can. Because I can't stop *looking* at her, letting her scent soak into me.

Fucking hell. I want to roll around in that sweet, musky perfume like a damned puppy. And it's softer now, muted.

When she's in heat – or when her emotions overwhelm her... I'm going to lose my damn mind for this omega.

When Fallon sucks her lower lip into her mouth, I nearly lunge, yanking myself back with a harsh swallow.

My lip to bite. I want my teeth in her skin, my mark on her.

Jesus fuck – tone it down, you absolute caveman.

No wonder Wilder ran. I don't blame him at all for not risking it.

"Um."

My attention snaps up from where I've been staring at her lips. Fallon fidgets, her fingers twisting in her dress as a small burst of her perfume reaches me, her scent deepening. "I'm ready when you are."

I nod. I can't speak. So I spin, heading toward the elevator as I clear my throat. "Follow me."

My mind is racing. But one detail keeps jumping out at me.

Her dress.

It's pretty – and I'm pretty sure anything would be perfect on my mate – but it's faded, worn. Noticeably so.

And Teddy already told us she was wearing a faded blue dress. *Yesterday.*

I hold the elevator door for her as Fallon slips past me, gifting me with another fragrant burst of orange blossoms as we walk into the enclosed space.

I immediately start breathing through my mouth, but it sounds ridiculously loud in the silent space. And frankly, a bit bizarre.

So I stop breathing altogether.

As the doors slide closed and I risk running out of oxygen, I sneak another look at her. Our eyes meet, and her lips part, a blush crawling over her face as she glances away without saying anything.

Speak, you idiot.

Blissful oxygen flows into my lungs when I open my mouth, a heavy wheezing sound slipping out that makes my mate jump.

Damn it.

"So...," I search desperately for anything that isn't a request for a lifetime commitment. "Have you ever worked in publishing before?"

This is good. I want to find out more about her, to know everything about this omega, and this is a safe space to start.

Except it's not. I catch the hitch in her breath, the way that the bright color drains away from her face. She starts nibbling on her lip again. "Not... not really. Are you... do you work with Teddy?"

I forgot to even introduce myself.

"Zeke." I croak it. "Zeke Quill. I'm the...the Chief Finance Officer. Here. At Ink & Quill."

She blinks. "You're Teddy's alpha?"

"No," I say carefully. "But I'm his packmate."

There's curiosity there that she buries, but I like the glimpse I get.

Ask me, I will silently. *Ask me anything you want. Talk to me, sweetheart.*

But as the doors slide open, she's still quiet.

"This way." She follows a half-step behind me as I lead her down the hall toward Teddy's office. My mouth starts to run away from me in my increasing panic, more words coming out than I think I've said in the last week. "We're pretty informal here. It'll just be a chat, especially with Teddy. One of us might sit in, since you'd be working with all of us, but it's nothing to worry about."

I can sense her tension rising, feel it in the way her perfume sharpens, fluctuating with her nerves. "All of you?"

Don't overwhelm her.

"Our pack," I clarify, resisting the urge to smack myself in the face. "The position is mainly to help Teddy, but we all have things we might need a hand with occasionally. The Quill pack makes up the leadership team here."

We pass Emily, and I pause, backtracking. "Fallon, this is Emily. The interview is to fill her position when she retires."

Emily smiles warmly, and it's enough to settle the omega by my side as they exchange greetings. Em leans forward, eyes twinkling.

"They'll try to wind you around their little finger. Don't let them, Fallon. I'll leave you my bat just in case you need it." Emily points to the baseball bat propped up behind her desk. "One good smack should knock some sense into them."

Fallon takes a small step back, her eyes sliding to me in silent question.

I blanch. "Just to be clear, she has *never* used that bat on us. It's just a joke."

Emily winks. "Always a first time."

Damn it. I can feel the heat rising on my face, but something in our exchange has Fallon relaxing, a smile playing around her lips. "I'll bear that in mind. Thank you."

I swipe a hand over my flaming face. "Let's go, before Emily gets us in any more trouble. Or starts chasing me with that bat."

A small huff of amusement sounds behind me.

Maybe the best sound I've ever heard. My chest puffs up – and jeez, I need to get a fucking grip because you couldn't even call it a proper laugh.

Deep breath.

It's only as I push the door open that I remember that I was supposed to message them when she arrived.

My bad.

20

FALLON

I hover behind Zeke as he leads me over to a closed wooden door. Emily gives me a discrete thumbs up when I glance over my shoulder.

An encouragement I desperately need, because this is well out of my comfort zone.

I look back to Zeke, taking advantage that he's facing the other direction. Zeke looks as though he'd be more comfortable in the forest than in an office, his head almost above the door frame as we reach the door. The deep green shirt he's wearing clings to his wide back, only highlighting the muscles that flex in my line of sight.

He might be the biggest alpha I've ever seen. But... he doesn't *act* like it. I can sense his dominance, the outpouring in the lobby enough for me to know that he could put me on my knees in a second if he wanted to.

But he's... gentle, instead of domineering. Almost a little awkward.

And he smells *really* good.

Discreetly, I lean forward and take a sniff. Woody cardamom, and... I take another breath, my inhale a little deeper. Liquorice? Maybe. Or star anise. Almost peppery.

A little closer.

Wow.

"Fallon?"

Zeke's low murmur interrupts my little breath-a-thon. My whole body stills as I slowly look up and meet his eyes.

My nose... my nose is buried against his back. The warmth of his shirt is pressed against my face. And Zeke... I don't think he's even breathing as he cranes to look over his shoulder at me.

I don't know who looks more mortified.

Oh – oh *no.*

I burst into flames. That's what it feels like as my legs skitter back, as if I might actually run from this moment which immediately flies into my top five Most Humiliating Moments of all time.

Top *three*, even.

Who the hell am I kidding? I have never been this embarrassed in my life.

And yet... my eyes slide back to Zeke's back. And a noise sounds in my throat.

A noise that sounds suspiciously like it could be a whine.

Want.

I wrench my eyes away with effort, ignoring the little stab of need, the urge to go back and plaster myself against the large alpha's back. My body is clearly having a moment, maybe because my heat is coming.

But how *embarrassing.*

And to top it off... I spy the open door over Zeke's broad shoulder. And the two males standing there, watching with avid interest as I slap a hand over my mouth.

Teddy is grinning, his arms crossed and his body completely relaxed as he leans against the door. But the male beside him... he's just staring at me, as if he can't believe that I'd do anything as unprofessional as shove my nose into someone's back and breathe them in like they're the air I need to live. His jaw is clenched, his arms at his side but tightened into fists.

Another alpha. Both he and Zeke are completely still, but I can *feel* them. The new alpha has a dominance level to rival Zeke's – if not even bigger, and I can feel it pushing at me, both of them responding to the perfume that leaks from my skin.

And *his* scent is just as alluring as Zeke's, although my brows drop as I try to identify it. It smells familiar, but I can't place it.

Even Teddy's warm, addictive chocolate scent is joining the party as he lets out a low whistle. "Well, this is a party."

"Teddy," the alpha says in a low tone. Admonishing him.

So this is Teddy's alpha. As he turns back to me, I take in his thick, inky black hair and the deep, deep blue of his eyes, so much so they almost look purple. Sloe, a little darker than the plums I used to love. A dark layer of stubble already covers his jaw, as if it's grown in since this morning, brushing over lightly tanned skin.

Not quite as big as Zeke, although he still towers above me. But as our eyes meet, my body jerks forward.

Holy hell, dominator.

I was wrong. This alpha's dominance is off the charts.

And I am... so fucked. I step forward, around Zeke, and it feels as though I'm in a daze, my body controlling every tiny movement as I edge toward him.

Just one sniff—

No. No more sniffing, Fallon.

I was about to lean forward and try to sniff another omega's alpha. My hands join together to cover my face.

If I stay really still, maybe we can rewind thirty seconds.

Or was it... more like a minute?

Heat prickles at the back of my neck, matching the one that appears at the back of my eyes.

I'm fucking this up already. I can't even behave in public.

Ellis was right. I am useless.

My breathing speeds up as I stumble back. "I'm sorry. I'm so sorry. This was a mistake, I'll go—,"

"*Stop.*"

I lock into place. The alpha doesn't bark, but the word is infused with enough dominance that he doesn't even need it. I want to roll over and show him my throat.

I stop, pinning my eyes on the floor. "I'm really sorry. I don't know what happened, but I didn't mean to overstep—,"

The words catch in my throat, and I cough.

"Fallon." My name is gentle on his lips, far more gentle than I expected. Or deserve. "Look at me. Please?"

This alpha doesn't demand. He asks, as he comes to a stop in front of me. A murmured request that has me tipping up my head just a little, enough to see his face.

My heart twists as he holds out his hand.

"My name is Fox Quill," the alpha murmurs in a low, patient tone. Waiting, those vibrant eyes not moving from my face. "And it's a pleasure to meet you, Fallon."

I can't look away from his gaze. Slightly hooded eyes lock me into place, his scent washing over me, and I suddenly realize exactly why the smell was so familiar.

Books.

Fox smells like *books*. Like walking through a bookstore, an afternoon curled up with an old favorite story and a hot drink, the library on a rainy day. Indescribable, and yet so perfect that I almost want to cry.

This pack is perfect. Teddy, Zeke, Fox.

And as I take Fox's hand, I can't stop the desperate, fleeting wish that they could be *mine*.

Fox draws back, his voice still low and comforting as he holds out his arm yet keeps a respectful distance.

He somehow brushes off my embarrassing episode with a nonchalance that has me following him into the office, past a beaming Teddy, without running for the door.

They're not yours, Fallon.

The scents are even heavier in here, a heady mix that makes my head spin.

I am in so much trouble.

21

FOX

I force my steps to remain even as I step away from my scent-matched mate.

Zeke hovers in the doorway, the look on his face as if he's been smacked with something heavy as he breathes deeply, watching Fallon.

But there's concern on his face too. She coughs again as I nudge her to take a seat. "Let me get you a drink."

I have to stay in control. The demand pushes at me, urging me to go to her. To scent-mark her, to bite—

Fuck. I spin away and move over to the bar that sits in the corner. Rowan catches my eye, amusement and a little worry there. He stays back, leaning against the far wall.

Her voice is small, but hoarse. *Is she getting sick?* "You don't need to do that."

"I want to." I don't mean to, but the slightest edge of a growl slips out.

I want to take care of her. Because I can feel the concern in Zeke's eyes reflecting back at me from my whole pack.

Something is *wrong*. From the deep circles beneath Fallon's eyes, to the shabby dress she's wearing, even her bare arms on a cold day. And she's trembling, a vibration in her muscles that might not be obvious to anyone else but feels like a fucking red flag that has me gripping the edge of the bar.

Her perfume flickers and peaks as I take a breath and turn back to her with a bottle of water in my hands. I let it soak into me, soothing the jagged edges of my temper. "Would you like a coffee?"

A tremulous smile. "I don't want to be a bother."

"Absolutely not," Teddy declares. He throws himself down beside Fallon, and my body tightens in very unwelcome places at the sight of them both, so close together. "We'll both have a coffee. Usual for me – Fallon, you want a vanilla latte? That's what you had yesterday, right? Or you can have something else. We have a fancy-ass coffee machine that Wilder treats like his first-born child, so we can do whatever you want."

She hesitates, but then she nods. "That sounds lovely, thank you."

Don't thank me.

I catch the growl before it slips free. The concept of being thanked by my mate for something so basic – or for anything at all – rubs me the wrong way.

A warm hand grips my shoulder. "Go do the coffee. I'll stay with Teddy and Fallon, okay?"

"Good plan," Teddy eyes me, his eyes tightening at the corners. As if he can sense how close to the edge I am. "No pesky alphas allowed for this interview."

My head jerks into a nod before I stride out of the room without another word. Zeke falls into step beside me as we head to the meeting room.

He staggers as soon as I close the door. "Fox – holy *fuck.*"

"I know," I rasp. Slowly, I sink into the first chair I reach. "She's—,"

"Perfect." Zeke sounds dazed. Awed, even. "She's perfect."

I can almost feel the dynamics of our pack shifting, small tugs in my chest as the bonds rearrange themselves. Making space for Fallon, although she doesn't wear a bite mark, the bond not fully complete.

Yet.

It won't be long. I don't know how long I can keep *this* up. Being around her for any length of time without biting her, without caring for her in the way a mate needs to – it's going to drive me insane.

I groan, swiping my hands over my face. "Wilder's going to lose his *mind*."

There's no getting away from it. If it's hitting both Zeke and I this hard, then the most unbalanced alpha in our pack is going to go full-on feral the first time he scents her.

And I don't blame him at all. My mate's perfume still lingers, the sweetest scent with a little musk that makes my fucking mouth water as I stand and move to the coffee machine.

Even that small trickle soothes me as I make the coffees. Zeke joins me, making a green tea for Rowan that we carry between us back to Teddy's office and knock.

Caring for my mate. For my omegas – *both* of them, never mind that Teddy isn't my destined scent-match. Rowan, too.

They're going to be trouble, the three of them. I know it.

My suspicions are confirmed in the gleam of Teddy's eyes as he opens the door and grabs the coffees from me.

His smile is as sugary-sweet as his scent. "Sorry. No hunky alphas allowed for a minute. Top-secret omega and beta discussions happening in here. Come back later."

He winks.

And then he *slams the door in my face.*

Zeke and I stare at the closed door for several long seconds. Zeke places his large hand on my shoulder. "He probably asked for a reason, Fox. We should give them some space."

But he still enjoyed every second of ordering me out of his office. Little shit.

Finally, I sigh. "We'll call Wilder. Work on a plan."

Neither of us move.

"Over there," Zeke says finally, pointing. I nod in agreement.

Where we can see the door.

22

— · —

ROWAN

"O kay." Teddy passes the coffees around, waving me over from my position against the wall. "Just us, okay? It's not fair to ask you to interview when you're surrounded by alphas."

Fallon glances up at me shyly, her hair a curtain around her face as I take my tea from Teddy and settle opposite her. "You're...,"

"A beta." My smile easy, I take a sip of my tea. "Name's Rowan."

"And *also* part of our pack," Teddy adds. He flops down beside Fallon. "We'll do a run-through, but you'll get the hang of it in no time."

Fallon curls her hands around her coffee, hunching over it. "Fox is your pack leader?"

I nod. "Fox is the pack leader, and he's the Chief Operating Officer here, so he manages day-to-day operations across Ink & Quill."

Slowly, she nods. "And Teddy—,"

"CEO," he drawls, but his shoulders straighten with pride. "I manage overall company strategy and direction, and Fox answers to me while we're at work."

Fallon looks surprised. "That's... unusual. Isn't it?"

I roll my eyes affectionately at Teddy. "Teddy is the CEO here, but Fox is our pack leader. So anything that falls under the company ultimately sits with Teddy, and Fox takes the pack issues. It works."

"Most of the time." Teddy laughs, his head tilting back. "We butt heads occasionally, but those are my *favorite* days."

Fallon's flushed cheeks deepen when he winks at her. "That... makes sense. I already know Zeke is the CFO. Finance, right? And you, Rowan?"

"He's a technical wizard," Teddy says before I can answer. "He should probably be working for the Secret Service or in some shadowy government organization, but I managed to keep him with me instead."

I grin. "I'm still waiting for someone to notice the SOS message on the roof. So I'm the Chief Technical Officer. All of our technology, our systems, apps, cyber-security runs through me."

"Each of the five of us has a role at Ink & Quill, and together we make up the Board, so we make major decisions jointly." Teddy bounces.

I see the moment it registers with Fallon, the way she silently counts in her head. "Wait. There's five of you?"

Teddy stops using the chair as his personal trampoline and casts me a wide-eyed look. "Uh. Yeah. So you haven't met Wilder yet, but you will. He's our CMO – heads up the design, marketing and advertising teams."

"You'll like him." I pitch my voice as reassuring.

"Yup." Teddy tilts his head with a coy look. "Wilder is crazy good at what he does. Has a real flair for the *dramatic*."

I yank out the cushion from behind me and throw it at his head. He ducks, laughing. "What?"

I shake my head, turning back to Fallon's bemused look and trying to find the words to explain. "So... Wilder is an alpha, like Fox and Zeke. But he struggles with some of his designation. Sometimes it's hard for him to regulate emotion."

Fallon glances between us, her brow furrowing at my clumsy explanation. "Okay?"

"He'll probably explain it to you himself when you meet." I glare at Teddy again, but he looks unrepentant.

"She needs to know," he points out, and he even manages to make it sound reasonable. "Wilder is a sweetheart, Fallon. Sometimes he gets a bit *caveman*, and he can't always control it. Nothing for you to worry about, but you should be aware."

"Feral," she says softly, and we both stiffen. "He... is that what it is? He has feral tendencies?"

I nod. And worry for my packmate has my brow knotting. "Is that... does that make a difference? He's well-respected here."

Not that it matters now. She's Wilder's scent-match.

But he deserves to have a mate who isn't scared of him, who isn't dragged into wanting him purely because of a bond.

If Fallon *is* scared of him, it's going to be much harder for both of them.

When Fallon shakes her head, both of us relax. "He can't help it, right? I've never seen a feral alpha, but I've read up about it before."

Teddy gives me a smug look, but I ignore it.

I don't need to say anything. Fox will pin him down and spank him before the end of the day – both for shutting him out and for discussing Wilder.

But I can't stop the thread of relief.

At least she knows now. Whatever happens when they meet, it hopefully won't be such a shock.

Teddy claps his hands.

"So," he says brightly. "We should probably discuss the actual job. It's yours if you want it, Fallon, but we need to iron out the details. Basically, you'll be my right hand – diary management, appointments, some admin. And the same for the rest of the pack. We'll start out light, and the role will grow as you become more comfortable with us."

Fallon's eyes grow wide. "You're just... *giving* it to me? The job, I mean?"

"Sure." Teddy shrugs. "I'm a good judge of character, Fallon. I think you're nice and you'll work hard, and that's all I really need. Obviously, we'll talk about your experience, salary expectations, working hours, et cetera. I know you have set hours you need to start and finish by. But... how does that sound so far?"

We both wait. I'm holding my breath as Fallon's face flickers with something indecipherable.

I don't think any of us considered what would happen if she *didn't* want the job.

Even Teddy is holding his breath as he watches her.

Fallon stares down into her half-empty drink. And she almost looks... guilty.

"Yes," she breathes finally. She looks up at us and any hint of whatever worried her is gone, her eyes shining. "I would like the job. Please."

23

— · —

FALLON

"Welcome to Ink & Quill, Fallon."

Teddy leans back in his chair and grins at me. "This feels like the start of a beautiful friendship."

My smile almost falters. I'd give almost anything for that to be true. The Quill pack – the way that they work together, care for each other – I'd give almost *anything* to be a part of that.

But I have my own pack.

And I'd give anything to be free of them.

In a few weeks, I'm taking whatever wages I can earn and I'm running.

I'll never see Teddy or the Quill pack again.

And I feel more settled in my decision as we sit and talk. Teddy and Rowan brush off my inexperience, my stumbled explanations of why I dropped out of school. Interested, but not pitying.

This is the right decision. Because as Teddy shows me to the door, throwing a joke over his shoulder to Rowan, the knowledge that's been bubbling somewhere in my chest grows until it physically hurts.

This is how a pack should be. Whatever the Smith pack and I have... it's not right. Today has opened my eyes to what an idiot I've been, to let things get to this point.

I have to get out.

As Teddy opens the door, he starts to laugh. "Have you been waiting there the whole time?"

The two alphas leaning on either side of the door exchange looks. Fox Quill runs his eyes over me, bright and assessing. "How did it go? Will you be joining us, Fallon?"

I bite my lip. Fox's dominance... it's like bathing in a warm pool. Protective. Caring. Something you can relax into. And I'm only getting the scraps of how Fox feels about Teddy.

Combined with Zeke's, it's enough to make my head swim.

Teddy doesn't realize how lucky he is.

Although as Teddy ducks easily beneath Fox's arm, I wonder if that's true. They're all so solid in how they interact. There's no uncertainty, no fear there.

"She's starting tomorrow," Teddy announces happily. "So don't do *anything* to put her off between here and the exit, please."

"I wouldn't do that." Fox doesn't smile, but his eyes warm. Sunshine and books. I keep my breathing light, in case I do anything else to embarrass myself. "We'll walk you out. Teddy, Wilder is calling your office any second."

"What—,"

Behind us, a phone starts to ring. Teddy sighs, but he bounces past me anyway. "I'll see you tomorrow, Fallon!"

Rowan slips past me with a smile. "I'll be the one sorting your equipment out, so I'll see you in the morning too. It was nice to meet you, Fallon."

Fox murmurs something I don't catch before he brushes his knuckle over Rowan's cheek. It's surprisingly intimate, and heat rises on my cheeks.

Feeling eyes on my face, I glance at Zeke.

He's watching me with interest, and I drop my eyes to the floor, wondering what he's just seen.

I'd better get used to it. I get the feeling this pack is this way all of the time.

As Rowan leaves, Fox turns back to me. "May we walk you out?"

"You don't need to." With Teddy and Rowan gone, their full attention on me, it feels... exhilarating, if not overwhelming. My lips part as Fox's gaze drops to my mouth, but he immediately glances away.

"I'd like to," he says a little roughly. "Both of us, if you'll indulge it."

"Sure." It's nearly a whisper.

The elevator doesn't help. In true alpha habit, they nudge me into place between them until they're all I can smell.

Zeke's arm brushes against mine, and I shiver.

Do not lick the alpha.

Fox clears his throat. Loudly.

I wait, but he doesn't say anything.

On my other side, Zeke's jaw is a tight line. He interrupts the silence. "Why don't you have a coat?"

My pulse spikes and both alphas tense, as if they can hear it. "Oh, I forgot it."

Zeke looks down at me, his eyes searching. I force a shrug. "I'm always doing it."

He nods, but his jaw is still locked. "You should wear one. It's going to be cold tomorrow."

If I had one, I would.

They walk me through the lobby, Fox holding out his arm to stop an over-zealous group from bumping into me until we reach the doors.

When I turn to them, I find them both watching me. Suddenly shy, my hand jumps up to my ear, pushing it behind my ear. "Thank you very much for the opportunity. I won't let you down."

Until I leave them in a month. And as Fox smiles, surprisingly gentle, I hate myself for the lie. "You couldn't let us down if you tried, I'm sure. How are you getting home?"

"Oh, I don't live far. I'll walk. Thank you!"

They both hesitate at that, but I'm already darting through the doors, before Zeke can bring up my lack of a coat.

I don't even feel the cold as I walk home, crossing the street to avoid the far-too-fancy Wordsmith building. It's barely a thought in my head, my smile spreading across my face.

I have a *job*.

An actual, paying job, in a publishing house.

My hand flies to my throat as if I can ease the ache.

Not the way I always planned. Not as an editor.

But I still feel proud of myself as I hurry home, stopping at the grocery store on the way. The house is silent when I let myself in, my pack still at work as I carefully place the change on the side with the receipt and unpack.

It feels a little surreal.

As if I no longer quite fit in this sterile kitchen.

There's no phone call today. The space where the phone used to hang on the wall is empty, and I busy myself by cooking a salmon dish for dinner. Ellis always pretends he hates it, even though he eats the whole plate.

I stop, my hands buried in the pastry I'll use to wrap the filets.

Steady, Fallon. One more month. That's it.

I can do a month. I *will* do a month.

And then there will be no more shouting. No more punishments. No more cold showers and no more pain.

As the food cooks, I drop my hand to my stomach.

The Quill pack would never let Teddy be in pain. Not for a second.

I deserve more.

Deserve far more than these alphas have ever given me. Even Rory, who acts like he loves me even as he stands back and lets the punishments happen, never saying anything. Never stopping it.

My newly-found steel lasts up until the moment I hear a key in the lock. Glancing at the clock, I stand, my hands finding the pocket of my apron as they appear, one by one.

Ellis doesn't even look at me. Doesn't apologize for last night, as Shaun tosses a package at me. "We're going out. Wear this."

I don't look at the freshly-cooked food laid out. Instead I turn over the package in my hands. "Where are we going?"

"For dinner." Rory slides his arm around my waist. I let him press his lips to my cheek. "With a potential new client."

"So don't fuck it up." Shaun's tone is tight as he counts the change from my grocery shopping, the receipt tight in his hand. "I want this author on our roster."

Confused, I look between them. "Why am I coming?"

I've never been to a business dinner with them. They've never allowed me close enough.

The three of them exchange glances. Rory pulls me more into him, until his chest is pressed against my back. "This author is an omega. She's not especially comfortable around alphas, so we told her about you. Figured she'd be more comfortable signing a contract if she met *our* omega."

He nuzzles into my neck, but my body doesn't relax into him. It tenses, my muscles locking.

I don't want him to touch me. But even with him pressing into me, it doesn't ease the ache that springs up in my abdomen. A throbbing, needy ache.

Not quite pain. But not nice.

Ellis slides in front of me. His fingers lift up my chin, holding me in place.

"You will not embarrass us," he says with a hard look. "You will not speak unless spoken to, and you will smile and make this omega feel at ease. Do you understand?"

How can I do that if I'm not allowed to speak?

He's still holding onto me.

"Say it," he prompts. "*I will not embarrass you, Ellis.*"

I wet my lips. "I... I will not embarrass you."

He drops my chin with a look of disgust. "Hard not to. Look at you. Pathetic."

Rory draws me behind him. "Go and get ready. We leave in an hour."

As he lets go of my wrist, the ache lessens.

Weird.

My heat is definitely on the way, my body going haywire with new symptoms. Shaun follows me down to my bedroom. "Any update?"

I don't look at him as I start opening the package. "No. It's coming, though."

He sighs. "First sign of a spike and we'll do it. We have too much happening at the office to deal with you right now. If we have to double dose you it won't be the end of the world."

Just a double dose of unpleasantness for me.

But that doesn't even register with Shaun.

***

The clink of cutlery, the low sound of a piano and murmurs of conversation echo as I reach for my glass.

The small drop of wine Shaun poured me is long gone, but I take a sip of water.

Across from me, the omega author I've watched my pack trying to woo for the last hour smiles at me. She's gorgeous, her lustrous russet skin shimmering beneath a sleek wine-colored dress. Nia Weeks tilts her head to the side, curiosity coloring her expression. "And what do you do, Fallon?"

Before I can respond, cold fingers cup the back of my neck. Shaun massages the skin a little too tightly as he smiles without showing his teeth. "Fallon enjoys being at home. She's quite a shy omega. Aren't you, darling?"

Forcing my own smile, I nod my head before Shaun can do that for me too. "Ah, yes. Not very exciting, I'm afraid."

"Nonsense," Nia says firmly. Ellis tops up her glass again, and she waves a hand in thanks. "I must say, I'm glad to meet you. It makes these alphas seem a little more human."

The quirky smile she gives them takes the sting out of her words. Across from where I'm tucked between Ellis and Shaun, Rory raises his hands with a wounded expression. "I'm hurt."

She laughs, deep and throaty. "No, you're not. Wordsmith is well-known for your ambition. And I want my books to do well."

"Well," Shaun says. "That's certainly something we can help with. I even brought a contract with me, in the happy event that we can persuade you to sign with us."

Nia's face flickers. "Interesting. I'd certainly be happy to take a look."

She rises from her seat. To my surprise, she turns to me. "Fallon. Would you be a darling and come with me to the bathroom? This dress is a little fussy."

Ellis grips my knee so tightly I feel his nails dig in. "Of course."

They don't say anything as they watch me go. But I can feel their warning wrapped around me like a leash as I follow Nia into the restroom. She gestures to a hook on the back of her dress. "Nightmare. I don't know why I picked this one for tonight."

"It's a beautiful dress." I unhook her, both of us disappearing into separate cubicles.

As I'm washing my hands, she comes up beside me. "Tell me something, Fallon. Should I sign with Wordsmith? They want a seven-year minimum contract with all rights, domestic, international, every format, to any books I write. There's money there, but not until I've sold a frankly *ridiculous* amount of copies for a debut author."

I still as Nia leans forward to check her lipstick. "Sometimes, we're so desperate to be what we want to be that we can make bad choices without realizing. And I've wanted to be an author since I was a kid. But I also want to be comfortable with my choice."

Our eyes meet in the mirror.

"I don't know much about how they work." My throat feels dry. "I'm not sure I'm the right person to give advice, honestly."

"But you're their omega." She flips open a compact and begins applying a cream over her cheeks. "Which in my view, makes you exactly the right person. I agreed to this dinner because I'm interested in who they are as people, and even after two hours of sitting at the same table, I *still* can't work them out. That's why I wanted to meet you."

I will not embarrass you.

"Don't sign with them," I say in a rush.

Nia stops. She doesn't say anything. She just watches me.

"You'll regret it," I say quietly. My heartbeat leaps inside my chest as I glance toward the door. "If the contract is bad, it won't get any better. Don't sign it, Nia. Don't sign with them."

"Damn." Nia snaps the compact closed. Her shoulders sag. "I thought this might be my breakthrough moment."

"You should try Ink & Quill. They have an omega CEO."

Her nod is considering. "Maybe I will. Fallon—,"

There's a knock at the door. "Fallon? Are you okay?"

Ellis's insincere voice filters through, and Nia and I look at each other.

I look away first.

"Fine," I say loudly. "Coming now!"

24

WILDER

I make it back to the office in time to catch Emily leaving.

Our teams line the hall, a line of farewells and cheers as Emily walks through with Teddy beside her. She's beaming as she clutches the ridiculously sized bouquet, but his eyes are suspiciously bright.

I stay back, against the wall as Teddy starts the clapping.

But she spots me. Emily passes the bouquet to Teddy and nudges her way through to me.

I swallow. "Sorry I wasn't there today, Em. I hope you have an amazing retirement. You've earned it."

Emily sighs. And I close my eyes as she wraps her arms around me, squeezing me.

"You're going to be a wonderful mate, Wilder Quill. Fallon is a very lucky girl – and you're a lucky alpha."

My eyes fly open. "How—."

Emily pats my shoulder. "Because I know *everything*."

She really does.

Fox catches my eye. He tilts his head in silent question, but I shake mine.

I'll wait for them at home. Even now, Fallon's scent is a faint echo from her presence today. My guts twists, squeezes as I turn and make a swift exit.

I can't fuck this up.

But I have a plan.

***

"This is a *terrible* plan." Rowan's face is a reflection of the whole pack as he stares at me. We've finished dinner, Teddy regaling us with everything new he and Rowan learned about our mate today. The three of us have hung on his every word as I tried not to get too jealous over the fact that they've all at least *met* my mate.

And I had to stay away. "You're going to make yourself ill, Wilder."

Fox pulls the packet toward him, inspecting the back as his lips press together. "I agree with Rowan. Hormone blockers aren't a solution, Wild."

"I'll lose it the first time I see her." I tug the tablets out of his hands. "I don't like it either. But if I take these the first time we meet, take a bath in enough de-scenter that it burns my damn nose, then hopefully I can avoid *mauling* her before we actually get to have a damn conversation."

That's my only hope. A combination of rut-blockers and bleach.

Wonderful.

Teddy glances between us. "I think she's sturdier than you realize. She can handle this. She even knows about your feral side, and she didn't *care.*"

Fox gives him a narrow-eyed glare at that. But I'm glad he warned her, just in case.

"It's not that," Zeke says quietly. "I don't like this either, but she doesn't know we're her scent-matches. If Wild loses it at the start then she's going to know before lunch on the first day."

"But why is *that* a problem?" Teddy presses. He shakes his head. "This is a *good* thing."

"Not when we still don't know her circumstances." I grip the neck of my beer, my fingers tightening until I force myself to release them. "I don't want to force her into something she might not be ready for, Teddy."

He folds his arms, throwing himself back in his chair with a mutter that sounds awfully like *damned stubborn alphas*. "So you're going to self-medicate? That shit will fuck you up."

"Just for the first day." My eyes move to Fox, pleading. "I think I can manage after that. But the first time... we only get that once, Fox."

He hesitates. And then he sighs. "First day only. Whatever happens after that, we'll deal with it."

"But you said it," Rowan points out. "You only get this once, Wilder. You'll be lucky if you even remember it."

But I won't traumatize her. Won't drag her off somewhere. Won't cage her in until my teeth can sink into her neck.

"It's not about me," I say finally. "She's the priority."

Fallon.

25

— · —

FALLON

Shaun is reluctantly pleasant on the way home. "You did well."

I stare out of the window. "Thank you for dinner."

Rory smiles at me in the reflection. "Did you enjoy yourself?"

When I nod, his smile widens. "Maybe you'd like some time in your nest tonight? It might not be a bad idea anyway, not if your heat is on the way."

I can't look at him. Instead, I give him the answer he expects. "Sure."

When we get back, I trail behind as Ellis yanks his keys from his pocket. He fits them to the keyhole, turning it and stepping back. "An hour."

I kick off the black heels they bought for me, padding inside on bare feet.

He shuts the door before I can say anything else.

Sighing, I look around.

I *hate* this space. Despise every damn part of it.

Omegas are supposed to love their nests. Maybe I'm broken.

The floor, a built-in mattress, feels too firm beneath my feet. The pristine whitewashed walls are too bright. The light above my head is even more so. The glare threatens to give me a headache as I settle down against the wall and draw up my knees, reaching out for the blanket I left in here last time and wrapping it around me.

My head bangs softly against the plaster as I close my eyes. I don't even have it in me to be bothered anymore.

One month, starting tomorrow.

And at least I have something else to wear now.

26

TEDDY

Fox tugs my lip free from where I'm chowing down like it's a chew toy.

He scowls at me. "Stop that. You're making me nervous."

I scoff, but I still push into him until I can slip under his arm and breathe him in. My favorite place to be. "Don't even try with me. Like you got any sleep last night."

He grumbles, but we both know I'm right. He tossed and turned, finally getting up around four and going to work in his office at home. Even Rowan was tetchy this morning, his normally cool mood frayed by the stress radiating from the three alphas in our pack. Especially Wilder.

Sighing, I slip into my chair and rearrange the gilded name on my desk again. Then my pens. Then I reach for the towering stack of unread manuscripts that I've been too afraid to touch in case they bury me under a mountain of paper.

Death by the written word.

What a way to go.

But Fox pulls me back, his hands firm on my shoulders. "She's not even late."

I start worrying at my lip again, glancing at the clock. "No."

I gave her the hours she wanted – the hours she needed, for reasons yet unknown to me. And that unreasonably annoys me too, because I've decided that I want to know everything about Fallon.

My fellow omega.

My omega twin.

Twinsies?

For one wild moment, I have a vision of us in matching outfits.

When my phone rings, I launch myself over the table to grab it. Lauren, back from her stomach flu. "Fallon is here for you, Teddy."

"Coming!" Fox is already moving for the door as I throw myself to my feet.

I wobble. My hand shoots out, brushing my paperwork.

My eyes widen as the stack of manuscripts teeters. "Oh, sweet baby Jesus, no—,"

It's like a slow-motion horror movie. One sheet slides from the pile, then a few. Ten. Twenty.

Seventy-five million sheets of paper topple onto me like a freaky paper avalanche, the rustling a clear threat. "Aaaaack!"

Firm hands drag me back from the line of fire. "*Honestly.*"

We both stare at the paper that now covers most of my office. I clear my throat. "Good job Emily's not here, really."

She'd definitely chase me with the baseball bat for this. She's spent the last six months bugging me to make the time to read them.

Which I want to do. Desperately.

But there's not enough hours in the day.

"This is an issue for future Teddy," I declare, gingerly stepping between sheets.

"Just hand them to the Acquisitions team," Fox grumbles as he follows behind me.

My tone is intentionally casual. "Well, I can't do that now. I have to sort them out first."

Maybe I can read a few pages while I'm doing it. Multi-tasking.

Fallon is waiting for us in Reception. Her blue dress has vanished, replaced by a sleek black dress and heels that show off her lower legs.

Beside me, I feel Fox slow, and grab his arm. "No mauling."

"Not even funny," he mutters. His scent jumps, spiking the air, but there's no sign of the need I can feel pulsing through the pack bond as he reaches for Fallon's hand. "Welcome back."

She smooths down her dress after they shake. "Thank you. I'm excited to be here."

I'm grinning widely as she turns to me. "I'm glad you're here."

Her smile is shy, but genuine. "Me too. I didn't expect you both to meet me."

"Teddy will take you around this morning," Fox explains. "You'll see the rest of us at lunch."

A casual, family lunch on my floor, in our space.

One where Wilder and Fallon can meet, and we can pin him down if we need to.

Fox glances between us. But it's me he settles on. His lips twitch up. "Try not to get into any more trouble before lunch."

My hand spreads across my chest. "Me? Trouble?"

My eyelashes have never batted so fast. Fox shakes his head, his expression softening as he lands on Fallon. "Have a good morning."

"Thank you." She leans forward, yanking herself back as heat suffuses her cheeks. Fox turns, but I catch his fingers curling into fists as he heads for the stairs instead of the elevator.

Fallon falls into step beside me. "Teddy – I'm really sorry."

"Why are you sorry?" I glance down at her. She's only an inch or two shorter than me, but I quite like being a little taller. Must be how the alphas feel.

She'd fit perfectly under my arm.

Her face is scarlet now. "Your alphas – the scents – I didn't mean to overstep. Especially yesterday. They're just a lot to get used to."

"I get it." I press the button for Human Resources as we get into the elevator. "They smell like snacks, right? Hard not to want a bite."

Her mouth opens, then closes. "You don't... you sound like you don't mind."

Ah. First hurdle.

Because if it were anyone else sniffing around my alphas – even Zeke and Wilder, I'd likely be a lot less friendly about it. I once full-on body tackled another omega who tried to touch Fox's ass. Launched myself into her midsection like I was one of the rugby players I saw at a game once, and I took that handsy wench down. It was freaking *impressive*.

I still remember the look on her face. *Yeah, bitch. Paws off.*

"Uh. We... we're pretty open."

The fuck does that mean, Teddy? She's going to think we're all swingers.

Not that there's anything wrong with that, but we are firmly a closed pack. Outside of our established relationships, we don't share.

I start chewing on my lip again. "Anyway. We'll get you registered with HR, sort out your salary and then go and see Rowan for your tech."

"Oh. Sure." But she shifts on her feet. "I... I meant to ask this yesterday. What happens if... if I don't have an ID? Do I need one?"

I turn down to her, my lips twitching. "Legally, yes. Don't panic if you forgot it. Is this where I find out you're some kind of secret sleeper agent? Do you have a driver's license?"

Fallon shakes her head. Her shoulders drop. "I should have asked this yesterday. I just... I thought I might have something at home, but I looked everywhere."

"Don't worry." We step out onto the floor. "We do need an ID, but I'm pretty sure you can make an application for one and give us the receipt, and then you've got a few months to get it in."

"Okay." Her voice is barely a whisper as she comes to a stop. "I didn't... I mean, I *really* didn't think. Because I don't have a bank account at the moment, either."

Alarm bells start to ring inside my head.

Gently, I take her arm and pull her into an empty side-room, closing the door behind us.

Fallon looks miserable as I close the door behind us and turn to her. "This isn't going to work, is it?"

"That depends." I lean on the table, crossing my arms. "Are you in trouble, Fallon?"

She looks so scared. And my heart nearly breaks for her, but I pull it back. In my head, I run through any explanations I can think of for her having no identification... *and* no bank account.

I wait as her eyes dart around the room. She swallows. "I'm not... I'm not a criminal, Teddy."

"Oh, sweetheart," I keep my voice low. "I didn't think that. But I'm a little worried. How old are you?"

"Twenty-five."

"Okay," I say slowly. "But... you went to college, you said? I know you didn't finish, but you would have had an ID for that – and a bank account."

Fallon nods. She looks as if she's chewing a damn hole in her cheek. "I don't know where my ID is. And my bank account...well, we have a pack one."

Every single muscle in my body turns to stone.

Fox immediately starts tugging on the pack bond, sensing the panic that floods my veins as I stare at her.

Fallon has a *pack*.

Fuck.

This whole situation just became a lot more complicated.

"Oh," I say finally. My voice is hoarse. "I assumed – I'm so sorry. I didn't see a bonding mark on you."

"I don't have any."

And now my emotions are seesawing all over the fucking place. Because scent-matching is rare. Not everyone finds their mate. And it's common to be bitten into a pack, when people are in a secure, loving relationship. Hell, omegas *need* to be bitten in, or it hurts them to spend too much time around a pack and not be part of it. Social ostracization on a biological level is no joke, and no decent alpha would mess around with it.

Like me. Even Rowan has a bite mark, despite not needing one. Fox insisted on it, that he was just as much part of our pack as anyone else. Rowan tattooed over the faded marks to keep them.

For an omega to be part of a pack, but not bitten—

"Fallon." My words are quiet, but they're vibrating with an emotion that I can't name yet. "How much pain are you in right now, sweetheart?"

She doesn't look me in the eye. "I'm fine. I promise. But the documents—,"

"Fuck the documents." I can't remember ever feeling this livid in my life. "Fallon. Your pack hasn't *bitten* you? How long have you been with them? Is this a new thing?"

But even as I say it, I know I'm wrong. Because more about Fallon is making sense now. The way she hunches into herself. The crinkle between her eyes that doesn't seem to go away, even when she's smiling.

No bonding marks makes all of this a lot easier. But I don't care about any of that, as I watch Fallon wrap her arms around her body.

Like she's hurting. Right now, in front of me.

"Seven years," she whispers. "Teddy... please don't tell anyone. *Please.*"

My hands grip into the desk underneath me, to stop me reaching from her.

Seven fucking years?

They're going to lose their minds.

Wilder and his nature will be *nothing* compared to the three alphas in our pack when they find out their scent-matched mate is tied to a pack that's kept her on the edges for *seven fucking years*.

I feel as though I'm going to lose my own damn mind. I force my voice to keep steady. "You don't want them to know you're working here? That's why you're not using their account?"

She nods. And I watch in horror as her eyes fill up. "I'm leaving. But... I needed a job. Some money to get away."

To get away.

This pack... they're not just ostracizing her. They're actively *hurting* her.

"Do they hurt you?" I ask quietly. "Outside of the lack of bond? Physically?"

She shakes her head. I should be relieved by that.

But there are many ways to hurt someone. And not all of them leave visible marks.

Fallon covers her face with her hands. Her shoulders begin to shake, and I jump off the desk as a sob slips out. "I'm so sorry, Teddy. I should go. You have enough—."

"Come here." I throw my arms around her and drag her into me, holding her tightly as she almost collapses. "And stop that. You're not going anywhere, okay? Does anyone else know? Who do you have, Fallon?"

Family. Friends. A damn neighbor.

But her small whisper nearly guts me. "I don't have anyone."

Wrong.

So fucking wrong.

"You do now," I say grimly. I grip her tightly. "You and I are going to my office. And we're going to work out a plan. Okay?"

She buries herself into me, gripping me so tightly that I wonder when the hell the last time was that anyone even *held* her. Even her cries are quiet. As if she's so used to holding them in that she can't make any fucking noise.

We stay there for... a long time. Long enough that Fox moves from tugging on the bond to calling me, over and over again.

I refuse to let go of Fallon until she's ready.

My eyes feel damp, and I close them, my hand gently rubbing her back. "We're going to fix this."

Fallon first.

And then I need to work out how to tell my pack that our new omega – and she is *ours*, no matter who has a mystical damn mating bond - is possibly traumatized far beyond *anything* we might have expected.

And hope they don't lose their minds over it.

27

FALLON

I can't stop shaking.

I didn't even last an hour. One hour.

Teddy keeps his arm around me as he leads me up to his office. The people who head in our direction get one look at the pair of us and spin around.

I'm leaking. My perfume is blasting, veering wildly from floral to deep, deep musk as I fight to get myself under control.

Teddy doesn't let go. His voice is a low, reassuring murmur as we stumble out of the elevator.

And I smack into a broad chest, the scent of books slamming into me.

I almost double over from the yank that comes directly from... me. Pushing me to step closer, to burrow into Fox, where it's safe.

What the hell?

"Fallon?" Fox has his hands on my arms, but I rip myself away from him, nearly falling in my haste to back away before I do something stupid. "What's happened? What is it?"

His eyes are wild, his hair sticking up as he pulls Teddy closer, his hand cupping his face as he reaches for me again. "Are you *hurt*? Either of you?"

The low, rough sound of his voice only makes it worse. Shaking my head, I back away from him and spin, darting into Teddy's office.

I'm panting, my eyes blurry from tears as I nearly slip on the paper littering the floor.

"Fallon." Fox follows me, Teddy murmuring as he stops me from falling. "Please. I don't know what's *wrong*."

He sounds... almost desperate.

I can't look at him. My whole body flushes with humiliation and need as I back away until my back hits the wall and I slide down, throwing my arms around my knees and curling myself as small as I can.

Trying to hide from his scent, when all I want to do is bury myself inside it.

The room goes quiet.

"Fallon," Teddy whispers. And it sounds – it sounds like he's crying.

Or I'm crying. Maybe both of us.

You're useless.

You idiot.

You thought you could do this.

But all you're doing is fucking things up for a pack who don't deserve it.

I need to go. To get away from them, before I cause any more of a scene.

But I can't move.

28

WILDER

"Here." Zeke fiddles with my tie. "You're going to be fine, Wild."

He looks just as nervous as me. Throat tight, I stare up at the building. "Fuck me, I hope so."

Because everything changes today. Just how much, I'm about to find out. My world will be rearranged by an omega who by all accounts is pretty fucking perfect.

I just pray I'm not going to lose myself.

Generally speaking, I know who I am. Wilder Quill. Witty, sarcastic as hell, lover of loaded fries, the written word and shitty detective movies from the eighties. Never more excited than when there's a crisis I can fix or a new author to promote.

Pack mate. Friend.

And now... *mate*.

But I've been called other names too.

Rabid. Feral. Broken. Beast. Animal.

I've been called many things over the years, and not one of those incidents bothers me as much as the potential of scaring Fallon.

I take a breath, feeling the bleach from the de-scenter burning my nose. At my wince, Zeke shakes his head. "You didn't need to go that far. The rut-blockers would have been enough, you idiot."

Yes, I did.

Burning my nose so I can't breathe in my mate's perfume... it's fifty shades of fucked-up. But I'll be bad enough just *seeing* her. If I could scent her, too, I'd rip the whole office to shreds trying to get to her.

I swallow back a surge of nausea which might be from the rut-blockers. That shit hits hard. My head is already pounding.

Fallon is going to see that side of me at some point.

But not today. Today, I'm wearing my best suit – tailored, designer, the best that I could get for her. I jiggle the fucking huge amount of flowers in my arms, and Zeke gives me the side-eye. "Did you have to? You're making the rest of us look bad."

I snort, wincing from the fire that laces up my nose. "It also helps to hide the scent. As if you haven't already started planning gifts."

He looks uncertain. "I don't know her well enough yet. What she likes."

"We will." We'll know every part of Fallon, and she'll know every part of *us*.

I've never been so fucking scared in my life.

But this – this is as manageable as we can make it. An easy, introductory family lunch. Just us. Our mate. And my burned nostrils.

I take one step.

And a surge slams through our pack bond, so strong that it smashes into both Zeke and I. I've never felt anything like it.

"What the fuck?" Zeke rasps. His face is pale. "What the fuck's *happened*?"

Breathe. I suck in a breath, willing my pulse to settle. But those emotions keep coming, a tsunami flowing into the bond.

Not my mate.

But a surge of panic, of horror. Of *pain*.

Teddy.

I did everything I could to dampen any physical trigger, but I can't control the Quill pack bond. Or the way that it controls *me*.

Zeke grabs onto my shoulder. "Wilder. Fox is up there. Teddy is fine. *Fight it.*"

Teddy is fine, I repeat frantically in my head. *Fox is there.*

But Teddy is scared, and angry, and so fucking sad.

And my mate – my mate is up there.

"*Wilder!*"

29

FALLON

And now people are shouting. There's so much shouting that I flinch, my whine rippling through the room as the anger threatens to weigh me down.

A door slams, cutting off the sensation.

And in the background, I hear a roar. A roar that sounds like fury and pain, and a crash.

Look what you've done to them.

Ellis... Ellis was right.

30

ROWAN

I burst out onto the top floor, bellowing his name and shoving through the opening doors without waiting. "Teddy!"

Today was the first time I've ever truly *felt* it. Through the faint bonding mark on my neck, I felt a surge of emotion from our omega, so strong that even a beta like me picked it up. That single pulse sent my heart into my throat, sent me running out of a meeting without a word and leaving a dozen people slack-jawed behind me.

And for good reason.

Because it's fucking carnage up here.

Fox and Zeke are on top of a roaring Wilder. He twists and bucks, snarling at them as he scrabbles to get closer.

To... *Teddy*?

Teddy shakes his head, holding out his arms as I rush over. "I'm fine. I promise."

He doesn't look fine.

He looks devastated. His lip is trembling, his hair everywhere as he rakes his fingers through it.

"It's not me," he rasps. "It's Fallon, Ro."

I turn to look behind me. Emily's desk, the one Fallon was supposed to use, lies in splintered pieces, the three wrestling alphas clearly more than enough to tear it to shreds. Fox is roaring, barking orders, but even *his* dominance can barely handle Wilder's beast on a normal day.

And this version of Wilder... I throw my hand out, sliding in front of Teddy as he locks his eyes on us and snarls. Even his eyes look darker, his teeth bigger.

"Jesus fucking Christ," I breathe. "What the hell happened? Where is she?"

"In my office," Teddy whispers. His forehead presses into my back, his cheek rubbing against me in a desperate, silent request for comfort. "She... I don't know where to start, Ro. And they don't even know yet. Not all of it. They felt the bond, but I haven't told them *why*."

My heart constricts, He's standing in front of his door. Blocking the way to Fox, Zeke and Wilder's scent-match with his own body. Protecting her. "Oh, Teddy."

"I don't know what to do." His words burrow into my back. I can feel him shaking, the pheromones in the room pulling at him. "I don't know how to help her. And if I tell them—,"

It's going to go from bad to worse.

Teddy's fingers grip my shirt, and he whines, his distress clear.

I reach around, dragging his fingers to thread with mine. "Can we go in?"

He nods against me. "I mean, I think so? But she wasn't moving. She just sort of froze up."

"Okay," I say gently, rubbing his arm. "We're going to go in and see how we can help, okay? Fox is managing things out here. But you need to be away from this too."

There's another crash from behind us, and I wince. But there's no way we can do anything against one feral alpha and two others losing their shit. If anything, Teddy's misery is making it worse. Fox's eyes lock onto mine, his face twisting in pain as he looks to Teddy before he jumps back in to try and help Zeke.

"I can help Wilder though," Teddy insists. "I've done it before."

But not like this. Never like this. Contact, *pack*, helps, but Wilder's rage is beyond constraint. The mating bond, newly established and erratic, is ramping his emotions up to unseen levels. *And* he's taken the rut-blockers.

Holy fuck.

I twist, keeping Teddy in front of me as I twist the door handle. "In. Now."

He dives inside without complaint, and I follow, slamming the door and locking it. The bellow that follows almost shakes the frame, and I wait to see if any of them try to come after us.

When nothing reaches my ears aside from the same noise, I turn.

Teddy is on his knees, his hand stretched out. "Fallon?"

She's shivering, huddled into the corner with glassy eyes. She doesn't look at either of us. "I'm sorry."

"I told you before," Teddy whispers. "No apologies. Okay?"

"But...," she glances at the door. "I made this happen."

When she shivers again, I rip off my hoodie. Crouching, I wait for her to notice me. "Hey, Fallon. You look cold, love. Can I put this on you? Or give it to you?"

Her eyes slide from me to the hoodie.

Beside me, Teddy is silent. When Fallon nods, he lets out a shuddering breath, close to a sob. "Fallon, they're not fighting because of anything you did, sweetheart. It was me. They felt something through the bond, and it made things... a little crazy."

Fallon doesn't reach for the sweatshirt, so I edge forward. She doesn't resist when I slowly reach for her arm, unfurling it and threading it into the warm material. "There we go. And over your head, okay?"

Tears are trickling down her face, her amber eyes swimming with them when her head pops out. "I caused so much trouble."

I don't move back. Instead, I keep her hand loosely clasped in mine, trying to rub away the cold. Her hands are like ice. "Teddy's right. You didn't do this. Wilder... well, we mentioned that he has some feral tendencies. It's all a bit heavy out there right now, but they'll be fine soon."

I hope.

This isn't the first time we've had a situation like this, but it's definitely the worst I've seen.

There's no way in hell I'll tell her that, though.

"Can I...," Teddy leans forward, his voice rough. Needy. "Can I sit by you?"

She shuffles over, and Teddy scoots into the vacated space, leaning against her. I take them both in, the way that Teddy presses against her, the steadying breath that Fallon takes.

As if they're pulling something from each other.

An echo of the scent-match, perhaps. It's interesting.

Because both of them start to relax, tucked up against each other.

Teddy shifts, holding out his hand.

I slide my body into place beside his. Teddy blows out a breath, his body relaxing further as I carefully slide my arm around him.

When my fingers brush against Fallon's shoulder, I yank them away. But a moment later, I feel it again.

I lean forward to see her eyes closed. She's curling herself into Teddy, and her head brushes my fingers. Gently, I stroke my fingers over her hair, trying to give her a little comfort too.

She pauses. And then she shifts a little closer, until the three of us are so closely pressed together that I wonder how Teddy is still breathing.

But none of us move away. I keep holding onto them, stroking Fallon's hair until the shouting on the other side of the door begins to fade.

I don't miss that it coincides with the perfume filling the air around us fading. The panic, the distress begins to fade. Replaced by an almost sleepy scent, drowsy and warm. Fallon's pretty orange blossom twists with Teddy's chocolate, the bitterness replaced by something sweeter.

I watch the door, waiting.

It takes a while, but there's a quiet knock.

Fox waits for a minute, waits for us to refuse him entry before he eases his head around the door. His tight jaw eases as he takes the three of us in - his eyes lingering on Fallon, then Teddy, before they slide to mine, full of apologies he doesn't need to make.

"We're okay," I say before he can ask. "All of us. How's Wilder?"

Fox swallows. Shakes his head. "Beyond devastated."

My heart hurts for him. Slowly, I move my arm away from the two sleeping omegas beside me. Both of them exhausted from the emotional barrage.

But it's my alpha who needs me. Fox lets out a shuddering breath, his face dropping to my neck as I wrap my arms around his waist. "She must think we're animals. I could *feel* her fear. So could Wilder. It was a mess, Ro."

I consider Fallon's words. "She wasn't scared of you. She was scared because she thought it was *her* fault."

Fox stiffens. "What?"

"And Teddy thinks it's his." I roll my eyes, even though he can't see me where I'm pressed against him. "Something happened between them. She told him something that upset him."

"Something I'm not going to like, so he wouldn't tell me," Fox finishes, his voice grim. "He stood in front of that doorway for her. God, *look* at them."

I'm realizing that Fallon seems to have that effect on our entire pack.

Even... even me. "They wouldn't settle without the other. It's an interesting dynamic."

I don't know any other scent-matched packs with two omegas. But now I wonder if there are any studies on the effect, on how the mating bond filters through.

But it's clear that the full mating bond – once Fallon is bitten in – is going to be a damn force to be reckoned with.

"Think I can go over?" Fox asks quietly. There's so much uncertainty in his voice that I pull back. He stares back at me. "Zeke took Wilder home. I just...I need to be close to them."

"Go." He shifts past me, and I watch as he crouches in front of Teddy. Slowly, he reaches out to brush his finger over his cheek.

When Teddy opens his eyes, it takes a second for his haze to clear. He and Fox stare at each other. And then Teddy looks down at Fallon, his face softening. His voice is a whisper. "I can't tell you, Fox. She asked me not to."

Fox's whole body tightens. "Teddy."

"She's not in immediate danger," Teddy murmurs. His eyes start to mist again. "But it's not good. She needs help, Fox. But she needs a little time, too."

We both watch our alpha, watch him wrestle with the words. I can see the strain in his face, the strain to push for more, to *bark*, even. He could yank the knowledge from Teddy in a second.

But that's not who Fox is. He'd never abuse Teddy's trust like that.

"Damn it," he breathes finally. He stares at Teddy. "You promise you'll tell me if I need to intervene?"

Teddy nods. "We do. But just... not until she tells us."

"Okay," Fox says roughly. I can see how much it hurts him to say it. His eyes travel across Fallon. Her hair, her face. He swallows. "Is there anything I can do now?"

"You're already doing it." Teddy's smile is sad. "But... Ro. She needs an ID. And a bank account."

I snap upright. "I can do that."

"Fuck." Fox shakes his head, sinking it into his hands with an exhale. "I'm going to struggle with this. I don't even know what the others are going to say about it."

When I move over to him, he leans back against my legs. "Tell me there's something else I can do. Anything. *Please.*"

Teddy prods him with his foot. "Go and get us some sandwiches. I'm hungry."

It's such a plaintive, normal response that a laugh unexpectedly ripples in the back of my throat. "God, I love you."

"That's because I'm very lovable. And handsome." Teddy sniffs. "Please, Fox. My insides are about ready to eat themselves. I need six inches of beef, *stat.*"

A small noise comes from next to him before we can respond to *that* statement as Fallon begins to stir.

She blinks at us drowsily. "Did I... I fell asleep?"

Clarity returns to her gaze, but Fox drops back down to his knees.

"Fallon." His voice is gentle, so gentle that I wonder how he can even manage it. "I'm going to get us some food, okay? What's your favorite?"

Teddy gives her an encouraging nod.

"I don't... I don't mind. Anything, really. Whatever's left."

I can almost see Fox puffing up in outrage, so I nudge him in the back.

Maybe more of a kick. "Get a selection, and we'll work it out. In the meeting room."

Now is *not* the time to tackle her about her sandwich preferences.

"Fox?" Fallon's voice is tiny. "I'm really sorry. About... all of it."

My alpha closes his eyes. His response is ragged. "Teddy has informed me that I can't ask you what's wrong. So I'm not going to, not until you're ready to tell me. But let me make one thing *very* clear, Fallon. Not one single thing about this is on your shoulders. Okay? And when you're ready to talk, I will be right here. But in the meantime, Teddy and Rowan are going to look after you, and I'm going to get you some food so *I can at least feed you.*"

His words trail off into something that *might* be a growl, and I kick him again.

A loving kick. A love tap.

Her eyes are wide. "Okay."

"Good." Fox rises to his feet. I just know that he's going to buy every single sandwich from the family-owned deli across the street and bring them back here so he can work out Fallon's favorite. "We can pick up the work side tomorrow, when you come back. For now, I just want you to rest with these two. Take it easy this afternoon."

If he can't fix what's wrong, he's going to go all out on the protective alpha front at every possible opportunity.

"Cool," Teddy breathes. "Movie day in the meeting room. I've been talking about doing this for months. Ro, get the projector."

I have work up to my eyeballs, and so does Teddy. Fox too. But in that moment, nothing on earth could stop me from running back down to my office and grabbing a projector.

There's nothing that can't be fixed with a movie and popcorn.

31

—·—

Fallon

I'm not breathing as I push open my front door a few hours later. I stand in the doorway for several long minutes.

I'm *waiting*.

Waiting for Shaun to jump out, for Ellis to be leaning against the counter. Or for Rory to be there with a sad expression on his face.

Because it feels like they must know. How can they not know something is going on, when I feel so... changed?

But the house is as empty and cold as it always is.

My body is singing, little streaks of electricity in my veins. I drop the groceries to the floor and step over them, going to the mirror.

Even my face looks different, a mixture of exhaustion and exhilaration. But my eyes are bright, shining, as I flick on the lamp and head back to sort out the groceries.

I wish I could talk to someone about it. About the chaos of this morning, and how my heartbreak settled into something closer to longing as we all curled together and watched movies. And Fox – I've never met an alpha like that. One who radiates dominance from every pore, yet bolted into the room with twenty different types of sandwich in his hands and blushing cheeks so I could pick one I liked best.

Yes, you have.

The thought has me smiling, the usual grief that threatens at the thought of my dad settling into something softer. Still painful, but appreciative.

They're still not yours.

My smile slowly melts away, but I cling on to the feeling in my chest as I get rid of my scent-soaked dress, throwing it into the wash and climbing under the shower.

No, they're not mine. But seeing how they are with Teddy – and even with me, a strange omega... it's giving me something I haven't had for a long time.

Hope.

There are better things out there than this. A better life. I just need to reach out for it. And now that Teddy knows I'm part of a pack, the guilt... it lessens slightly. At least he knows that I'm planning to leave, to run.

But he's keeping it from his alpha for me. And I find myself hating the idea of splintering their pack in any way, even though Fox seemed to work with it.

The frown stays on my face as I dry myself, slipping into my only other dress and start dinner with my teeth sinking into my lip.

I get to go back tomorrow.

The thought has me smiling at the Smith pack when they come home, even Ellis. His eyes narrow, but he doesn't say anything, doesn't complain as he eats dinner and leaves again for a late meeting.

I push myself back from the table, clearing the empty plates. "I have a bit of a headache. I'll clean up and go to bed."

Shaun follows me over to the sink, his cold fingers feeling my forehead. "You have a slight temperature. Any heat spikes?"

When I shake my head, he backs off. But Rory takes his place, crowding me against the counter and taking the plate from my hands.

"I don't want you to take the suppressants. I think you should have a proper heat, Fallon."

His hands settle on my hips, and my body turns to ice as he starts running his fingers through my hair. "It's not a good time."

"For who?" He places his teeth over the pulse in my neck, grazing my skin before he pulls away. His face is flushed, a ruddy red. "You don't *do* anything. We'll decide when it's a good time."

The jab doesn't even register.

I don't want him to touch me.

The pain that follows me everywhere doesn't react to his touch. If anything, it grows stronger as Rory's hands cup my skin. My breathing speeds up. "Please, Rory. I don't feel very well."

I don't. My lie becomes true as he reaches down, lips pressing to my collarbone. The feel of his tongue makes nausea swirl in my stomach. "I'll make you feel better."

It sounds like a threat.

But a hand grips Rory's shoulder, pulling him back. "She said she's not well. Go to bed, Fallon."

And for once, I'm actually *grateful* to Shaun as he hauls Rory away. Rory snaps something at him that I don't catch as I dart out of the kitchen and to the bathroom.

My tears mix with the running water as I grab a cloth and wipe over the area where his mouth touched me, bending over the sink. I don't stop until my skin is a deep red, and I can't smell him on me anymore.

I've never had that response to Rory before. Apathy, certainly. Numbness. Sometimes even relief, his touch at least staving off the dull pain that hounds my every waking moment.

But never this violent surge of repulsion that sends me scurrying into my bed, yanking the covers over my head and wrapping myself up.

I stare at the door until my eyes force themselves shut.

32

WILDER

I hear him come in, but I don't stop. I keep hammering the bag in a one-two motion. My knuckles are screaming at me to stop.

I can't stop.

That's the fucking problem.

Fox jumps up, ducking his body between the ropes to get into the ring. "If you want to fight, I'll work it out on the mat with you."

"Because we haven't had enough fighting today." My tone is sarcastic as I keep hitting the bag.

I thought this might help. Help to work off some of the energy still buzzing around my body. But all it's doing is making me more aware of just how much damage I can do.

How much damage I did today.

I pull my punch just in time, yanking my arm back as Fox slips between me and the bag, folding his arms.

I bellow at him. "For fucks' sake. I could have hit you!"

Fox only raises his eyebrow. "Could you?"

Sweat is dripping from me. I got rid of my ripped suit as soon as we got back to the house, tearing it off and shoving it into the trash, replacing it with a pair of gray sweatpants.

I don't even know what happened to the flowers. Scattered and crushed all over the sidewalk, probably.

That's what happens when you try to be civilized.

Nothing but a damn animal after all.

"I'm not in the mood for a pep talk, Fox. We're a little past that, don't you think?" I start unwrapping my wrists. "I'll run it out."

"You need to meet Fallon."

I stop with my back to him. My chest is heaving, my body covered in sweat. "Not a good idea."

A realization I've been adjusting to for the past six hours, locked away in our gym under the town house.

Alphas like me don't get nice things. We don't get gentle mates, not unless we want to hurt them – which I don't.

We don't get a happy ending.

"Today wasn't your fault." Fox follows me to the running machine. "The scent-matching does ridiculous things when it first appears. You know that. Add in Teddy, and it was always going to be a clusterfuck. But it wasn't your fault. It wasn't anyone's *fault*, Wilder."

"Tell that to Emily's desk. Or to Zeke's sprained wrist." I set a punishing pace.

"That was me," Fox points out, exasperated. "I elbowed him. He's been icing it, and it wasn't that bad."

But none of it would have happened if it wasn't for me.

"Listen to me." Fox smacks the button on the treadmill, slowing it. "She needs you, Wild. Fallon needs you. You hear me? Our mate? She needs you, asshole. Pull yourself together."

My muscles turn to stone. "What the fuck is that supposed to mean?"

He has my full attention now. Fox sighs. "Something is wrong. She's in trouble."

He holds up a hand, his words a bark. "*Control it.*"

I wrestle the vibrations that wrack my body into submission, pinning them down. "Like it's that easy."

"This is," he says quietly. "Fallon has a difficult home life. Teddy knows more, but she has asked him not to say anything to us and I've agreed, unless she is in immediate danger."

My fists clench. "What the *fuck*, Fox? Why?"

He looks tired. "Because being Fallon's scent-match does not entitle us to trample all over her and force her into sharing things she's not comfortable with."

And he hates it. I can see it in the rigidity of his shoulders, the tightness of his jaw. "I don't like it any more than you do, believe me."

He swipes a hand over his face. "That's what the surge in the bond was. Teddy finding out. We're going to get her out, Wild."

My pack leader eyes me carefully, but I force myself to stay still. To listen to this information about my mate. "But I need you. *Fallon* needs you. So tomorrow, you're coming to the office, Wilder. You're going to meet her, and once you do, it's one more obstacle out of your way. You would have been fine today if it wasn't for the bond surge."

I swallow. Hard. "I can't stand the idea of hurting her, Fox. It's tearing me apart."

He considers. "You think I'd let you anywhere near my mate if I thought you were a danger? You think *Zeke* would encourage you to meet her?"

"I—," I stop.

Fox smiles slightly. "Tomorrow, Wild. It's another day. We'll be better prepared this time. And I think that once you meet her... you'll find that your world starts rearranging itself. You might be surprised by your own reactions."

He turns to leave.

"What's she like?"

My longing colors the air around us with my scent. It bursts out of me along with the question I'm desperate to know the answer to.

Fox glances over his shoulder. "She's fragile, at least at first. Quiet. Sweet. But she's resilient, Wild. She didn't bat an eye at the carnage. All she was worried about was what she was doing to *us*. I have a feeling Fallon is much stronger than any of us are giving her credit for."

My lungs feel like they expand. I take a deep, satisfied breath. "Our mate."

"Yes." Fox heads for the door. "Pull your head out of your ass, get an early night, and you can see for yourself."

33

FALLON

"You came back!"

Teddy's words are muffled as he buries me beneath a hug that threatens to suffocate me. At my choking noise, he draws back, his cheeks tinting red. "Sorry. I'm just happy you're here. God, you're cold."

I'm back in my blue dress. I notice Teddy sweeping his eyes over it. His lips tighten, but he doesn't mention it. "So, we're going to actually show you some of the ropes today. Rowan will be down later to help with tech, but for now we've got some meetings to do."

"That sounds great." His happiness is infectious. I can feel my smile stretching my cheeks, unfamiliar but welcome as I follow him into the elevator.

Teddy leans against the wall. "I completely get it if you say no to this, but I couldn't stop thinking about it last night. Would you – would you share your address with me? I promise it won't go any further. I just...,"

He stops. Swallows. "I couldn't stop thinking about... if you didn't come back. Or if something happened, we wouldn't be able to find you."

My heart clenches at his worry. A warmth sweeps over me. But I'm not sure. "Teddy...,"

"I *know*." He wrings his hands. "But it really would help me sleep at night. And I'm a real grump when I don't get enough sleep. So think of it as a favor to everyone else in the building."

He's so smooth, I barely realize I'm nodding until he smiles widely. "Great."

My eyes narrow slightly. "Do you always get what you want?"

He winks at me. "Stick around and find out."

The shrapnel from the alphas yesterday has disappeared. A new desk sits in its place, and I run my fingers over the aged walnut. "This is beautiful."

"Zeke picked it for you." Teddy ducks into his office as I take in the huge, comfortable-looking chocolate brown leather seat. I could curl up inside it and still have space left over.

I can hear Teddy rummaging around, his voice carrying. "You'll see him later. Fox booked us a lunch meeting. And you can actually *meet* Wilder instead of just listening to him snarl from the other side of the door. He's a sweetheart, I swear."

Teddy looks worried as he reappears, his laptop under his arm and a pair of glasses pushed up into his hair. In his fitted pale green suit, he looks ridiculously handsome. "I swear, you've got nothing to worry about."

My brows crease. "I'm not worried. Wilder is part of your pack, right?"

I can't imagine any member of this pack not being... perfect.

He examines me, but then he grins. "Great. Coffee first, then meetings. Brace yourself. I can be a bit of a whirlwind."

He really isn't kidding.

My head starts to spin after two hours. We dart from meeting to meeting, Teddy somehow charming everybody he meets as he covers everything from the company accounts to a new strategy campaign.

I keep looking around for members of the Quill pack, but I don't see any of them.

"I bow down to your skills," I murmur after we leave. My head hurts, but in a *good* way. I feel as if I'm stretching muscles that have never had a chance to be used, the notebook Teddy gave me already filling up with notes I'll need to go back through.

He's a machine. An intelligent, charming, witty machine in a beautiful package designed to make people think he's defenseless. But Teddy has a spine of steel. I'm actually a little awed. "How do you get so much *done*?"

No wonder you never stood a chance, Fallon.

He only winks at me before he returns to the e-mails on his phone, his fingers flying across the screen. "By the skin of my teeth and a little magic, really. This floor is my favorite, though. I might need you to drag me out."

The door opens to a dark wooden floor. Across from me, the walls are rammed with bookshelves. There must be thousands, all of them romance. It looks like a rainbow, the titles arranged in a cascade of beautiful color that takes my breath away.

Teddy spreads out his arms. "Welcome to Editorial, Fallon."

I step out in a daze. Laughter and the scent of coffee fills the air, people waving to Teddy as they stroll past. Spread out down the hall are small spaces designed for reading, comfortable chairs and huge cushions. Some people are curled up in them, flicking through manuscripts and making notes on tablets.

"What do you think?" Teddy is watching me closely. I turn, trying to get it all in and failing.

"This is amazing," I whisper. Emotion threatens to choke up my throat.

Because for years, all I ever wanted was to work in a place like this. It looks exactly how I imagined it.

Better.

"Fallon!"

At the sound of my name, I turn. Fox is strolling up the hall. He smiles crookedly at me, his hands buried in the pockets of his suit. He's not wearing a jacket, and my eyes drag over the way his violet shirt clings to his chest before I tear them away to stare at the books again. "Welcome to my kingdom."

Teddy sniffs, but there's amusement in his voice. "Fox oversees Editorial, amongst other things. But he's very protective over it."

Of course he does. Even his scent fits here, and I quietly take a breath as he comes closer. It settles into my chest, and I relax as his grin widens. "Has Teddy overwhelmed you yet?"

My tongue is glued to the roof of my mouth as I stutter a response, and Fox's smile warms his eyes. He extends a hand. "Come on. We're doing the quarterly Acquisitions briefing. Teddy likes to pretend he's still an editor and join in."

I turn to Teddy. "You were an editor?"

He blushes, tugging on his sleeve. "I *was* an editor. I did a joint degree in business and worked my way up in another publishing company. It's how we all met."

Fox's whisper brushes my ear, making me shiver. "He keeps a stack of unread manuscripts in his office that he never has time to read."

On his other side, Teddy sighs. "One day. Although they're currently spread out across the floor. I'm too scared to touch them."

"I can do that." The offer slips from my mouth. "I'll go through them later and reorganize them for you. If... if you like?"

"Thank you." Teddy blows me a kiss. "You would be my hero."

We slip into the meeting, and Fox settles me into the chair at his right. Teddy takes the one on his left, exchanging good-natured banter with the others around the table. There's six of them, and I shrink back in my seat at the curious looks.

"This is Fallon," Fox introduces me. His hand settles on my shoulder, gently squeezing. "She's new, and we really like her, so try to find the manners I know some of you have somewhere, *please*."

An older male, tall and lanky with a short beard and kind eyes laughs. "I lost mine when I walked through the doors of this place."

Leaning forward, he holds out his hand. "Ed Burrows. Nice to meet you, Fallon."

He shoots a sly look at Fox, wiggling his eyebrows. "Look at me, setting a good example."

Smiling, I reach forward and shake his hand. "Fallon Matthews."

Ed's head tilts, curiosity lining his face. "Fallon Matthews, you say? You wouldn't be related to Rick Matthews? He was a damn phenomenal author."

Teddy waves a hand. "Don't *hound* her, you animals—,"

"He was my dad," I say quietly. Beneath the table, my fingers twist and clench.

Silence falls over the table. Even Fox stills, although Teddy only glances at me, his eyes heavy. As if he already suspected.

"Well, shit." Ed leans back in his chair, his smile softening into something sadder. "You've got greatness in your blood, kid. I was truly sorry to hear he'd passed. You're joining our team?"

My throat tightens at that. Fox settles next to me. "For now, she's just observing and helping us out. So let's get started – we have a lot to cover and not enough time."

I start when his fingers cover mine under the table, where nobody else can see. He squeezes, gently, stopping the twisting motion before he pulls away. "Maggie, you can go first."

***

"How did you know?" I ask Teddy on our way back up to his office.

My mind is buzzing from the editorial meeting, the talent in the room *insane* as they debated the merits of new authors and pushed for budget allocations.

I caught Ed Burrows watching me several times, but nothing that made me feel uncomfortable. It was... sadder, somehow.

Teddy shifts. "That day we met in the café... you had that copy of *The Light in Us*. It was a first edition cover. And I've read it so many times that I could reel the dedication off by heart. I didn't know for sure, but it made sense."

"I love that copy," I say quietly. "It was the first one he got, and he gave it to me."

"You know," Teddy says gently. "Ed Burrows worked on *The Light in Us*. He was part of the editing team."

My breath catches. *Oh.*

Teddy studies the mirrored reflection opposite us. "You wanted to be an editor, didn't you? That's why you started studying English."

"Yeah." I wrap my arms around myself. "Things don't always work out the way we plan them, though."

"They rarely do. But maybe different paths show up at different times. Sliding door moments," he says thoughtfully. But he doesn't say anything else as we step out. "I'll grab a coat. I have a rack of them here, so you can borrow one of mine, okay? No arguments."

"Okay." I stare down at the floor. Thinking.

About Ed Burrows. About my dad. And about sliding door moments. Small, inconsequential decisions that change the path of our lives for better or for worse.

"Don't be nervous." Teddy drapes a coat around me, the same one he lent me at the café. "Looks better on you. If it makes you feel any better, Wilder is probably far more nervous than you are right now anyway."

"Why?"

He offers me a smile. "Because we're all a little bit in love with you, Fallon Matthews. Come on. Fox will come with us, but the others have been out of the office this morning."

He's joking. I *know* he's joking, but my stomach still flips over at his words, a heavy weight settling inside my chest.

We're all a little bit in love with you, Fallon Matthews.

And for a moment, I allow myself to wish that he wasn't joking at all.

34

WILDER

"You're fine," Zeke says gruffly. "For the love of fuck, leave your hair alone before it falls out."

We're seated in a booth in one of the Italian restaurants we frequent. The owners, an elderly beta couple who've been married since the year dot, give us a wide berth when normally they'd be over here chatting.

It could be the waves of panic pulsing from me like a damn warning beacon.

"Wilder." Even Rowan looks stressed. "Breathe."

"I am breathing." I rake my hands through my hair again, trying not to think about how much they're shaking. "Kind of."

The bleach is in full effect today. I double-dosed on the de-scenter compared to yesterday, even running it around the base of my nose. My nose is bright red, but I don't particularly care.

Much.

Zeke stiffens next to me. "They're here."

Both of them swing to me. "Will you *stop*? You're going to make me lose it if you keep looking at me like I'm going to bite you."

My palms are sweating as the bell above the door tinkles. It's quiet today, only us in the back and a pair of older women seated in the window.

This is it.

Fucking breathe, you idiot.

Ow.

On second thoughts, don't breathe.

Fox arrives at the table first. He shrugs off his coat, hanging it on the coat rack beside us before he turns around.

I hear her before I see her, my eyes fixed to the table.

A low, throaty murmur. Her voice is deeper in person than I thought it would be, but there's a sweetness to it that catches my attention.

My *full* attention.

Oh, god.

Silently willing the semi that's just erupted in my pants to go down, I take a breath before thinking and freeze.

Nothing. Just bleach.

Rowan gives me a small thumbs up as my shoulders almost collapse in relief. "Hey, Fallon."

Zeke murmurs his own greeting beside me. "Fallon, this is Wilder."

She hesitates. "Hello, Wilder."

Look up. Look *up*.

Swallowing hard, I force my head up. My hands grip the padded leather beneath us.

My mouth goes dry. I couldn't speak if I tried.

Because my scent-matched mate is *nothing* like I thought she would be.

But she's everything I never knew I needed.

Fallon is taller than I imagined, her body lithe but with curves faintly visible beneath her blue dress. My eyes drink her in, taking in the wind-rustled sheet of dark hair that drops down to her waist, pulled forward to hang in two sections on the other side of her face. It looks like silk.

And her face – deep-set amber eyes that show a dozen different colors blink at me, surrounded by inky dark eyelashes and a sloping nose tinged pink at the end with the cold. Her lips, the lower one plumper than the top, twitch into a small, uncertain smile.

My mate is flawless.

My mouth is hanging open.

Say something. Say anything, you idiot.

Rowan leans forward and casually slaps me across the back of the head. "Earth to Wild."

I snap my mouth closed. "Hey. Um. Fallon. Hello."

Whoever voted for me to be named *Wittiest Colleague* at the joke staff awards last year was clearly having a great laugh at my expense.

When I don't say anything else, Fox shifts. "Why don't we sit down and take a look at the menu?"

Teddy slips in beside me and Zeke. Fallon takes the middle beside Rowan, Fox slipping in beside her.

Directly opposite me. Our eyes meet, and she glances away, her cheeks flushing. When she starts to nibble on that plump lower lip, I jerk forward just as Zeke slams his hand down on my knee. Teddy casually leans his arm behind me, his fingers twisting in my hair and tugging.

Hard.

The small bite of pain yanks me back. I lift my menu so I can't see Fallon at all, but then drop it again, because not seeing her suddenly feels fucking *unacceptable*.

I'm in the shit. Massively so. Lifting the menu again, I turn to Teddy. His brown eyes are wide, the disbelief clear on his face. *What the fuck are you doing, Wilder?*

Help me, I mouth desperately.

And then I turn back to Fallon as if she's the fucking light and I'm a moth.

Kill me now.

35

FALLON

I'm struggling to breathe as I stare down at my menu. The delicious-looking choices swim in front of my eyes, fading.

Wilder Quill is... *intense.* And all of that attention is solely focused on me, his gaze lingering on my face.

He's just as big as Fox, broad-shouldered and tall. He lifts his menu up and I take the opportunity to snatch another glance at him, taking in the way his muscles flex in his arm as he pushes back deep chestnut hair. Deep blue eyes suddenly lift to mine.

Jerking my flaming face away, I turn to Zeke. He's watching me too, but carefully.

Zeke looks like he wants to take care of me.

Wilder looks like he wants to devour me.

And Fox... I sneak a glimpse at him. He looks like he wants to strangle someone, his jaw ticking as he stares over at Wilder.

I bite down on my lip, and Wilder *groans*, a deep sound ripped directly from his chest.

"Okay!" Teddy says brightly. "What are we having?"

I'll take a main course of everyone at this table.

Because good god alive, they're all freaking delicious. It's like they went through the *hot male* catalog and picked out only the best candidates for the Quill pack.

An elderly woman brings over some bottled water, and I almost snatch my glass when Fox pours it to press against my hot cheeks.

"Are you warm, Fallon?"

I shake my head, yanking the glass away. They're all watching me with matching looks of concern. "No. I'm fine. Absolutely great."

"Are you sure?" Teddy asks earnestly. "Because we can ask them to put the air-con on."

He sounds sincere enough, but his lips are twitching. He looks as if he's about to... *laugh*?

I'm saved from my embarrassment as the owner returns to take our orders. When I choose the smallest item, Fox glowers at me. "You don't want that."

My chest flutters. "I – I didn't bring my purse."

I'll need to dip into Shaun's grocery money just to cover this.

Rowan leans forward. "You liked the chicken club yesterday, right? They have an amazing chicken pasta dish here."

Fox orders it before I can say anything, reeling off a ridiculously long list of food that has my eyes widening. "You can try a little of everything, see what you like."

"Don't argue with him," Teddy says drily. "He'll order more to make a point."

"It only took you five years to work it out." They both smile at each other, and the affection between them makes my chest ache.

"Fallon," Zeke says softly. "How has your second day been?"

This, I can answer. "It's been... great."

We fall into talk about Ink & Quill, and I almost forget where I am as I lean forward, making an animated motion with my hands.

"The Editorial department was *amazing*. All those books on the wall and listening to everyone talk – it was incredible. Better than I ever imagined."

In my excitement, I nearly tip over my glass. They're all staring at me, and I stop. "Um. Sorry."

"No," Wilder says quietly. "Keep going."

My cheeks start to burn. "I've only had one morning. But I'm going to help Teddy with his manuscripts this afternoon."

Matching looks of surprise. I glance around, wondering what I've missed.

Rowan leans in. "Teddy never lets *anyone* touch those manuscripts."

The omega in question looks prim as our food starts to arrive. "Well, Fallon is an exception. Obviously."

As we eat, I'm cornered on all sides by alphas determined to feed me. Zeke spoons some of his risotto onto the edge of my plate, his cheeks pinking. Fox is adamant that I try everything, his eyes fixed on my expression as if he's taking notes.

And Wilder... Wilder holds up his fork. "Taste?"

Our eyes meet, conversation fading. He looks nervous as he offers some of his steak. "I haven't used the fork yet. But it's delicious. Maybe you'd... maybe you'll enjoy it."

His blue eyes seem to darken as I lean forward. I don't think I could stop myself if I tried. Wilder is... magnetic, almost. And a low thrum of approval sounds in his throat as I open my mouth, wrapping around my body and urging me closer.

Wilder gently slides the tines into my mouth, watching avidly as my lips wrap around the fork. "Good girl."

He's... *purring*?

My whole body softens unexpectedly, my bones turning liquid as I press my legs together. "It's... it's really good."

I mean it. The steak almost melts in my mouth, the garlic and olives working together as I press my fingers over my mouth and stifle the moan I want to make. "Thank you."

He stares at me. And without another word, he reaches forward and swaps our plates. "It's yours."

Oh. Wow.

This is... I stifle the urge to fan myself in case Teddy makes another joke about the air-con, but I'm starting to melt.

This pack is melting me. Beside me, Rowan is a solid, reassuring presence. "You doing okay?"

"Yeah," I whisper back. "Are they... always like this?"

"Worse," Rowan murmurs with amusement. "You'll get used to it."

How could anyone ever get used to *this*?

He clears his throat, keeping his voice low as Teddy draws the others into a conversation. "When we get back, we'll sort out your documents. I can register you at a new address and they'll be sent there. Nobody else has to know, okay?"

I stare at him, my heart pounding. "You can do that?"

He shrugs. "It's pretty easy. But you'd need to be registered somewhere new, unless you're happy for them to be sent to your current address."

I bite my lip. "Somewhere new is fine. But how?"

"You can use ours." He squeezes my hand, reassuring. "None of us will mind, I promise you. If you're comfortable doing that."

"Yes," I whisper. "Thank you, Rowan."

He only shakes his head. "No need."

I catch Fox looking at me when I turn back to my food. But he only smiles. "Okay?"

I tuck my hair behind my ear. "Yeah."

Maybe... *better* than okay.

Better than I've been in a long time.

I can almost feel it, then.

A flicker, deep in my chest. It starts to glow as Fox orders the whole damn dessert menu, insisting that I try them all.

A flicker of *light*.

36

TEDDY

I crash into Wilder, wrapping my arms around him in elation. "You did it."

He starts laughing, ragged and low as I bury my face into his chest. But I can feel his relief. "Yeah. Now I just need to work out how to be around her without bleach being a defining component."

He squeezes me tightly. Rowan has taken Fallon off to work on her documentation, and we've headed down to the marketing floor, Zeke and Fox following.

"She's perfect," Wilder says reverently. "Just like you said."

I almost bounce on my feet as I step back. "And she likes you. All of you."

They all stop to look at me.

"She does," I insist, spreading my hands out wide. "I can tell. Can't you?"

It's in every interaction she has with them. "She's going to realize it soon. About the scent-matching."

I'm surprised she hasn't already, but then again, if her home life is as bad as I think it is, I'm not surprised.

Something tells me Fallon has no idea what it's like to be with a pack who truly *cares*. It breaks my damn heart to see the way she lights up with every interaction. And I'm as determined to show her as the three alphas who converge on me with questions tripping over each other.

"Enough." I have to laugh at the desperation in their faces. "This is a *good thing*."

Fox studies me. "And you're still not going to tell us?"

I shake my head. "That's for her to decide."

He sighs, but he nods. "Go on up with her. We've hounded her enough for one day. She liked Editorial, though. Maybe she could start coming to the morning meetings if you can make it work."

I beam at him. "This is why I love you. You get it."

It's clear that Fallon has a connection to that part of the publishing world. I fully intend to nurture it. "Ed wants to work with her, doesn't he?"

And Ed is the best editor we have.

Fox nods. "He has an intern vacancy coming up since we promoted Maggie. He was fairly close to Rick Matthews, by all accounts. I think he tried to reach out to her before, but he never heard back. And then she disappeared, and fell under the radar."

Another path. Another possibility.

Wilder's eyes widen. "Rick *Matthews*?"

"He was her dad." My brows draw together. "I'm going to ask Rowan to look into that side of things, you know."

Because *The Light in Us* was possibly the biggest-selling adult fiction book of the decade. And yet Fallon doesn't seem to have anything to show for it.

It doesn't seem right to me.

"We'll find out," Zeke says quietly. "It's something we can do for her."

Damn straight.

37

FALLON

I t starts with a sudden, heavy tug in my abdomen.

I'm lying in bed, staring up at the ceiling. Ellis, Rory and Shaun came home from work late enough that I wrapped up their dinner and went to bed, grateful for the distance as I curled myself into the bedding.

The usual dull ache feels a little sharper tonight. A little more bite to it.

I turn onto my side, kicking off the covers.

I'm too damn *hot*. Sweat dampens the back of my neck, soaking into the pillow behind me as I press my arm against my forehead, feeling the heat before I even touch it.

I'm burning up.

I twist around again, drawing up my knees. My scent feels heavier, too. It soaks into the air, musky orange with the sweet, spicy scent of nutmeg.

My hips rotate. And my eyes fly open, as I hear voices coming from the kitchen.

No.

I drag the bedding over me, trying to ignore the heat as I curl up, gripping my stomach.

Just a spike. That's all it is. A precursor to the heat I've been putting off for seven years.

Every year, the pain gets worse.

There's a knock on the door. "Fallon?"

Rory.

Another twist digs into my abdomen as I fold over, my teeth snapping together to hold back my moan. My scent hasn't reached the hall yet. But if he comes in here—

I'm panting when the door opens. Flinching back, I scrabble against the headboard, shaking my head.

"Fallon." Hands on my face. "It's me."

Blearily, I peer at Shaun. "I... I need—,"

The strain of my perfume shows on his face. "What do you want to do?"

I bang my head back. "Meds."

I need them. Shaun shifts in place, his eyes darting to the door when I whine. "I'll get them, okay?"

He disappears, the door closing behind him. It feels like hours before he appears again. I cower beneath the covers as he comes closer, my legs shaking. "*Please.*"

I slide my bare arm out in silent request.

I don't want it. Don't want it here, in this house. Not with *them.*

The faint prick of the needle is nothing compared to the need dragging my body down. "It takes a few minutes."

I'm shivering. I'm so *hot*, but I can't shake the cold that settles into my bones. A cool cloth covers my forehead, and I push against it with a sigh. "Helps."

"You're going to feel like shit for a few days." Shaun stands, his eyes sliding over my swaddled body as I poke my head out from beneath the covers.

I wet my lips, my voice rasping. "Don't tell Rory."

He's never pushed me before. But this time... I don't think he'll be happy. Shaun glances around the room, grimacing. "Hard to hide it. But... I won't say anything."

"Thank you."

After he leaves, I wait for the pain to subside. Slowly, my scent begins to lessen, the hormone blockers getting to work.

But the pain doesn't stop.

It never stops.

38

ZEKE

I'm humming as I step out onto Teddy's floor, gripping the gift bag in my hand.

It's perfectly acceptable to give a new colleague a welcome gift. I glance down again, taking in the pretty notebooks, the set of sleek, colorful pens the sales assistant assured me any omega would adore.

I probably didn't need to add the cardamom-scented candle, or the silky teddy I couldn't leave behind. It nudges the gift from something professional into... something else.

But I couldn't help myself. I'm desperate to spoil my mate, and this is nowhere near enough. But it was enough to quiet the churning of my stomach after a sleepless night spent tossing and turning.

First, I was too hot. Then too cold.

Then my damn stomach started to hurt.

Maybe there's a bug going around.

Teddy is attending a networking meeting this morning, Fox and Rowan accompanying him, so there's nobody around as I wander up to Fallon's desk. Her head is down, focused on her new laptop that Rowan set up for her yesterday. "Fallon?"

She doesn't respond. And as I get closer, I catch a small pulse of perfume that has me slowing.

Because it smells... bitter, almost. *Twisted*.

I'm across the room in a second, kneeling beside my mate. "*Fallon*."

Her skin is waxy and paler than usual, a faint sheen of sweat on her forehead. My heart feels as if it's about to burst out of my chest as I stroke a damp strand of hair away from her forehead. Her temperature is sky-fucking-high, and panic has my heart pounding in my chest. "Fallon, love. Can you hear me?"

She murmurs something, and I lean closer.

"Hurts." It's a faint whisper, but enough to have my vision darkening until white spots dance in front of my eyes.

My mate is in pain.

"I have you." My voice is hoarse as I stand, lifting her up and into my arms. Her head lolls against my chest. "You're going to be okay. I'm going to get you a doctor, okay?"

I don't take the elevator. Instead I sprint for the stairs, my feet pounding as I carry her down. Her weight is nothing, feather-light as I cradle her. Startled faces flash past us.

"Move," I roar, and a gaggle of people break apart as I race past them. My phone starts to ring, the bond pulsing. Blood thunders in my ears.

She's so pale. Her fingers curl into my shirt, a small whine that rips open my fucking chest coming from her. "Okay, baby. I know it hurts."

I burst out onto the street and start running.

A mist coats my vision.

"I'm taking you home."

39

WILDER

I'm on my feet before the pulsing of the pack bond truly registers.

Please, God, not again.

My breath ripples out of me with a shudder.

Keep it together.

I run into my marketing director, Emma, on my way out. She stops me, her face pale. "Wild. You're going after Zeke?"

I shake my head, trying to stave off the tension in my muscles. "Why?"

She hesitates. Emma's seen me lose my shit before. She phrases her words carefully. "It... you should go home. Now. Don't speak to anyone on the way apart from Pack. Everyone's okay."

"Thanks." I duck past her, pulling my phone from my pocket.

Fox answers on the first ring. He sounds out of breath. "I'm on my way home."

"Why?" I snap. "What the hell happened?"

When he doesn't say anything, my tension shoots up. My voice deepens. "*Tell me.*"

"Fallon," Fox breathes. "She's okay, Wild. She's not very well. Zeke called the doctor, and we're on our way back now."

But I'm already running.

40

FALLON

I curl myself up against the warmth.

Try to bury myself in it, to get away from the pain. It radiates inside my body; sharp, stabbing spikes that have me whimpering.

"Fallon." A low voice says my name, sounding desperate. "The doctor is on the way."

I don't need a doctor. Whining, I push myself closer, nuzzling into him. "*Touch*."

It's a plea. A plea ripped from somewhere deep inside as I appeal to the alpha holding me.

This is the *right* alpha. And I need him to touch me more than I need to breathe.

He sets me down into a cloud of soft, amazing-smelling bedding. I burrow into it, breathing deeply, my hand already reaching out.

When I don't find him, my whine ripples again. "Don't leave me."

My face feels damp. A small, shuddering sob sounds in my chest, my tears otherwise silent.

"Fallon." A gentle hand on my face. The alpha sounds distraught. "You're breaking my heart, baby."

I pull myself up and forward, beelining for this alpha with the woodsy scent. He tenses beneath me as I throw myself into him, burying my face in his neck and inhaling. "*Touch*."

At my guttural words, a huge hand covers my back. It soothes the burning even through my dress, so I push myself closer. "More."

"Fallon." But he does what I ask. I soften against him as his hand strokes over my back. His fingers spread across my neck, holding me. And he starts to vibrate against me, the low, purring sound comforting me in ways I don't know how to express.

I just push into him, silently asking for more until that pain starts to recede. Heat and ice and burning dampens into a familiar ache, low in my stomach.

Murmurs around me. I pull away from the cold touch of metal, the alpha holding me still. "Let the doctor look at you."

I don't like the metal. But I obediently stay still, letting them poke and prod at me until they go away and I can curl back into the alpha with a sigh.

This is much better.

41

Fox

I stride into our house, Teddy and Rowan on my heels. Wilder is in our reception hall, talking to the doctor we keep on retainer for Teddy with a strained expression.

But he hasn't lost himself, hasn't given in to the animal inside him. Relief almost has me stumbling as Doctor Miersen turns to face me. "Your mate is fine, Fox."

"*Thank god.*" Teddy goes to push past me toward the stairs, but Rowan pulls him back.

"Wait." We all look at the doctor.

He shifts under our stares. "The omega – Fallon, is it? I believe she's under the influence of heat-blockers. Nasty things."

My heart flips over. "*Heat-blockers?*"

Wilder looks as angry as I feel, a tic appearing in his jaw. "I didn't think heat-blockers caused a reaction like this."

"Normally, no." The doctor pushes up his glasses. "But if someone takes them over a particularly long period of time, they can cause chaos inside the body. Add in proximity to her scent-matches, and you have a perfect storm waiting to happen."

"How do we help her?" I take a step closer, my fists closing. "What do we *do*?"

"Zeke is already doing it." Miersen points to the ceiling. "Hold her. Ground her through touch. She'll likely tell you what she needs through body language. Not much to be done for the pain, unfortunately, but she should be fine in a few hours. You may find that it comes back in short bursts. And given that she seems to have been taking these on and off for a long time, it's possible that your interactions may bring on a much stronger heat than she's experienced before. Heat-blockers weaken over time. It's only delaying the inevitable at this stage."

We all stare up at the ceiling as if we can see her.

But I can feel her. *Scent* her. It fills the air around us, drowning the usually potent scent from Teddy and filling it with oranges and nutmeg.

"I will say," the doctor says carefully. "I found some elements during my examination that suggest she has not been well cared for, more generally speaking. Some vitamin deficiencies. And her pain tolerance is well above normal levels, which suggests long-term—,"

"Pack ostracization," Teddy whispers. His face is pale. "That's what you found."

The atmosphere plummets as we all turn to look at him. He sways in place. "Fox—,"

My voice is hard as I turn back to the doctor. "Is he right?"

Pack ostracization.

He hesitates. "I... believe so. Quite a severe case."

Being part of a pack, but permanently on the outside, looking in. For anyone, it would be difficult, but for an omega, it's emotional abuse on a scale I can't think about, because if I do, if my fucking scent-matched mate has been subjected to that—

Forget Wilder. I'll tear this whole damn house apart.

No.

I'll tear *them* apart. Whichever assholes had a treasure like Fallon and let her fucking *wilt*.

The roar rips from my throat as my knees slam into the floor. I slam my hands over my face, trying to keep myself together.

Wilder. I have to keep myself together, to keep him together.

Rowan throws himself down, his hands on my face and his voice urgent. "We're going to her now, Fox. She's going to be fine. Okay? We're her pack. Her real pack. You, Wilder, Zeke, you're her mates. Not... *them*, whoever they are. We're going to be everything she needs, and she's *never* going to feel that way again."

"I don't know," Teddy interjects. He sounds tearful. "I don't know who they are. Fox, I'm *sorry*. She didn't want me to tell you, not yet, and I couldn't break her trust like that. I didn't realize it was this bad."

I can't respond. The agony in my chest spreads.

My mate has been hurting for... a long time. In the same city. Within the same fucking radius. And I had *no* idea.

Teddy whimpers, a matching echo of his agony reaching me through the bond. "Fox, *please*."

I can't breathe. But I hold out my arm as he dives for me, his tears soaking into my shirt. Teddy babbles apologies into my neck, the devastation in his voice clear. "What do we do?"

"Wilder," I rasp. "Where is he?"

Rowan stiffens. "He was here—,"

I explode into motion past them. Taking the stairs three at a time, I race up them, following the scent of my damn *mate*.

I slide to a stop in the doorway of Zeke's bedroom.

Fallon is asleep. She's curled up against Zeke's chest, his arms wrapped around her. He holds a finger to his lips in a silent message, and I nod.

This room is *soaked* with her scent.

Wilder... Wilder is pressed against Fallon's back, his hand tangled in her hair and his body curved protectively over hers, his arm banded over her waist.

And the eyes that gleam at me... there's nothing of Wilder in them at all.

42

WILDER

M^{ate}.

43

FALLON

The room is dark when I wake up. Blinking, I huddle into the warmth of the alphas on either side of me, breathing deeply and letting the comfort soak into my aching muscles.

Wait—

I almost catapult out of bed – or I would, if a heavy band of muscle didn't yank me back down. I'm rolled onto my back, and the breath rushes out of my lungs as I stare up into the furious face of an alpha.

It's not fear that fills me as my eyes widen.

I lick my lips, and he follows the movement with an almost lupine gaze. My voice is a whisper. "Wilder?"

My breath catches when he lowers his face. The light brown stubble on his chin scrapes my neck as he nuzzles into me, his breath hot against my skin.

When I shiver, he follows it up with a rasping lick, directly over my pulse.

My body turns into flames. I slam my legs together as my underwear dampens, my back arching lightly.

The alpha above me smiles. But I can't see Wilder there at all as he inhales deeply. A rumbling sound echoes around us.

Approval.

"Fallon?"

I turn my head to the side at the panicked whisper, earning a displeased growl from not-Wilder. Zeke's eyes are wide. "Sweetheart. Be *very* careful. Wilder's not thinking clearly right now."

My brows crease. "He's not going to hurt me."

I don't know how I can sense it, but I can. Zeke murmurs a low curse, but he doesn't stop me as I lift my fingers up to Wilder's face. His eyes almost close as I stroke my fingers over his cheek, but I can still see the gleam there. I slide them into his hair, stroking him carefully and listening to the low purr that sounds in his throat.

"Hey," I whisper. "Um. I need Wilder back for a second. Please."

His lips peel back in a silent snarl, eyes opening wider. Vehement disagreement.

He shifts, covering me a little more as his nose drags across my cheek.

Carefully, I wrap my arms around him. Press my face into the crook of his neck, and I take a breath.

Wilder's scent is earthy. Resinous. A little like vanilla and toffee, but with a musky scent beneath.

Myrrh.

And as I breathe him in, letting his scent soak into me, Wilder whines.

And I know.

"Mate," I whisper. Wilder stiffens. Beside me, Zeke does too.

They're my mates.

The awareness trickles into me. Not in a bolt of lightning. But in a steady, solid reassurance that fills up my lungs with air and causes tears to prick at my eyes. A huffing noise comes from Wilder as he presses his lips to the tear that escapes.

My face crumples.

And I throw my arms around his neck, holding onto him. "I'm sorry. I'm sorry it took me a while."

My emotions battle inside my chest. There's fear, fear of the darkness lingering around us and what that means. But there's joy, too. Such overwhelming, oxygen-stealing *joy* that I don't even know what to do with it, except to hold onto Wilder and sob into his neck.

Because there's a space for me here, with them.

Something shifts, the frantic energy in the air around us fading. Wilder rolls until I'm on top of him, his arms wrapped around me. "Mate."

And it's hoarse, and ragged, and a plea. "*Mate.*"

And when I look up, I know it's the real Wilder staring back at me. He shudders when I reach up and brush my thumb over his lip.

"Yes," I whisper. My smile grows, from a small, fragile thing to a beam. "*Yes.*"

I press my cheek against his chest and look at Zeke, drinking him in.

My mate, too.

His green eyes are glistening. "Hey there. You feeling better?"

He carried me here. Zeke *ran* with me, ran like his heart was going to break as he raced to get me where I would feel safe.

"Thanks to you," I murmur. Feeling shy, I half reach out my hand. But he gently snags it, presses it to his heart.

I can feel the thump of his heartbeat beneath his chest. Strong, steady. Sure.

Curling my fingers over it, I smile at him. "Good job."

"You scared me." He swallows.

I scared *him*. This alpha, the biggest I've ever seen, who cradled me so carefully.

My heart feels as though it might burst.

"*Mate*," I whisper. Testing it out.

Zeke suddenly looks unsteady. "Not until you're ready. I can wait, Fallon. I don't want to rush you—,"

His words cut off as I shift, Wilder reluctantly releasing me.

I press my lips carefully against Zeke's. I want to test this too. His lips are warm beneath mine, exquisitely soft. They part slightly, but otherwise, he stays frozen.

And I smile against my stunned mate's mouth. "You can kiss me back, you know."

He's careful. Zeke slides his hand into my hair, reverence in his every movement as he takes over, tasting me. Learning me, exploring my mouth as if he'll never forget this first time.

This is what it's supposed to be like.

This is what it should always be like.

I'm breathing a little heavier when I pull away, moisture swimming in my eyes. The darkness threatens to press in, and I blink.

"I... I have to go."

Two matching growls are my only response.

And a snarl, as the door flies open. I lock eyes with my third, scent-matched mate, my gaze widening as he storms across the room.

And Fox is *furious*.

"Over my dead body are you going *back there*."

44

— · —

Fox

I have always had the most control in this pack.

Always.

But now I can feel it fraying, strands falling away from my grasping hands like trying to hold onto fucking air, as my small, perfect, petrifyingly fragile mate faces off with me in the middle of our living room.

It's not the meeting I always imagined.

Teddy and Rowan are curled up against each other on the sofa opposite, mouths agog as they watch Fallon cross her arms. "I have to go back, Fox."

My mate is magnificent.

If I wasn't so scared, I'd be in awe of the way she doesn't back away. Her head is tilted to display her neck, her eyes down, but she doesn't back off, doesn't shy away from the anger filling my every muscle.

Because she knows I'll never hurt her.

Or because she's used to dealing with worse situations.

That thought sends fury snaking down my spine in a red-hot burst of fire.

Fallon knows we're her scent-matched mates now. I can almost see that knowledge wrapped around her, in the way she sneaks glances at Zeke and Wilder, both leaning against the wall. I could see it in the way she looked at me when I stormed in, no fear in those amber eyes as I started yelling.

Even Wilder is more fucking chill than I am. He doesn't look happy – far fucking from it – but his eyes are soft on our mate, drinking her in with growing admiration that wars with fear.

That knowledge is the sole saving grace keeping me from a full-blown alpha fucking *tantrum* as I cross my hands behind my back to stop myself reaching for her. "But *why*?"

She shifts. "I need to get something."

I can't stop myself anymore. My hands grip her arms, gentle, but I don't give her a choice as I slide them up until I can cup her cheeks.

"We can buy you whatever you need," I breathe. "You have full access to all of the accounts, Fallon. Empty them, if you want. You can fill this whole house with anything you want. But you're not going back there."

It's killing me, that steadiness in her eyes as she slowly lifts her hands to cup mine. Still a little hesitant. Just the soft touch of her hands has me ready to drop at her knees and beg. "*Please.*"

She's not going to change her mind.

And I can't – won't – force her to stay. A line so absolute in my mind that I'd slit my own throat before crossing it.

I will never force my will on an omega. Not unless we're in a consensual situation, or they're on the verge of death.

My lips press together, considering.

"Fox," Teddy says softly. "This is not the time."

"They've never hurt me physically," Fallon says again. She's said it over and over again for more than an hour as we've stood here and argued, as if the word on the end of that sentence makes a single fucking iota of difference. She swallows. "It's not like that."

I have to close my eyes. I can't look at the expression in her eyes anymore.

"Tell me," I say roughly. I keep hold of her hands, gripping them like a lifeline I desperately need. "If they have never hurt you, Fallon... why do you look so *scared*?"

Because she's radiating with it, every time she mentions her home. She freezes.

My voice drops. "How they hurt you... I care about that. And I want to know every part of it, Fallon, but it doesn't matter to me nearly as much as the fact that they hurt you in the first place. Emotionally. Mentally. However they fucking hurt you, it doesn't matter. Only that they *did*."

Sticks and stones don't break my bones, but words will never hurt me.
They had a bad day.
It was a one-off.
Bullshit. All of it.

She doesn't say anything, and I dare to hope that I'm getting through.

"Pack ostracization takes place over *years*." It still guts me to even say the words, but I force them out. Trying to get through to her. "That is not nothing, Fallon. We don't even know what effect that will have on you going forward. And I know that this scent-match is new and we have a lot to work through, but believe me when I say that the thought of letting you walk out of here and back there is *ripping me apart*."

Fallon stares at me, pain creasing her face.

"One night," she whispers. "There won't be an argument, Fox. I'll go home and go to bed. We don't even share a bedroom. And tomorrow, when they go to work, I'll get what I need and walk out of there."

Small hands on my chest. "I will come... *home*. And I promise that I won't leave again, but I can't leave this behind."

Home.

Her voice stutters over the word as if it doesn't quite fit yet.

It will.

Teddy shifts. "It's the book, isn't it?"

We all stop to look at him. Fallon presses her lips together, but she nods. "I can't leave it behind. It's the *only* thing I care about, Fox. It's irreplaceable."

I suck in a breath. "Whatever book it is, I will—,"

"My dad gave me this book." She beseeches me with her eyes. "It's the only thing I have left of them. I don't have anything else. Not even a photo. I cannot lose it."

Rowan starts to frown, but he doesn't say anything as Teddy murmurs something in his ear. He nods.

I'm flagging. Turning, I glare at Zeke and Wilder. "Well?"

Wilder hesitates. He looks as if he still doesn't believe she's real. "Fallon... I agree with Fox. But this isn't a dictatorship. It's your choice."

Damn him for agreeing with me. "Zeke?"

Zeke crosses his arms. He pins his gaze on Fallon, eyes unrelenting. "I'll drive you to the house. And I'll wait outside. All night, until the morning when you'll get back into my car and I'll take you away from there with anything you want to bring. If you need help, you flick a light switch on and off and I'll smash through that door so fast they won't even see me coming."

He takes a breath. "But I'd prefer to go now and just get it for you. I don't give a fuck about whoever's in there."

"Wow." Teddy's stunned whisper drops into the silence. "Mated, grumpy Zeke is *sexy*."

"*Teddy*," I growl. But... I consider it. I still hate the idea, but—

"I can cope with that," I say begrudgingly. "We can all go."

"Just Zeke," Fallon whispers. She looks up at me as hurt flickers in my chest. "Not because of – just in case. Please."

Her eyes travel to Teddy. Then Rowan. They flicker to Wilder next.

My heart constricts. She's worried – about *us*?

"How many are there?" I ask roughly. She holds up three fingers, and Zeke nods.

He'd annihilate three alphas if he had to. Particularly the type of alphas who get their kicks from tormenting an omega.

My temper threatens again, and I have to turn away from her pleading expression. If I don't, I might steal her away and lock her in a room until I know she's safe.

And that's something I refuse to do.

"Nobody will ever hurt you again," I say quietly. "Including me. So if you need to go, go. But we'll be ready to get you out."

A small hand slips into mine, and squeezes. She's smiling at me, uncertain but a small glow about her. "Thank you."

"What did I say?" I squeeze back. "Never thank me. I never want you to feel grateful to me, Fallon."

Her eyes soften. "Then what do you want?"

Everything else.

I expect her to go, but my mate shocks me. She takes a step away before inhaling and spinning back around.

She hits my middle like a feather, almost bouncing off before I grab her to keep her steady. Her arms wrap around me tightly. "I won't be long. And when we get back – we'll talk."

She sighs when I drop my cheek to her head. I'm so damn tempted to scent-mark her, but I hold back.

I don't want them to scent it on her. And once I start, I won't be able to stop. "Try not to... to let them get close. They might scent us."

My eyes lift to Zeke's, and he nods at me.

He'll take care of our mate.

But as she walks away from me, it feels like she's tearing my heart out.

45

ZEKE

I turn off the engine where Fallon directs me. My truck is parked up the street, but my eyes land on the house she points out.

It looks nondescript. A little shabby, even. As though nobody bothered to spend any money on the outside. I'm desperate to know what the inside looks like, to imagine how Fallon spent her days before she met us, but I swallow that urge.

"You can still change your mind." My tone is a plea as I turn to my mate. She's staring out of the window, that fucking dress that feels like a symbol of everything wrong with her world covered up with one of my hoodies.

She looks small, and terrifyingly breakable. But her spine is like steel as she casts me a smile. "They don't scare me. Not anymore."

Nodding, I glance at the house again. Curiosity prickles at me. "Who are they? What do they do?"

Fallon shakes her head. "Later. I – I need to get inside. They'll already have questions."

My lips press together at that. The time we spent arguing – every minute made it worse for her. None of us realized she had to be home by a set time until she confessed it to me a few minutes ago. "I can walk up there with you right now. They won't say a single damn thing to me, sweetheart."

"No," she whispers. "I don't want an argument, Zeke. I don't want to see that, or hear that. It's one more night sleeping under that roof, and I'll never see them again. I can slip away without any arguments, and I'll leave them a note to tell them."

Her voice shakes.

"And you're... okay with that?" I keep my voice as gentle as I can. She wouldn't be the first person to want to stay in a situation that causes her harm, as awful as that truth is. Not that I would ever let that happen to Fallon, but it's worth broaching now.

"Yes." Her eyes are shining. "I didn't expect any of this, you know. I sat in that restaurant yesterday, and I – I wished you were mine. That I could be part of something, instead of always on the outside."

My heart hurts. "You're going to be the center of our world, Fallon Matthews. I promise."

"Don't make me cry," she breathes. Her fingers brush my cheek. "I'll see you tomorrow morning. You don't need to wait."

"I will be right here," I rumble. "Where's your room?"

"On the other side, facing the back."

Damn. "Remember what I said. Get to a room on this side and flick the lights on and off. But either way, I'm coming through that door tomorrow morning if you don't come out."

She nods. Points. "That corner is the kitchen. Living room on the other corner and R— *one* of their rooms in the middle."

My muscles lock into stone, my hands clamped around the wheel.

"I have my own bedroom," she says gently. "That's never been something they've used against me. They've never hurt me that way."

"Then why the heat-blockers?"

Her face flushes. "I never wanted them near me during my heat. I fought them the first time they tried. Apparently, I nearly lost my mind. I don't know why. They began getting me the medication after that. It wasn't forced on me."

I can't hear anymore. "Go now. We're losing time."

My voice is guttural. "If you don't come out, I'm coming in. Okay?"

She takes a breath. "I know. I trust you."

Such a simple gift, handed over as if she doesn't have every reason never to trust an alpha again. But she's gone before I can respond around the tightness gripping my throat, the faintest scent of orange blossom and my folded hoodie on the side the only sign she was here at all.

I watch as Fallon moves down the sidewalk. She doesn't look back.

I wonder if she's aware of how her shoulders tighten, how her arms lower to grip her body like protective armor.

The steering wheel cracks under my grip.

My mate disappears inside that dilapidated house.

And all I can do is *wait*.

46

FALLON

The door is unlocked.

They never forget to lock it behind them. *Ever.*

And as my hand touches the brass handle, it feels as though someone's thrown a cold bucket of water over me, submerging the warmth I've felt today and burying me beneath the coldness that emanates from beyond the door as I push it open.

My pulse slows to a crawl as I step through.

No use in avoiding it.

Zeke is outside. He'll be here in a moment.

The thought should reassure me, and it does – *it does*. But Zeke is one alpha, against three. And the thought of him getting hurt... it tightens my lungs until I think I might pass out.

I've held on for seven years.

I only have to hold on until tomorrow.

And my mates are waiting for me.

I pause for a second, letting that thought soak in, snatching the strength it provides.

I can do this.

They're waiting in the kitchen, seated around the table. Several empty bottles litter the counter, but there's no—

No dinner on the table.

I stop in the doorway. And Ellis smiles at me. A small, curved twist in his lips that makes me take a step backward.

Coming home at this hour is bad enough.

But... the grocery money.

The money Shaun leaves me every morning, just enough and never too much, is tucked away in my desk at work.

And in the pandemonium of today, I completely forgot about it.

"Not so fast." Rory has his fingers around my wrist. He tightens his grip, dragging me forward. "Where the hell have you *been*, Fallon?"

Anger threads his words. "I was—,"

"No dinner on the table," Ellis remarks silkily. He tips his bottle to me. "No groceries in the cupboard. You must have had *quite* the adventure today, Fallon. Why don't you tell us about it? We have nothing better to do than sit here and wait for *you*, after all."

My cheeks feel hot as Rory tugs me into a seat. He doesn't sit. Instead, his hands land on my shoulders, gripping me. "Rory, that hurts—,"

"Where have you been?" He *roars* it, directly into my ear. I slam my hand over it and flinch away, but his nails dig into my shoulders and drag me back until my back slams against the chair, almost winding me.

"I—," I fight to take a breath. "I was—,"

"Don't bother," Shaun says quietly. Ellis shoots him a sharp look, but he ignores it. "We know where you were."

Any wind is sucked directly out of my sails. I feel my skin pale, grow clammy. "What?"

In response, Shaun slides his phone across the table. "Quite the scene from our fellow publishers today. Maybe you could fill in the gaps."

I stare down at the video. My heart jumps into my throat and stays there.

Oh, Zeke.

His face desperate, Zeke bursts out of the Ink & Quill entrance. He's cradling my body in his arms, people stopping to stare. He doesn't pay them any attention before he bursts into a run, disappearing out of view.

"Watch," Rory says tightly. When I try to look at him, he grabs my chin, dragging it back to the video. I watch as Wilder follows him out a few seconds later. He lifts his phone to his ear, his fingers running through his hair before he takes off after Zeke.

My eyes close as the video cuts off.

"I don't think any lie you could tell could possibly be as interesting as *that*," Ellis says coolly. His eyes glitter with delight. "But feel free to try."

"You're a liar, Fallon." Rory's fingers dig in tighter. "All this time we've looked after you. And this is how you repay us—,"

"Looked *after* me?" I suck in a breath, my fingers clenching on the table. "Is that what you call it?"

Everyone stills. Even Rory, his disbelief tainting the air.

"Why do you have such a nice office?" I demand.

I can't look at them. Can't meet their eyes. But I pin my gaze on the table, and I let it all out. All of the questions burning inside my chest.

"Why do we never have any money, but you have your name in solid gold letters on the wall of your fancy building? Why do I count pennies when Wordsmith is one of the biggest publishing companies in the *country*? Where did the money for that even come from? Because you didn't have any money when I first met you."

But I did.

I did.

And I was an idiot; a blind, grieving idiot for far too long. I let my light go out, lost myself in the numbness and let them take it all.

I let them take *me*.

"What happened to my house?" I keep going, when they don't say anything. The heat of my anger scorches through the cold, burning it away and leaving fire in its wake. "My parent's house? My things? My bank account? My identification? My *life*?"

I'm breathing faster now. "You stole it. You stole my identity. My family's legacy. You *stole* it."

"We didn't steal it." Rory's voice is hoarse. "Fallon. How could you think—,"

"Then explain it." My voice is rising. "Tell me how you did it. Because for the life of me, I don't understand. But then again, I'm just a useless, ugly, frigid excuse for an omega. Aren't I? Maybe I need another *lesson*."

"You little—," Ellis stands, his face purpling. "You haven't seen a damn lesson yet."

Shaun grabs his shoulder. "Sit the fuck down, Ellis. Jesus."

Ellis sits. And Shaun disappears. I can feel Rory's stare burning into the back of my head, but I stay silent until Shaun returns.

He slams a document down in front of me. "That's a signed Power of Attorney form, Fallon. Tell me – whose signature is that?"

The rock in my stomach becomes heavier as I stare at the paper.

At *my* signature. "I don't remember—,"

"You signed it the day after your parent's funeral," Rory says softly. Even his touch softens, his fingers rubbing at my shoulders. "You were so overwhelmed, Fallon. You begged us to help you. So we did."

I don't remember begging them for anything. And I certainly don't remember *this*.

"We bought you a house." Ellis smirks. "We made sure you were taken care of. And if we used some of those funds to keep you warm and fed, then you'll find that legally, we've done *nothing* wrong. Not in the eyes of the law. Because you're not capable of making these decisions. So we make them for you."

I don't say anything.

Not for a long time.

"Now that's out of the way," Ellis says finally. He taps the darkened screen of Shaun's phone. "What's this?"

Rory tenses again.

I press my lips together, and I say nothing.

"Tell us." And at Ellis's bark, my spine locks into place.

I can't stop the words. Ellis's bark tears them from me, pulls them out into the heavy space between us. "They're my... scent-matches."

I'm not sure if I even want to hide this from them now. I lift up my chin. "And they're better alphas than any of you will *ever* be."

The silence stretches on. Finally, Ellis shrugs. "Interesting. But ultimately, it doesn't matter."

I tense as he and Rory exchange looks over my head. "I'm leaving. You can't stop me."

"But we can." Rory's hand slides to my neck, clamps down on it. "We have a signed document that says we have the ultimate say over your welfare, Fallon. You're not going anywhere."

Panic floods my system. "You can't *do* that—,"

"Yes, we can." Rory rips me from the chair. I struggle against him as he keeps a tight hold on my neck, pulling me across the kitchen and into the hall.

My hand stretches out, reaching for the kitchen light switch, brushes it—

Ellis gets in my way. "We've decided that you're a little out of control, Fallon."

"A bonding mark," Rory says tightly. "Your heat is coming soon. As soon as it does, I'm putting my teeth in your neck and an end to this. With a mark and a Power of Attorney, you won't be going anywhere."

But Shaun—

I don't say anything. I don't tell them that he already gave me the medication to stop my heat. I can't see Shaun at all.

Instead, I fight. My nails rip into Rory's wrist, his face as he pulls me down to my shitty excuse for a nest. He's breathing heavily as he shoves me through the door, and I land on the mattress. "You'll be staying in here until your heat hits. However long that is."

I stare up at him wildly. "You're insane if you think I won't fight this. I'm done, Rory. I want to leave. Now."

He shakes his head, a sad smile appearing on his face. "I don't know where this attitude has come from. But that won't be happening. We're going to get past this, Fallon. You'll see."

Ellis appears next to him, and my eyes drop at what he holds in his hands. He turns it over in his hands, inspecting it with a sneer.

My single copy of *The Light in Us*.

I inhale raggedly. Slowly, my hands raise. "I'm sorry. I'm so sorry – *wait—*,"

Oh god, oh god—

I lunge for my father's book.

"*Get back.*"

My body yanks back, my knees landing with a bang at the order.

"I don't enjoy this," Ellis says evenly. "But you have to learn that actions have consequences, Fallon. *Watch.*"

He puts his hand to the cover of *The Light in Us*.

And he tears it from the binding.

I would have chosen a knife. It would have been cleaner than the agony that tears into my chest as I watch Shaun rip my father's book to pieces.

Page by page. He rips them out, crumpling them and tossing them into the room around me.

And he makes me watch every single one.

I can't see by the time he throws the rest of it in. The tears have blinded me as I rock back and forth.

"There," he says cruelly. "At least you have something to read while you're in here. If you can fit the pages back together, that is."

I reach for the page closest to me, smoothing it out with trembling fingers.

For Fallon,
My unofficial editor and my brightest light.
This book is what it is because of you.
May you always shine.

I grip onto that page tightly.

And I find the words buried deep in my chest, pulling them out into the light. "You're frightened. *Weak*."

Ellis snorts. "How exactly do you work that out?"

"Because," I stare down at my father's words. "Any decent being would never have done this. After all you've taken from me, you decided to take this too. Because you're *scared*, Ellis. You're scared that you can't control me anymore. And you're right."

My eyes are dry. Gritty, but dry as I pull myself to my feet. "My mates – my *real* mates - are going to rip you apart. One day soon, I'm going to watch you learn your own lesson. Because actions *do* have consequences, and when you face yours, I'm going to be watching."

"They're not your mates," Rory snaps savagely. "You made a mistake, Fallon."

"Yes, I did." I snap right back at him. "You're right."

And I put every ounce of fear, anger and pain that these alphas have caused me into my next words until I'm screaming them. "Letting you into my life was the worst mistake I ever made. But I'll never make it again. Now get the *hell* out of my fucking awful excuse for a nest, since *I paid for it*. You manipulative, abusive, weak, *thieving* excuse for alphas."

Rory stumbles back. "I don't even recognise you right now—,"

"*Because you never knew me!*" They saw a shy, nervous omega in a new environment. And then, when I was grief-stricken and terrified, they manipulated me into doing what they wanted.

But I'm not that omega anymore.

I hold onto my flickering light as tightly as I can.

I'm sorry it took me so long to find it again, dad.

But I've found it now, and I have no intention of letting it go out. "*Get out!*"

I yank off my shoe and fling it at them. Ellis slams the door shut, and my shoe bounces off it uselessly. I tug the other one off as well, just to hear the satisfying *clunk* as it hits the doors.

I wish it was their heads.

But I made my point. Seven years too late, maybe, but still.

I wait until my breathing slows before I start to gather up the torn pages. I carefully shuffle them into a pile, settling back against the wall.

My heart hurts as I take in the ripped, jagged edges. But I sort through them anyway, carefully putting them back in order of the numbers in the corner of each page beneath the bright light.

And I wait for my mate.

He's gonna lose his shit.

47

— ·· —

ZEKE

"Anything?"

"No," I mutter. "For the sixth time, *no*."

The sixth time this hour.

I can hear Teddy's feet treading a hole into the carpet at home. "You haven't seen anything at all?"

"Teddy, it's the middle of the night." I don't move my eyes away from those windows. "Hopefully she's in bed and everything is fine. You should get some sleep too."

That's what she wanted. But the more I stare at that house, the more my chest feels tight. The harder it is not to go in there and carry her out.

He sucks in a breath. "As if I'm going to sleep when Fallon is there. I haven't slept for two damn *days*, Zeke."

I can feel how hard the guilt is hitting him, for not telling us sooner. "I—,"

My passenger door opens, and my hand slams out as a figure slips inside. I pull my punch back just in time. "Fucking hell, I nearly took your head off."

Fox pushes back the hood of his navy sweatshirt and hands me a coffee. "We can both pretend that's true if it makes you feel better."

"Oh good," Teddy says in my ear. "You got my package. Careful, he bites."

"Teddy sent you?" I ask as he ends the call.

"It was a mutual decision. Wild is with them." Fox leans forward. "Which one is hers? Have you seen anything?"

Silently, I point. "Nothing. Which is supposed to be a good sign."

Fox nods. And then he settles back, his arms crossed.

The hours crawl by. Neither of us talk.

It's still dark out when a light flips on in the kitchen, filtering through the closed blinds. We both stiffen, waiting.

But it doesn't flicker.

My heartbeat thumps in my ears. "Good sign, right?"

My pack leader says nothing. We can't see anything else. The blinds are too thick for us to see any silhouettes.

Another hour passes. The sunrise begins to crest over the trees, spilling light over the street in front of us.

And then the door opens.

We watch as a red-haired alpha steps out. He stops, turning to say something over his shoulder, tugging at the sleeve of his suit.

Frowning, I stare at the alpha who follows him. Broad, stocky, blonde-haired. The red-haired alpha is laughing, clapping him on the shoulder.

Neither of us say anything.

The third and final alpha is tall. Dark-haired. He pauses on the doorstep, looking over his shoulder. He says something to the blonde alpha, who shakes his head, gesturing at him in a clear *hurry up* motion.

Fox and I watch in silence as they walk off down the street.

"Was that—,"

"Wordsmith," Fox's voice is like stone. "Fucking *Wordsmith*."

The Smith pack. Our closest competitors. The assholes who set Teddy up and bully the omega authors on their roster into signing ridiculous contracts that they can't escape from.

My hand moves to the door, waiting for them to turn the corner.

And then we're out. Our feet thud down the quiet road as we race to Fallon's house, jumping up the steps. I turn to check behind us as Fox pounds on the door. "*Fallon!*"

But there's no answer.

Fox doesn't wait. Doesn't hesitate. He lifts his boot and kicks the door open, slamming into it as it flies off the hinges with a crash of splinters and wood.

"Fucking Wordsmith."

His voice is full of anger and disgust as we move inside slowly.

Fallon's home is... empty. There's no photographs, no knick-knacks.

Several coats are hanging up in the small hallway.

My mate doesn't have a coat, but these assholes have coats to spare.

I start building up a picture of her life, and every piece feels like a rock settling on my chest, cutting off my breathing. "Fallon!"

I call her name again, echoed by Fox as we move through. A few empty beer bottles are stacked on the side, but the pristine white kitchen is otherwise empty.

There's no color here. No vibrancy. No *life*.

I'm here, baby. Where are you?

We walk silently down the hall, pushing open doors. The three alphas each have their own room, easily identifiable by the scents that spill through the doors. Their possessions litter the spaces, comfortable-looking beds and personal items dotted around.

"Zeke." There's no expression on Fox's face at first glance. He disappears inside a room, and I hear the furious sound of him swearing. "Do you see what I see?"

I pause in the doorway.

Our mate's scent soaks the room. There's a depth to it that tells me that this is *her* bedroom, layers built over time.

"Did we miss her?" Fox mutters. He spins, as if he missed something the first time.

I don't say anything. I can't.

If I open my mouth, I might lose it.

Fox shifts past me. I hear him moving down the hall, but I can't move.

The bed is small, tucked into the corner of the room. Slowly, I move toward it. My fingers graze the bedding.

Where are the blankets? The pillows?

Only a single, thin comforter sits on top of the bedding.

Jaw clenching, I move over to her dressing table, sending a silent apology for going through her things before I yank it open.

It's empty. There's a hairbrush. Some deodorant, and a few Kirby grips for her hair.

Every drawer is the same.

There is nothing to suggest an omega lives in this room.

I'm breathing faster now. Fox appears in the doorway as I rip open the doors to her small closet. It's fucking *tiny*, far too small for an omega. This wouldn't even hold Teddy's *belts*.

We both stare in.

"Empty," I say flatly. The black dress we've seen her in is hanging up on the side of the closet, but there's nothing else.

Fox reaches inside, crouching as he picks something up. When he stands, he holds out the torn piece of material. From a blouse, maybe.

His voice is deeper than I've ever heard it, a molten anger leaking from every pore that floods the air around us. "Find her."

I'm praying as we spread out again. That she doesn't use that room much. That everything is in her nest.

She wouldn't be the first omega to forgo a bedroom altogether, or to keep one just in case.

But I know. I know that's not what we're going to find.

When we find the locked room, I'm the first one to slam my foot into the door. This one is tougher than the entrance. *Reinforced.*

And it locks from the outside.

Fox grabs my shoulder, but I shake him off and I *go* for that fucking door, rage a snarl in my throat. He pushes me to the side, and then we're both hitting it with the force of two furious fucking alphas scared for their mate.

My mate is on the other side. And when I get in there, I'm taking her away from this horrible, cold place and we will not look back.

Never again, I vow. She's never going to feel like this ever again.

Never again.

48

FALLON

I'm waiting for them.

They burst through the door in a tangle of scent and anger. It flows around me, and I inhale sharply, my back pressing against the far wall as they stop to look around.

Zeke recovers first. "Fallon."

I offer him a weak smile as he crosses the room and drops to his knees in front of me.

"Are you hurt?" he demands. Zeke's hands land on my shoulders, gently checking me over. "If they touched you—,"

"They didn't." I glance around him at Fox. Fox's eyes are darker today, a violent shade of purple that swirls with his anger as he stares at the shelves. "I'm fine, I promise. I knew you'd come for me."

Zeke inhales. And then he gently urges me into him until he can wrap his arms around me. I sink into his chest, my fingers gripping his sweatshirt.

"I don't think I'll ever get used to this," I whisper.

It's still new. A weird blend of the familiar and the very *un*familiar. As if I should know every part of him, but I'm still learning. Playing catch-up with the scent-matching.

"You will," he says gruffly. He runs his hand over my hair. "God. This fucking house."

I duck my head at that, but he lifts my chin. "You have *nothing* to be ashamed of."

"Fallon." Fox says my name slowly. "Tell me this isn't your *nest*."

"Um." Swallowing, I pull back from Zeke and go for my hair, fiddling with it. "Technically, but I've never—,"

Fox storms over to the shelves. Inspecting them as if something might magically appear on the empty strips of wood. "It's empty. There's nothing in here, Fallon."

I start chewing on my lip. "Yes."

"Where do you nest, then?" Zeke asks me. He glances around him, taking in the wide, open space, the bright light above our heads. "Nothing about this nest is suitable, love. And we saw your bedroom."

Oh. I half-shrug. "I... I learned to manage without it."

They both pause.

"What?" Fox comes to me then. He crouches in front of me, cupping my face. "What does that mean? Can you explain it to me?"

"I...," I wet my lips.

Why do I feel so *ashamed*? "I've never had a proper heat. I kept pushing them back. And then... I just stopped feeling the urge, eventually. It's fine. Really. Can we go, please?"

"This is not fine." Fox doesn't let me look away. "Listen to me, Fallon. None of this is fine. *Nothing* in this house is okay. So we'll take you home, and we'll go from there. I want to get you out of here as quickly as possible. How does that sound?"

"Okay," I whisper. I shiver again, and Fox is immediately ripping off his hoodie and bundling it over my head.

"We'll get you some new things too. A damn coat, for starters."

I give in to the urge to rub my face against the soft, warm material. I think I'd prefer to stay in their clothes.

When I finally emerge, Zeke is frozen.

His voice is a rumble as I follow his gaze. "Tell me they didn't do that, Fallon."

I swallow. Harder, this time.

I didn't think I had any tears left. The burst of strength I found last night dissolved into never-ending sobs as I tried to piece *The Light in Us* back together.

But at the horror in their faces, I find some more. My face drops into my hands. "I tried to fix it."

But Fox is there. He scoops me up, pulling me close and letting me bury my face in him. I breathe him in, the scent so familiar to that of my ruined book that I only cry harder.

"We'll fix this." I can feel his heartbeat thundering against my ear. "I promise you, Fallon. I'm going to fix this."

And as much as I believe he's going to try, it doesn't lessen the pain inside my chest. "I don't need to take anything else. That was it."

Fox was right. I shouldn't have come back.

"You don't *have* anything else." Zeke follows us, *The Light in Us* cradled gently in his hands. "But that's going to change."

49

WILDER

Teddy is snoring lightly, his face buried in my arm.

And on my other side, Rowan has his head tipped back. His glasses threaten to slip off his face, his laptop still glowing in front of him with the research he spent the whole night working on. He doesn't move when I shift, carefully lifting the laptop away and replacing it with a blanket from the back of the couch.

Pack.

I *need* my pack, need them more than most. They're my anchor, my family, what stops me from tipping over into that darkness *all* of the time, instead of just when it gets too much.

I've spent more time feral in the last week than I have in the past *year*.

My eyes don't move from the door. I'm waiting for her to come home, tension coiled in every muscle.

My mate. A mate that I've spent very little time with, thanks to the other side of my sparkling personality.

Teddy shifts beside me. His words are sleepy. "They're not back?"

"Not yet." I wrap my arm around him, rub it gently. "Go back to sleep, Teddy bear."

He doesn't, though, He curls his legs up and we both wait together. "So, did Fallon really like the Wild Side?"

I slant him a narrow-eyed look. "I don't know. But she didn't run away screaming."

I'm not entirely sure what happened. I'm semi-aware of what's happening when the feral part of me takes over, but it's more of a foggy day than clear sunshine.

Although... I could scent her. Something that happened while I was out of it made my mate *slick*. I can still almost taste her on my tongue, a memory that goes straight to my knot.

My breathing starts to deepen, darkness creeping in.

No. Back the hell off. She's both of ours, asshole.

Shit. If I start losing control when all I'm doing is sitting around, I'm in a heap of fucking trouble.

"Jesus, Wild." Teddy jerks upright. He sounds mortified. "Please tell me that's not for me. I know I'm hot, and we'd do great things together, but I'm a one-alpha, one-beta omega."

I spring upright as if my ass is on fire. Rowan jerks awake as I skitter across the room, cupping my cock over my jeans. My cheeks are burning. "Of course it's not for you!"

"Awh," Teddy offers me a shit-eating grin. "Is it for Fallon? That's kind of adorable. A *little* teen-boy coded, but cute."

"Can we please stop talking about this?" I growl, willing my erection to deflate as quickly as my ego. "And if we could stop using the word *little* to talk about my cock, I'd very much appreciate it."

"I'm confused." Rowan stretches, yawning. "Since when does Wilder have a little cock? I always assumed you had the goods, Wild. Feral alpha, feral cock. All that jazz."

"I do not have a little cock!" I bellow. "Don't put that shit out into the atmosphere. It's bad juju!"

They both start snickering.

"Stop it," I snap. "My cock is completely normal-sized. Not too big. Not too small. Just right."

Teddy nudges Rowan. "You be Daddy Bear, and I'll be Mommy Bear. Wild is *clearly* Baby Bear."

They both collapse into laughter.

"Honestly," I mutter. But Teddy is eyeing me even as he grips his stomach, and I pause, suspicion creeping in.

The little shit winks at me. "Has he gone now?"

Sneaky, *sneaky* omega. My mind is clear, my fading embarrassment the only unwelcome presence. "I love you, Ted."

He sighs happily. "I know you do. Now please stop poking us in the eye with that damn thing and go and think filthy thoughts about your mate somewhere else."

Rowan's cheeks pink, and Teddy straightens, his mouth hanging open. "*Rowan Quill*. Have you been thinking filthy thoughts about Wilder's mate too? Without me?"

"Teddy," I snap. But my eyes slide back to Rowan. He doesn't look at me, grabbing for his laptop like it's a security blanket. "Ro?"

He shifts, the color spreading down his neck. "It's only because... I'm picking up echoes from Fox. That's it."

"You sure about that?" I ask, keeping my words soft. "Because you know it doesn't matter within the pack."

Our packs are an extension of us. It wouldn't bother any of us if Fallon chose to be with Rowan or Teddy too. Or both.

Whatever she's comfortable with.

Teddy sighs. "She fits under my arm."

We both turn to him, confused, and he shrugs. "I've always fitted under your arm. Or Fox's. Or Zeke's. I'm smaller than Ro. But Fallon... she fits perfectly under *my* arm."

I suddenly have a vision of a set of Russian dolls, largest to smallest.

He fiddles with the arm of the couch. "I want to protect her too, you know? And she's really pretty. And a sweetheart. And I just...,"

Teddy glances at Ro, teeth sinking into his lip. He looks more uncertain at that moment than I've ever seen. "I know that she'd still be Pack, even if we weren't together. But I've been wondering what it would be like. If she was part of *us* too."

"Yeah," Rowan rasps. They stare at each other. "Although you said it far better than I did."

Teddy sniffs. "See? I told you you'd be head over heels for her."

Rowan rolls his eyes. But a smile creeps over his lips. "You're always right. But I'm definitely head over heels for *you*, Teddy Quill."

Damn. They're adorable.

The door slams, and the three of us spin to the doorway.

My breathing starts to speed up as Fallon pads into view. She's kicked off her shoes, Zeke and Fox flanking her protectively as Teddy and Rowan jump up.

She's almost swallowed up beneath Fox's hoodie, her inky hair trailing down her body on either side in a tangled mess. My mate shifts on her feet. "I'm... back?"

The soft hesitant words are almost a question.

I stay where I am as Teddy and Rowan move over to her. Breathing the fresh, sweet scent of my mate in, trying to adjust.

But that darkness wants in, pushing and shoving against my brain, demanding entry. He knows she's here, too, and he *wants* her.

Mate.

Not now, I will desperately. *Just give me a damn fucking minute.*

Fallon's eyes fix on me, wide and sweet and questioning. "Wilder?"

She takes a step, and I hold up my hand, hating myself for stopping her. I can feel my damn lip curling up, dropping my face as I pant through the effort of holding my feral side at bay. "Just – just give me a minute, love."

"Fallon," Fox murmurs soothingly. "Why don't we go to the kitchen? He just needs to adjust."

He murmurs something else, and a growl ripples from me, the tension ratcheting up.

But my mate takes another step. Her brow furrows, as if she can see the struggle between us. "But he's *hurting*."

I don't know how she can sense the rippling pain inside my body as two halves fight for dominance. The scent-matching, perhaps.

"Fallon." I groan her name. "*Go*."

Fallon holds my eyes. I can feel them changing, flickering between electric blue and something wilder, brighter.

"It's okay," she whispers. "Let him in."

"Oh, shit," someone mutters.

My mate holds out her hand.

And I lose myself.

50

FALLON

I can see the pain in his face as it contorts. Wilder's eyes flicker from human to inhuman, too quickly for me to track.

It's like he's fighting with *himself*. Like he's hurting on the inside, too.

I know what that feels like.

"Fallon," Fox whispers. "I need you to back up."

A slow, curling growl comes from Wilder's mouth as Fox touches my shoulder. Fox's hand drops. "Now, Fallon."

Another growl.

But I shake my head, edging forward. "But he's hurting."

He's pushing down this part of himself for my sake, and he doesn't need to. I know he's not going to hurt me.

Wilder is my mate. And maybe he needs to trust in himself a little more.

Carefully, I hold out my hand. Wilder's head tilts to the side warily.

"It's okay," I whisper. "Let him in."

His eyes flash molten gold.

Behind me, Teddy inhales. "Oh, shit."

"Back up," Fox snaps. "Give them space."

I'm caught in those eyes. Wilder takes a step forward. Another, his gait prowling.

He looks... *bigger.* And I swallow. "What do I do?"

Nice one, Fallon. Bring out the feral alpha and then start asking questions.

"Don't run," Teddy breathes to the side of me. "Don't *move.*"

"Why?" My voice is a whisper, my gaze locked on Wilder.

"Because he'll chase."

Something flickers in my chest at that. Something *primal.*

My hand raises to splay across my stomach as Wilder tracks the movement, his head tilted and eyes glittering. He releases a low, almost pained grunt.

As if he can sense how much it hurts.

"We'll get him," Zeke murmurs. He and Fox come up behind me, Wilder baring his teeth at them in response. "Don't worry."

But I'm not worried. I'm *curious.* And maybe a little... excited.

Oh, god.

Wilder's nostrils flare.

"Wait." I throw my hand out, not looking away. "Please. He... this is part of him. He can't keep it trapped away."

It'll consume him.

I can feel the alphas behind me silently debating as Wilder edges closer, his gaze flicking between us.

Slowly, I shake my head. "Just let him do what he needs to. He just wants...,"

Me. He just wants me.

And as I think it, Wilder *lunges.*

Strong arms band around my back, taking me off my feet. The floor disappears beneath me as he snatches me up with a roar.

I can hear yelling behind us as he takes off. Wilder is impossibly fast as he grips me tightly, darting up the stairs with me over his damn shoulder like some sort of trophy.

Oh, fuck.

I'm gasping as he heads through a door and places me down, surprisingly gentle. "*Wilder.*"

Footsteps. More shouting.

"I'm okay!" I yell, and he flinches back. I don't look away from my mate. "Just give us a minute!"

This is his room. It's drenched with him, with vanilla and toffee notes, and I breathe in, trying to relax. My hands curl into soft bedding as I swallow.

He just... watches me.

"Okay," I whisper. To myself, and to him. "I'm here, Wilder. What do you need?"

My mate uncoils his body in a loose, almost feline movement as if he can understand me. I lose my breath as he nudges me down, following me into the bedding as he presses himself against me.

He's not wearing a shirt. Heat floods my body as I'm pinned beneath him and he drops his face to my neck, inhaling. "*Oh.*"

This... this is nice.

He's scent-marking me. Wilder rubs himself against my neck as my breathing speeds up. This is what he did before.

Comfort. That's what it feels like. And after a night spent in that horrible, bright room, it's what I need.

As if he knows, Wilder cages me, his arms on either side of my face. Boxing me in. The blinds are closed, creating the feel of a small, cozy space.

Safe.

"Yes," I breathe, watching him. "This is what I needed. This is...good."

I raise my hands, pressing them over his back as he rumbles against me. His skin is heat and silk, muscles flexing as he pushes himself up onto his elbows.

His golden eyes flicker to my mouth.

And heat, glorious, prickling heat floods my body. Pushing the pain out.

I don't know if he can understand me. But I tilt my face in a silent offering and wait.

Fingers curl around my throat, stroking the skin gently. But he holds me as his lips cover mine, soft but unyielding as he swallows my moan.

His approving growl, directly against my mouth, makes my toes curl.

With him pressed against me, I don't move. I can't, as Wilder shifts. His lips travel across my face, my cheek, down my neck.

I've never felt anything like it. There's nothing cold about this. This is pure fire, racing through my limbs as I shift beneath him. Searching for more as I tilt my head and try to follow him, a small complaint sounding in my throat. "More."

When his hand pushes up underneath my dress, beneath Fox's hoodie, I see stars.

Wilder spreads out his hand, almost covering my stomach as he strokes my skin, still holding my neck. His thumb brushes the hollow in my throat as his fingers glide over my belly.

Petting me. He's... *petting* me.

My bones turn to mush, sinking down into his bedding as he watches every flicker on my face.

Not enough.

My scent wraps around us, mixing with Wilder's in the air as he breathes in.

His eyes flicker again. Gold, to blue, to gold.

Wilder tugs his hand out from beneath my clothing, pulls his hand from my throat, and I whimper at the loss of contact. But he only moves his hands to the bottom of Fox's hoodie.

The tearing sound rips through the room, and my eyes widen as he rips it straight up the middle without blinking.

Wilder looks down at my blue dress and *snarls*.

I hate that dress too.

I hold my breath as his hands lower. He doesn't stop, doesn't wait, doesn't ask.

He rips it from my body, baring me to him.

My bare breasts rise and fall, my nipples pebbling as I still. Cool air sweeps over my skin.

And Wilder... his eyes travel over my body as if he can't imagine anything more fascinating. The noise he makes is pure pleasure.

An alpha male, inspecting his mate.

My moan locks inside my throat as he puts his hands on me. He starts with my legs, his hands sweeping over them. Higher. He fits his hands perfectly into the indents of my hips, moves them up to cover my breasts and squeeze.

I twist my hips. My slick has already started, wet heat between my legs as I voicelessly plead with my mate.

But he's already shifting down, pushing my legs apart.

At the first, hot swipe of his tongue, I come undone. My cry echoes into the room, the burst of slick making Wilder growl directly into my pussy.

Woah. Zero to seven hundred and fifty.

He slips his hands beneath my ass, lifting my hips into the air and feasting. I kick my legs into the air, my mate's grip unrelenting. He doesn't let me move an inch, and I buck as his tongue thrusts directly into my pussy, hot and thick and *holy fuck, if this is the start, what will his knot feel like—*

My thoughts become jumbled as he holds me in place. My hands find their way into his hair, and when I tug, Wilder pushes his head toward me in silent request for more. My hold tightens as he thrusts faster with his mouth, my pussy riding his face as he drags me impossibly closer.

His name is a prayer and a scream on my lips. "*Wilder*!"

I soak his face, thrashing and begging, deep in my throat as he holds me steady.

Both of us are breathing heavily when he sets me down. He chases me up the bed, a hum in his throat, and I wait. I can feel him, feel the heaviness of his cock as it pushes against my bare skin inside his jeans.

I swallow. I'm not sure I'm completely ready for that.

But Wilder only rolls me to the side, curling himself around me. Warm breath huffs against my neck as he drags me in until our bodies are pressed together.

His hand slips over my stomach again, gently stroking.

But he doesn't move. Doesn't do anything else.

He just... holds me.

My hand raises to stroke along his arm. A rumbling purr comes from his throat.

I fall into a half-doze, breathing in the comforting scent of him against me. When he shifts, putting space between us, I roll over to face him.

This is the more human side of Wilder. Blue-eyed, no trace of gold to be seen. He stares at me, his mouth opening and closing. "Fallon. I... fuck. I'm so sorry. I don't know what to say."

I reach my hand up to stroke his cheek. "He only wanted to help, I think."

Wilder swallows, his eyes searching my face. "And – did it—,"

I nod. I didn't need to think. Or worry. Just *feel*.

"He's a part of you," I murmur. Almost shy, I place my hand over his chest, feeling his heartbeat. "I don't mind if he comes out, Wilder. As long as I get both of you."

He closes his eyes. "You have me. But I'd like to spend some time with you *without* him, at some point."

I have to smile at the irritation in his voice. "We have time."

Now I'm here. With them.

Wilder groans. "God. I can *taste* you. I can even... kind of remember it. But it's fuzzy."

Flushing, I duck my head. "He didn't do anything else."

And I'm glad. Because that first time... that belongs to Wilder and I. And I have to wonder if part of that side of him knew it.

His lips brush my forehead. "Like you said. We have time."

51

TEDDY

I point. "That one is for her bedroom. The others are for the nesting area. But leave them by the door, please."

Fox snarls as he hefts another box, and I waggle my finger at him. "No complaints. We need to burn off that energy of yours."

Because the two alphas lugging dozens of boxes up and down the stairs are wound as tightly as the knot of a damn anchor. And instead of taking advantage of the heavy hormones, dragging my alpha upstairs and encouraging him to ride me like a rodeo, I'm directing their energy into taking Fallon's new things upstairs.

Possibly the only thing that might have stopped them kicking down Wilder's door.

Zeke jogs down the stairs, picking up another box. "It's quiet now."

He takes a deep breath. Chokes. And the edges of the box crumple beneath his grip. "I keep forgetting not to do that."

Because Fallon's scent is saturating this place. Sweet and spicy and *sexual*.

The Wild Side apparently knows how to treat an omega.

But at least the moaning has stopped.

I make a mental note to get *all* of the bedrooms soundproofed. Mine, Rowan and Fox's already are, but we clearly need to prep the whole house now.

Not that I minded listening. Apparently I have a little auralism in me.

You learn something new every day.

Whistling, I cast my eyes over the boxes still left.

"How much did you order?" Rowan is tapping away on his laptop. I gave him a pass on helping, since he's researching for Fallon. The little frown he gets between his eyes when he's angry is deepening by the minute, but he pushes his glasses back, rubbing over his face before glancing over the chaos. "Is there anything left in stores worldwide? National blanket shortage?"

"Ha ha." I glance at the boxes again, considering.

It doesn't feel like *enough.*

Fox puts down the box, staring at the ceiling. "I should—,"

"Nope," I smack my lips together. "Hopefully he's come out of it by now. Give them some space."

Because I can only imagine how hard Wilder – *our* Wilder - is freaking out.

Things must be upside-down when I'm the damn voice of reason.

"I don't understand this," Rowan mutters. His fingers fly along the keyboard. "There should be a hell of a lot of money attached to Rick Matthew's estate. But there *isn't.*"

On the stairs, Zeke turns. His brows knot. "Her... the alphas she was with."

Fox stiffens. "You think they *took* it?"

"Who?" Rowan and I are looking between them now. Fox sighs.

"I should have said earlier. But my mind is... not where it should be. Fallon was with the Wordsmith pack. Rory, Shaun and Ellis Smith."

"What?"

"What the hell?"

Rowan and I both burst into questions at the same time.

"I don't know," Fox grits out. "We haven't had any time to talk about it. And I don't want to hound her for details."

"Details about what?"

Fallon tiptoes down the stairs, Wilder behind her with a sheepish look on his face. She's wearing his shirt, all bare legs and hair and shyness as she reaches the bottom.

She looks...*edible.*

Fox and Zeke look dazed as they head directly for her.

I can't say I blame them. I feel like I've swallowed my own tongue. Rowan slips his hands around my waist, burying his groan in my neck. "We're in trouble, aren't we?"

Hell yes, we are.

52

FALLON

Everyone is staring at me.

I swallow, backing into Wilder and tugging at the edge of his shirt, trying to pull it down. His hand reaches up to stroke my back. "I didn't mean to interrupt."

Teddy shoves between Zeke and Fox. "You're definitely not interrupting. We were just taking some of these upstairs."

The room is littered with boxes. "I didn't even see these earlier."

Teddy winks at me. "They arrived while you were screaming Wilder's name."

I couldn't stop the blush if I tried.

"What?" Teddy protests when Zeke flicks him in the ear. "We all know I have zero off-switch."

"Not quite true," Fox murmurs. And then *Teddy* flushes.

I find myself very curious to know what could possibly make Teddy blush, but Rowan clears his throat. "Fallon. I... I hope you don't mind. But when I was setting up your address change, I noticed something. About... your dad? And his estate?"

My body stills. Rowan swallows. "I'm sorry. I didn't... I'm overstepping."

Slowly, I shake my head. "No. I mean- I don't mind. But I think I know what happened. Could we not talk about it right now, though?"

I don't want to lose this feeling. I don't want to think about the cold house I just left, or the pack who stole my life.

"They've taken enough from me," I say, trying to make them understand. "And I know I need to think about it, but this is my first day here. And they can't have this too."

And it's been so long since I felt anything close to *safe*. I don't want the Smith pack in this space, not yet. For now – for today, at least – I want to pretend that they don't exist at all. And that I'm just an omega, getting to know her scent-matched pack without any other baggage following me around.

"Of course," Rowan says gently. "If and when you're ready – I can help with whatever you need."

The simple offer tightens my throat. "Thank you."

"*So!*" Teddy claps his hands together. His eyes are twinkling, and the alphas around me exchange looks that suddenly make me feel a little nervous. "Can I show you your room?"

***

Good god of all things omega.

Open-mouthed, I stare as Teddy wanders around the huge space, happily chatting away as he pauses to inspect random items. "I know it's ridiculously *cream*, but you can pick whatever color palette you want and we'll match the accessories up."

He stops. "Fallon?"

I shuffle forward a few steps. My bare feet sink into the thick, cream fluffy carpet. It feels like heaven. "I... don't know where to look first. The bed is kind of giving me performance anxiety."

The bed is huge. I didn't even know they made beds that big. It stretches from one side of the wall to the other with no space on either side.

You could fit ten alphas in that bed.

Teddy grins, but there's understanding there. "Nobody else comes in this room but you. Not without your permission. Even my nest is off-limits to everyone without my say-so."

"Even Fox?" I ask curiously.

"Especially Fox." He tilts his head. "We all need our space sometimes. And it's easy to get *alpha'd*. You just sort of fall into doing whatever they want without realizing, because you're so damn needy for them. Fox usually notices first and puts me in time out until I have my head screwed back on."

Slowly, I perch on the edge of the bed.

We're so easy to take advantage of.

"Fallon?" Teddy sits next to me. "Too much?"

"No." I sigh. "But... I wish I'd found you all sooner."

Like seven years ago.

When Teddy's arm wraps around my shoulders, I lean into him. His chocolate scent feels closer to brownies today. Warm and welcoming. "Me too. But I'm glad you're here now. Wanna look at some blankets?"

My lips twitch. "I'd like that."

He drags me down onto the floor and starts digging through a box. He pulls out a variety of different blankets, holding each one up for my inspection.

"The first one was fine," I protest. I don't want him to go to all this trouble for me.

He lowers the thick quilted purple comforter in his hands and glares at me.

"Fallon Matthews," he says slowly. "It's okay to choose something you like. And it's okay *not* to like something. We're omegas, sweetheart. It comes with the territory. Fox would be terrified if I started choosing the first thing on the menu every time because I didn't want to make a fuss."

I bite my lip, thinking about his reaction at the Italian restaurant. Fox ordered nearly every item on the menu. And then there were the sandwiches.

"There are plenty of downsides to being an omega," Teddy murmurs. "But this? Liking pretty things? Soft things? This isn't one of them, Fallon. This is one of the *best* parts. We're allowed to be a little demanding. It's part of who we are."

He gently tosses the purple blanket at me. I gather it in my arms, tracing my fingers over the pretty pattern stitched into it. "I used to love this stuff. But it's been a while. I almost forgot how much."

His smile is sad. "Then I'll help you remember."

We work through several piles of boxes. And slowly, my little pile grows. First the purple blanket. Then a huge checked soft fleece blanket which reminds me inexplicably of Zeke. And two more. One blue. One gold.

My hands linger on a silky bronze sheet. It feels more like a luxury scarf than a blanket. I glance up, my eyes catching on Teddy's hair. It shimmers in the late afternoon light.

Neither of us say anything when I add it to the pile, but he's smiling. And when he passes me a second sheet, emerald-green like Rowan's eyes, I add that to the pile too.

Zeke pokes his head around the door at some point. "I'm not coming in, don't worry. But I brought coffee. And snacks."

His eyes linger on me when Teddy goes to grab the tray. "You okay?"

Shyly, I nod. "Teddy's looking after me."

"Good." Zeke smiles. "We'll be downstairs if you need us."

This is... nice. More than nice. The best day I've had in a long time.

We gorge on delicious coffee, courtesy of Zeke, and little honey cakes from a bakery Teddy loves. I feel a spark of excitement grow as we keep working through more boxes.

The shelves around us fill up with knick-knacks. Gorgeous-smelling candles, and pretty trailing plants. I fall in love with a chunky little set of jeweled glass candlestick holders, adding them to a spot where they'll reflect the light. And then there are the fairy lights.

So many fairy lights.

I sigh. "This feels like building a nest."

Teddy looks up. "Well, you have a nesting space too. It's on the top floor, next to mine. Different rooms, though."

"I don't need one."

He frowns. "You want to use your bedroom? We could split the space in two—,"

"Um." I fiddle with a tasseled scatter cushion, pulling my fingers through them. "I don't nest."

Teddy blinks. "I have a feeling I'm really going to hate whatever reason you have for this."

Playfully, I narrow my eyes at him. "It's not a big deal. I just stopped getting the urge a few years ago. I honestly don't think about it much now."

Only sometimes, when I let myself think about my *old* nest. The one I had before I left for college.

I liked that nest. Loved it, even.

Keeping hold of the cushion, I wander over and set it on the giant bed. "It's honestly okay, Teddy."

He mutters something under his breath. "Have you ever had a nest?"

I nod. "I was just thinking about that one."

"Tell me about it." He stretches out on the bed, tugging me down with him. "Please?"

He's impossible to say no to.

I stare up at the ceiling. "We had this barn that my parents converted into a space for me as I grew older."

"Cool," Teddy breathes.

I have to smile. "It was. We had an office on the ground floor that I shared with my dad. My bedroom was on the first floor. And there was a ladder leading off it that went into the attic, and I built my nest there. I used to like cozy spaces. Darker ones. The roof was really low, and I put these pretty jeweled sheets over the ceiling, draping them, and then I had lights in between. And these comfortable people-sized cushions on the floor. Lots of greenery. And where there *were* walls, my dad built these low shelves so I could keep my books in there too. I slept in there most of the time."

"It sounds amazing," Teddy says softly. "Hard to beat."

My throat tightens. "Yeah."

53

Fox

Arms slip around my waist as I'm chopping herbs. "She's in the shower."

Teddy sinks into me when I turn, seeking comfort I need to give, just as much as he needs to receive it. "Did you have a good afternoon?"

It was so fucking hard to leave them be, to not skulk outside the door. But I forced myself downstairs. The smell of garlic and oregano permeates our kitchen.

"Yeah." His words are muffled. "She's almost forgotten how to be an omega, Fox. They took it all from her. And I'm so fucking *angry*."

I have to force myself not to react, to not let my fury bleach the air. "They're going to pay for it."

Something I'm still considering. But if I hated Wordsmith before, it's nothing to how I feel now that I know exactly how they forced my mate to live.

Teddy sniffs the air. "Smells good. What are you making me, pack leader?"

I poke his nose. "*Us.* Lemon chicken and garlic roasted potatoes with feta cheese."

He feigns a moan. "You're going to spoil us."

"You're already spoiled." But Fallon isn't, and I intend to change that. "Exactly how it should be."

He kisses my chest. "In that case, I'm going to make us cocktails and chill out in my nest before dinner."

I pause. He only does that when he's feeling low. "Teddy."

"It's not that," he says softly. "I'm just... I'm sad for her. And I don't want to hound her, so I'm going to lose myself for a while. I'll take Rowan up with me. Call us when dinner's ready?"

I rub my thumb along his cheek. "Of course. And you'll call if you need me."

It's not a request.

After he's disappeared, I finish preparing dinner and slide it into the oven to cook. Wilder and Zeke aren't back yet from their errand, and I check my watch, wondering where Fallon is.

I lean against the counter and cross my arms.

Fuck it.

I take the stairs two at a time.

Teddy and Rowan are up in the attic. I veer off down the hallway on the first floor, passing Fallon's new bedroom. There are enough *things* scattered everywhere to last her for the next ten years at least, thanks to Teddy, but no sign of my mate, the door left open.

I slow as I reach the bathroom and check my watch. The door is closed, steam curling from underneath.

Teddy went upstairs forty minutes ago.

Maybe she likes long showers.

She can spend as long as she likes in the bathroom. Turning to leave, I hesitate. Something makes me reach out and tap on the door. "Fallon?"

There's no response. More steam appears, along with the scent of the shampoo Teddy probably picked out. It matches Fallon's scent, works with it.

But there's something else underneath it.

My hand is pushing open the door before I bother stopping to think. "Fallon—,"

She doesn't look up. She's sat on the floor of the shower, water cascading over her and her face buried in her knees. Her wet hair covers her like a damn shroud.

But I can *just* hear her sobs above the rushing of the water.

Fuck. Her quiet cries threaten to break my fucking heart. I rip the shower door open and ease myself down onto the floor next to her. The hot water pelts down over my head, my shoulders, soaking my shirt and jeans in seconds as I brush her shoulder in silent question.

What do you need?

I don't want to assume. Bad enough that I've invaded her shower, but there's nothing on this goddamned fucking earth that could make me turn around and walk away from my mate in pain.

She's had enough fucking pain in her life.

Fallon doesn't say anything. But my mate curls herself into me, still shaking with the force of her near-silent cries, and I inhale in silent relief that at least she'll let me give her this. Sliding my arms under her, I lift her onto my lap, Fallon's legs facing sideways and her head against my shoulder. Her arm comes up to wrap around my neck.

Nothing I can say can take her pain away.

But I hold onto her tightly, my hand cupping the back of her head as I gently rock her. "I've got you."

I don't expect her to respond. But we sit there for a long time. Long enough that I smell the unmistakable scent of burning in the air before Teddy's head slides around the door a little while later.

He hesitates. But when he goes to leave, Fallon makes a noise, deep in her chest. My mate holds out her hand, and Teddy dives in next to me, his hand lifting to stroke her hair as he cuddles into her.

And that's where we stay.

54

ROWAN

"You didn't come to bed last night."

Fox keeps his voice low as he leans against the counter. Pressing my lips together, I consider my words carefully before I flip another pancake out and onto the stack.

"Fallon was struggling," I say finally. Gently. "I didn't want to overwhelm her. So I stayed in the nest for the night."

Putting the pan down, I cross to the pantry and stick my head in. "Can you remember where we put the raspberry sauce?"

"*Rowan.*" Fox barks my name. He doesn't grab me. No, my alpha manhandles me into the damn pantry and pulls the door shut behind us.

"Fox—,"

"Listen to me." I shiver at the bark that infuses his tone. Shit, he's *angry.*

But it's not fear that races through me as Fox presses himself against me. His hands grab my cheeks. "You are not a fucking substitute, Rowan Quill."

I roll my eyes. "I know that. You idiot. We're going to have to—,"

But he's *really* angry. Fox snarls and slams his mouth against mine, his hand wrapping around the nape of my neck and dragging me into him.

My moan filters out when he rips his mouth away, his mouth dropping to trace the edges of my tattooed bite mark.

"You're mine." He purrs it against my skin as I tip my neck back to give him more access. "We may have some things to work out, but that will never change. Do you understand me? You, Fallon, Teddy - you are not interchangeable to me, Ro. You're all different people, and I have more than enough fucking love for all three of you."

I start chewing on my lip, and the grumpy male pinning me in place tugs it free with a growl. "Stop that. Or I'll replace it with my own damn teeth, and I have to go to work. Tell me you understand, Rowan, or I'll call in sick and spend the day making sure you never question it again."

I swallow as my cock stiffens, forcing it down.

He has to go. He's covering for Teddy today. All of us missed yesterday, and the work still stacks up, even with the brilliant team at Ink & Quill around us.

And Teddy and I are planning to spend some more time coaxing Fallon into feeling comfortable here, without the pressure of the alpha's presence or the scent-match overwhelming her.

And what a fucking presence it is. I could drown in it as Fox towers over me. "I understand. I just didn't want to push her too quickly, Fox. That's all. We need to be gentle with her, okay? And that includes easing her into the dynamics of this pack."

And I still think it was the right decision. Alphas might be possessive assholes, but omegas can be territorial. And a newly-mated omega that's coming to us from a terrible situation... what kind of asshole does he think I am?

Honestly.

"I'm not about to emotionally shove her into something before she's ready," I breathe. I poke him in the chest. "My decision had nothing to do with you, or how I feel about you. It was based on how I feel about *her*. Okay?"

Fox frowns. "Oh. I thought...,"

"It's not all about you, you know." I drawl the words, but a smile pulls at my mouth as I lean up to kiss him. "This was fun though. Feel free to shove me in a pantry anytime."

He's blushing now, a little embarrassed. "My emotions—,"

"I know," I say patiently. "You're all over the place. So is everyone else. But it'll settle, Fox."

Although probably not until Fallon has her first heat with us, whenever that is. That's when pack relationships tend to be set in stone, bonding marks given and accepted.

You can't hide *anything* during a heat. If there's anything – or any*one* – an omega doesn't want in their nest, they'll sure as hell let you know it.

Fox goes to push the door open, and I lean back against the wall, waiting.

He slams into it, bouncing back. "What the hell?"

"It locks from the outside," I murmur, trying to stave off my laughter. "I did try to tell you."

He bangs on the door in irritation. "I feel like a teenager. Who designed this, anyway? What if one of us gets trapped in here and dies of starvation? And why haven't we tried this for Wilder?"

"It's a *pantry*, Fox. And you'd never lock Wilder in here. Did you often get locked in pantries as a teenager?"

The smile he flashes me over his shoulder is nothing short of *wolfish*. "Next time, I'll show you what I learned in them."

I'm laughing when the door swings open. It catches in my throat, and I start to cough.

Fallon's smile tugs at the corner of her mouth, growing into a grin. "Were you... locked in the pantry?"

Fox hauls me out with him. "Very possibly. Don't go in there and shut the door. It's too late for us, but not for you."

And Fallon *giggles*.

Fucking wind chimes and orange blossoms.

From the table, Teddy is watching us with fascination. "God, Fallon, you really are his scent-match. Because that joke was *terrible.*"

"Brat," Fox snarls. But it's good-natured as he presses a kiss against Teddy's lips. "Do *not* get into any trouble today."

Teddy pouts. "Not even a little bit? Teeny-tiny?"

I watch Fallon's mouth fall open as Fox cups Teddy's neck from behind, tugging his head so Teddy is looking up at him. "If you want me to bend all three of you over the edge of my bed, tie your wrists behind your back and spank you at the same time, then do whatever you want."

"Well," Teddy breathes. His eyes are lit up with excitement. "What an incentive. Get out. We need to brainstorm immediately."

I glance at Fallon again to see how she's taking their banter. Her cheeks are flushed, hands gripping the table.

And even I can pick up on the scent that flares up in a fresh, sweet burst, mellowing into a spiciness that almost tickles my tongue.

I don't think she's against the idea.

Fox's eyes heat, and Fallon fidgets in place as he strides around the table. He tips up her chin, pressing a soft, testing kiss against her lips. "Rowan will get you a phone and add our numbers in. If you need me for anything – no matter how small – I want you to call me. Promise me."

It's not a bark. He doesn't need it, his dominance more than enough to have Fallon tilting her neck just enough. "I will."

He doesn't hesitate. She gasps as his lips press against the spot she's unintentionally offering him. And I catch his low murmur as Fox straightens, his thumb brushing her skin. "That's where I want my bite. Have a good day, mate."

None of us say anything as he strides out. The front door bangs in the distance.

Teddy blinks first. "We should totally make a list."

Fallon sinks her head into her hands. But she's grinning. "Where did the others go?"

I try to focus on something else. Anything other than the picture Fox created for us before he left. Heading back to the stack of cold pancakes, I frown before deciding to reheat them. "They're working on a top-secret project."

Fallon looks curious, but she doesn't ask. I hold up the plate before slipping it into the oven. "What's your pancake choice? I like raspberry syrup."

When her eyes widen, I glance down. "Did I spill something?"

"No," she says, smiling. "I like raspberry syrup too."

"Fallon." Teddy jumps up, heading for the coffee. "What did we talk about yesterday? Consider me your personal omega coach. Is it *really* your favorite?"

"It is!" Fallon protests. And then she pauses. "With... marshmallows?"

I grin. "I can do that."

After breakfast, I head to my own office and grab her a phone. She stares down at it. "I haven't used one of these in a while. This... model."

"I'll show you." I nudge her over to the couch, talking her through set-up and security. As I'm adding our numbers in, she looks around. "Your home is lovely, Rowan."

I pause. And so does she. Fallon laughs quietly, shaking her head. "My... home now, I guess?"

Relaxing, I keep going. "We can change things up. None of us are particularly fussy about décor. Maybe Teddy, but he hired someone in because he never has time for anything."

This is the most time I've seen him take off in years, aside from our agreed pack holidays.

She starts to nibble on her lip. "I... what do I do? Here? Is there a list anywhere?"

I jerk my attention from the screen, frowning. "What kind of list?"

She shrugs. Her hand drops to pick at the artsy hole in her dark jeans. At least she's dressed in something different today, the mountains of clothes Teddy ordered finding their way into her closet to pick from. The gray band tee she chose is knotted at the waist, a pair of thick fluffy socks on her feet and her dark hair pulled back into a sleek French plait. "Cleaning, maybe? Or I can cook."

"Fallon." Setting the phone aside, I take her hands in mine. "You don't have to *earn* a place in this house. That's not how we work. Besides, you have a job at Ink & Quill. We're just taking some time to adjust, that's all."

"So, they won't mind if I work?"

God, I hate the uncertainty in her voice. But I can fix that, right now.

"Teddy is the *CEO*," I remind her. "He's our boss, Fallon. At work, he calls the shots. And he's damn fucking good at it too. Fox is in charge here, but I promise you that *nobody* in this pack will ever stop you from doing what you want to do. You don't even have to work at Ink & Quill, if you'd rather work somewhere else."

She nods slowly. "Okay."

"And it's not about earning your way. We all pay a token something into the Quill pack account each month, but the profits from Ink & Quill are more than enough to cover everything we could possibly need." I study her face. "Okay?"

I want to tell her what Fox and Teddy are planning, but I don't want to ruin the surprise either. "Here's your phone. You're all set."

I make sure her tracking is linked to the family app and switch it on before I hand it over as Teddy bounces in.

"I have a list," he announces, waving it around. "Three rounds of spanking, coming up."

"He's joking," I say quickly.

Teddy's face falls. "So I can't put purple hair dye in his shampoo? He'll rock the matching hair and eyes look."

I bite the inside of my cheek, hard. Fallon looks as though she's not entirely sure if he's serious.

"Cut nipple holes in every single shirt he owns?"

Fallon chokes.

Teddy sighs. "Final one. We all pretend we got drunk and pierced our—,"

"*No!*" Fallon and I shout together. She starts laughing.

Teddy sighs heavily. "Damn. Looks like we'll have to play board games after all."

He winks at Fallon, and she frowns. "Board games?"

"Don't tell me you've never played Cluedo." He clutches his chest. "Your board game education begins now."

55

FALLON

I can't breathe for laughing.

Teddy is face-down on the floor, his arms and legs twisted at ninety-degree angles as Rowan draws a line of chalk around him on the wood of the hallway to imitate a crime scene. "Fallon, you're a genius."

"An evil genius," Rowan declares, straightening up. "They're going to lose their shit. I'm supposed to be the responsible one."

"We're *definitely* going to get spanked for this." Teddy's eyes look bright as he scrambles to his feet and smirks at us. My laughter fading, I lean forward and press my hand against his forehead. It burns beneath my touch.

"Teddy, you're hot. Like, *really* hot."

Rowan spins, dropping the chalk. Teddy offers both of us a smile. "It's fine. Not my heat. Just... a warning sign."

"Already?" Rowan is counting back on his hands. He clenches them into a fist. "Damn. Two weeks out."

Teddy winks at me. "Brace for impact."

Rowan grabs his arm. "I want to take your temperature."

"I'm fine, Ro." But Teddy sits himself down at the kitchen table as Rowan pulls some cold bottles of water out of the refrigerator, handing one to Teddy and one to me before he starts rummaging in a cupboard.

I take my time drinking, letting the questions gather in my head.

"You can ask." Teddy is watching me. "I'm an open book, Fallon. Ask me whatever you want."

"Although you might regret it," Rowan adds. He shoves a thermometer into Teddy's mouth. "He's an over-sharer."

I play with the label on my water, unpeeling it and sticking it back on as I think.

My own heats... I've been putting them off for years. And now, whenever one decides to appear, it's going to be *big*.

I blow out a breath. "Does... does everyone help with your heats? Wilder and Zeke too?"

Teddy drums his fingers on the table as Rowan tugs the thermometer free. "Sometimes, but probably not like you're thinking. Normally only a kind of... helping hand, if Fox or Rowan start running low on energy. Wilder and Zeke always get out of the house when it starts, but they stay close, and then Ro calls them back if we need them. But that doesn't always happen."

I nod. "Makes sense."

Although now I'm picturing all of them... *together*, and it's not helping my thought process in the least. Rowan's cheeks flush lightly, as if he can picture the same thing I can.

I pull myself together enough to phrase my next question, although it doesn't quite fit the format. "I wonder if our heats will sync up."

Teddy's eyes light up. "I would *love* that."

He sounds so delighted by the idea that my shoulders sag in relief. "You would?"

"Fallon," he gives me a stern look. "We're pack. Family. The more the merrier. Although Fox would lose his mind."

"Definitely a rut situation," Rowan murmurs. "God help us all."

My mind blanks. "Wait – what?"

Fox goes... into *rut*?

Teddy grins. "Yeah, our pack leader can go a little off the rails sometimes. Wilder is the one with the feral side, but if Fox loses it, he really loses it. Like... *lock us in the bedroom and ride us for days* loses it."

Teddy leans forward as if he's sharing a secret.

"One time," he purrs. "We had a heat and a rut at the *same time*."

Teddy sighs, but his eyes flicker with heat that echoes in my own body even as he winks at me. "Death by fucking – what a way to go."

And the longing that hits me at his words... it physically *hurts*.

So much so that I lean forward, wrapping my hands around my stomach. Both Teddy and Rowan appear at my side within a second.

"Fallon." Teddy bends to look into my face. "You okay?"

"I'm—,"

Another burst of pain. Like claws raking across my inside, and I gasp with the strength of it. It feels as if my body is reaching for something. Desperately. "I don't know."

A wall of heat slams into my stomach, roiling and flipping it as my body bursts into flames. And between my legs—

My whine rings out before I can stop it.

"Call Fox," Teddy snaps out. He's not smiling now. "Call all of them."

I start to protest, but another wave rolls over my body. My breathing increases as Teddy carefully lifts me. "What's happening?"

As he curls me against him, both of us suck in a breath. My perfume bursts out in a cloud that coincides neatly with the pulse that slams into my pussy. I clench my legs desperately. "Teddy."

"I know," he breathes. He's jogging up the stairs, Rowan behind us. He's talking into the phone. "Tell them I'm taking her to my nest."

I shake my head, biting back another moan. "That's your space—,"

"And I want you in it," he says firmly. "Unless you want your bedroom?"

I shake my head before I even realize I'm doing it.

I'm not functioning well enough to take in the full splendor of Teddy's nest. But I can see enough to spot different levels as he strides in. And there's greenery everywhere, what looks like a full-size, actual tree in the corner, branches overhanging the main space. Hammocks are strung up, wide and comfortable-looking, but he gently places me down into a pile of snug, welcoming blankets that are saturated with his scent.

He sucks in a breath when I bury myself into them, panting. I'm too hot, and not hot enough. A hand grabs mine when I start tugging at my clothes, pulling off my tee. "Fallon. Do you want us to help you? We can wait—,"

I shake my head frantically. Another pulse of slick slides into my underwear, another pulse of perfume. "N-no. Touch me. *Please.*"

I *need* them to touch me.

"Okay," Teddy breathes. I peer up at him and Rowan.

Rowan looks pale. Unsure.

"You don't have to," I whisper. And I want to cry even as I say it. "I can wait."

"No!" He drops down beside me. "God, Fallon. I want to, sweetheart. Teddy too. But are you *sure*?"

I don't answer. Instead, I grab his hand and drag it down. Rowan groans, low in his throat as I squeeze his fingers around my breast.

"Okay," he breathes. "We're going to make you feel better, Fallon. Okay?"

Yes.

"Please, Rowan." I squeeze harder, but it's not enough. "It hurts."

56

ROWAN

S he's hurting.

Unacceptable.

Fallon cries out when I reach down to press a kiss against her bare skin. Her hands are scrabbling with her jeans as she fights to get out of them, and I gently bat her hands out of the way, flicking open the button and dragging them down her legs until I can peel them off.

Her perfume, her *slick* – the slick of a needy, desperate omega – hits me in a rush of dopamine, nutmeg and oranges and a rich, sweet scent that has me breathing deeply. Teddy swears behind me, wrestling with his own clothes.

"Fuck." I groan the word as I take in the soaked state of her cream panties. "You're fucking beautiful, Fallon."

I don't waste any time. Leaning forward, I yank off her underwear and spread her legs open, exposing her puffy, swollen little slit to us. Fallon moans, lifting up her hips. "Rowan. Empty."

I want to lick. To spend hours gorging on her, bringing her to the edge over and over again.

Next time. And there *will* be a next time.

Fallon Matthews is about to learn that I might not be an alpha. And maybe I'm not her scent-match. But I'm hers all the same.

I belong to Teddy. To Fox. And now to Fallon too.

The knowledge settles into me as surely as she slips into place, right beside them.

Perfect.

I press my fingers against her entrance first. "What do you need, baby? Fingers or cock?"

My cock is straining against my own jeans, and I palm it roughly with one hand as I push two fingers inside her, testing. The tension in her body lessens slightly, and I add a third, sliding them in and out and watching them disappear inside her clenching cunt.

Goddamn.

Teddy stretches out beside her, and my throat threatens to close up as he nudges her face to the side. Her forehead is dotted with sweat as she goes straight for his lips, pressing into him as he holds her steady.

And her pussy grips my fingers like a fucking vice.

"That's it," I coax her. "Let Teddy fuck your pretty mouth with his tongue, Fallon. And I'm doing the same with my fingers. Your pussy feels so fucking tight, love."

I silently wonder at the marvels of omega biology. Because no diagram on this planet could explain how Fallon is going to be able to take her alpha's cocks, let alone their knots.

My cock is no slouch in that department, either.

I pull out of her, drinking in her breathy little moan as Teddy plays with her breasts. He tweaks her nipples, tugging on them gently, his hands roaming over her as he pets her while they're playing. Settling her.

She tears her mouth away from his, her eyes glassy. "*Cock,* Ro."

I nearly lose it at the sweet sound of my pack nickname on her lips. My cock is already rock solid and weeping for her, a bead of cum welling up on the end that I swipe my finger over before rubbing it into her little swollen clit.

I like knowing that I'm on her skin.

Fallon bucks under me as I grip her thighs and settle between her legs. Teddy moves his mouth down her body, sealing his lips around her nipple and sucking on them loudly. "Fuck me, you taste like Christmas, Fallon. This is my new favorite flavor."

She pushes her breast further into his mouth. Fallon's hair is trailing loose from her plait, strands clinging damply to her skin as Teddy suckles at her. Her amber eyes are hazy and full of yearning as she watches me rub my cock up and down her soaked pussy, covering myself with her.

She whines, pushing into me. "Now."

I'll never say no to her. I'll never deny her anything.

I push into her heat slowly, my eyes on her face. She tips her head back, her expression pure pleasure. "More. *Harder.*"

Teddy's fingers dance over her clit, rubbing and flicking. "You heard our omega, Ro."

His voice... he sounds almost drunk. Drunk on Fallon, his own eyes hazy as he returns to her mouth, tasting and sipping as if he can't get enough.

And as I pull back and thrust the full length of my cock into her, feeling her body accommodate mine in a silky, hot wetness that has me roaring louder than any alpha, I know exactly what he means.

I will never get enough of *our* omega.

Fallon's back bows, her scream pure rapture. "*More.*"

Everything. I give her everything, setting a pounding pace into her body, my fingers sinking into her soft skin as I drink in her cries, her moans, my name on her lips.

I take it all and I demand more.

I slow just enough, changing to shallow thrusts as Teddy lifts Fallon and slips in behind her, settling her back against his chest as I lift up her legs, nudging them over my shoulders.

Fallon's head lolls against Teddy's shoulder as he pulls her damp hair away from her face. The three of us are pressed so tightly together, Fallon between us, that I can't stop my speed from picking up. Teddy sucks on her neck, imitating a bonding mark that has her screaming and twisting, her pussy clamping down so tightly around my cock that I lose control entirely. Ropes of cum, fucking *endless*, erupt from me, filling up her sweet little pussy as Teddy smooths his hands over her skin, licking at her neck as I sag over her, my cock still buried inside her as I carefully lower her legs to the soft floor.

I don't... I don't quite understand what just happened.

Nirvana.

"Fallon," I choke, suddenly desperate. I stay where I am, reaching for her and cupping her face in sudden panic.

What if she didn't like it?

What if it was just for this moment?

If all I can be is a replacement on standby, I'll take it. But I think... I think it would break my heart every single day to not be able to call her *mine*.

Teddy reaches out, strokes my face in quiet reassurance before he glances down at her. "Steady. She's just coming around. Aren't you, love? You did so fucking well."

He presses his lips to the side of her head as her eyes flicker. "There we go. Rowan is worried about you, I think. Did we break you?"

His words are soft, infinitely gentle, but I can sense the concern there, too.

We're not her alphas. This isn't instinctive for us. We don't automatically know what she needs.

And if we got it wrong—

Fallon stirs. A small, sleepy smile curves her lips as her eyes blink open. And it's Fallon watching me, not an omega in the middle of a heat spike. "Come here, Ro."

My heart twists inside my chest as I lean over her. She brushes her lips against mine once, twice. And then she twists to do the same to Teddy.

I press my face against her stomach, my words rumbling against her skin. "This should be interesting to explain to Fox."

Teddy's amusement fills the room. "He's going to be so damn jealous he wasn't here."

As if on cue, Fox's voice bellows up the stairs in the distance.

Something about a crime scene?

The three of us stare at each other. Fallon winces as we hear footsteps outside, and the door flies open.

"Where's my mate?"

"Why the fuck is there a crime scene by the front door?"

"Fallon—."

The three of them come to an abrupt stop.

Silence.

I casually try to hook a nearby blanket to cover us with my foot as they get a good look at my bare ass, stretched out over Fallon with Teddy behind her. Our bodies covered in sweat and slick and the scents of the two omegas filling the room.

"Panic over," Teddy says smoothly. "We took care of it."

Someone moans when he drops a kiss on Fallon's smiling lips. Possibly our pack leader. "I should have written a full paper on what I define as *trouble*."

Definitely heading for a spanking.

57

WILDER

After the unexpected shock of racing home to tend our mate during her heat spike – and finding Rowan and Teddy doing a pretty fucking phenomenal job of it instead – my body feels too tightly-wound to go back to the office.

I work from home instead, taking calls from my team, from various publishing industry press organisations, and trying not to think about the fact that Fallon's sweet scent – her fucking slick – is *everywhere*.

When I can't cope with it anymore, I go looking for her. Teddy and Ro are curled up in the living room, Rowan still looking a little stupefied.

I don't blame him at all. "Have you seen Fallon?"

Teddy points up. "She needed to sleep it off."

Makes sense. Omegas need more rest in the build-up to a heat, and we all know that Fallon's is going to hit her with the approximate force of a freight train.

I keep my footsteps quiet as I ease her door open. But she's not here. Her bed is rumpled as if she kicked the blankets off.

Frowning, I glance over my shoulder, my eyes lowering to the ground.

What the hell?

The hall stretches out away from me and dotting the floor at regular intervals... are *blankets*.

I bend to pick the first one up.

Then the second.

It's like a little omega trail. My lips start to tug up as I follow it, my heart twisting. "Fallon?"

There's no response. I pick up another three blankets before I reach the final one.

It's right in front of my bedroom door. I nudge the door open.

My smile grows soft as I follow yet more blankets over to my closet. Tiny little shuffling movements are coming from inside.

My mate is possibly the most adorable thing I've ever seen in my damn life.

She twists, her amber eyes wide as I take the scene in.

Because Fallon is nesting. *In miniature.*

And inside my closet. The walk-in space is filled, every inch of floor space taken up with blankets and shirts. I recognise Fox's favorite hoodie as Fallon shifts it around with a little crease between her eyebrows, until she's happy with the position.

And then she moves onto the shirt I was wearing... yesterday. She buries her face in it, breathing in.

"Hey," I whisper gently, not sure what I'm working with. I kneel a short distance away, giving her space as she turns to me. "Little mate. What are you doing?"

Her gaze snags on the shirt I'm wearing. It's an older one, a soft pink flannel worn by years of use. She stares at it for so long that my fingers drop to the buttons. "You want this? You can have it, baby."

Fallon can have whatever the hell she wants, because I can't cope with the *cuteness*. My breathing stops as my mate crawls out of my closet and straight onto my lap. She buries her face in my chest and breathes in, a cute little growling sound vibrating into my skin.

Fuck. Me.

Carefully, I stroke her back. She shuffles, making a little huffing sound. "You like that?"

Her cheek is rubbing against my chest as Fallon pushes herself into me, her knees sliding to either side of my hips as I kneel there.

I cast my eyes upward, mentally praying for self-control as my hormone-addled omega rubs herself against me, more little growls falling from her lips as I pet her and she stretches out like a kitten. Her exposed neck is a damn beacon, and she shivers when I press my lips to it.

If she was fully aware – or if she was wearing my bonding mark – I'd already be knot-deep in her, giving her exactly what she needs.

But for now, I keep running my hands over her in petting movements as my mate wrestles me out of my shirt with an almost freakish amount of strength and pulls it over the vest top she's wearing. It swamps her, but she smiles up at me as if I've handed her the damn moon.

And then she curls up against my chest and falls asleep.

58

— · —

FALLON

I can't look at Wilder without blushing.

Which is a little awkward, because my mate hasn't stopped watching me since we sat down for dinner. Wilder's lip tugs up when I catch his eye, and I nearly burst into flames.

I climbed him like a damn tree. Wrapped myself around him.

I ripped his shirt off.

And I'm still wearing it. I can't bring myself to take it off, the flannel so warm and comfortable that I'm definitely planning on sleeping in it tonight.

And he held me for hours as I slept, curled up against him.

My whole body warms.

Fox adds some more stir-fry to my plate, and I lose myself in it. My other mate is a phenomenal cook, I've realized. And he loves it – even though he's the pack leader, even though his dominance overwhelms everybody else in the room.

Nothing makes Fox happier than caring for his pack, and I adore— I stop, flushing.

I think I might adore Fox Quill. In a starry-eyed, love-struck omega kind of way.

In a forever kind of way.

In fact...

I sneak looks around the table. Wilder's grin grows as I skate over him. He's almost glowing, the same way he was after I woke up.

As if nothing gave him more pleasure than holding me as I slept. Beside him, Teddy and Rowan are arguing with laughter in their voices over a book. Teddy throws his head back, his laughter warming the whole kitchen.

And Zeke. Zeke... is watching me. He was nearly late to dinner, running in just as Fox was dishing up the food onto plates. His white shirt is pushed up past his elbows, his beard trimmed.

He's so handsome that my throat nearly closes up.

This pack is *mine*.

And I'm starting to believe it.

"You okay?" he asks softly. Zeke doesn't push. Never asks for more than I'm willing to give.

He never actually asks for anything. My heart softens.

"I am. I'm...happy. What happened to your hands?"

He drops his fingers from his beard, flushing deeply. Both hands are covered in tiny little cuts. "Oh. I did it at work."

My brows knot. "I didn't realize finance was so... stabby?"

He chuckles, but Fox clears his throat. "Fallon. How would you feel about coming back to work tomorrow? No rush, but if you're ready."

My eyes dart to Rowan. He offers me a small smile.

It's a gentle but unmistakable *I told you so* smile. "Yes. Absolutely. Teddy, I can make a start on the manuscripts?"

Teddy looks as though he's chewing on his tongue. "Yes. I mean, absolutely. Although...,"

His voice trails off, and he glances at Fox.

I shrink back in my seat. "You don't... you don't want me working with you?"

He bolts upright. Everyone does, as he holds out his hands with a panicked look in his eyes. "*No!* Fuck, Fallon, that is not it at all. I would *love* to work with you. Fox, tell her. *Quick.*"

I blink away tears.

"Fallon," Zeke says gently. He shifts in his chair and I immediately slide from my own, curling up in the warmth he offers as he strokes over my hair. His words are a low, soothing rumble. But firm, too. "This is nothing for you to worry about. Listen to Fox."

"Sorry." I bite down on my lip as I turn to him. I'm all over the place.

Fox's eyes are soft. "You know I manage the Editorial department, Fallon."

The bookshelves. The *atmosphere.*

And the longing, for a lost opportunity.

"You remember Ed Burrows?" Fox taps the table. "He's one of our best editors."

Slowly, I nod.

Fox leans forward. "We run an intern program at Ink & Quill. There are spaces available all over the company. But Ed has a space coming up for an Editorial intern. And he would very much like to work with you."

My breath catches. "But... I didn't even finish college, Fox."

I barely remember those days. Only that Rory took me into campus one day, and when we walked out, I'd given up my place.

Next year, they had said. *Such a shame. We can support you.*

But I never went back.

Another thing I let them take from me.

"The program also accepts those with relevant lived experience," Fox says softly. "Ed himself told me about the work you did on *The Light in Us*, Fallon. Your father was so proud of them. He said your suggestions made it a much stronger book, and you were still a teenager then. Ed worked with your dad, you know."

Zeke wipes wetness away from my cheeks. "But—,"

"No buts," Fox says quietly. His purple eyes don't look away from me. "No conditions. No expectations. You deserve a chance, Fallon. A chance to try again and to be the person you want to be. That's what this is. There's no favoritism. You'll answer to Ed, not us – and he's a fantastic mentor, but he has high expectations."

"Life has a habit of getting in our way," Teddy says. His face is serious now. "You don't have to take it, Fallon. None of us mind what you choose to do. And if you want to be my office manager, you'll do an amazing job at it. But I really think you should be an editor instead—,"

Rowan jabs him in the side.

"Yes," I breathe through my tears. I half-tumble off Zeke's lap, and he steadies me before I rush around the table to Fox. "Yes. Please."

He smiles broadly. "You know, I'll still technically be your boss. But I don't get involved—,"

I throw my arms around his neck, pressing my lips against his. His arms wrap around me, and he deepens it until I'm smiling against his mouth. "Sorry, boss."

Laughter.

And it bubbles up inside me, filling up my light with sheer, perfect happiness.

Different paths. New opportunities.

I bury my face in Fox's neck, breathing him in.

Hope.

59

Fox

My hand jumps out from beneath the bedding, grabbing Teddy's wrist as he sneaks past me.

He lifts the back of my hand, kisses my pulse. "I have a breakfast meeting. The others are heading in early too. Bring Fallon with you."

Nodding, I let him leave. Only Fallon and I are left, her back a warm, soothing weight against my chest, my arms wrapped tightly around her.

My mate.

I stay there for long minutes, breathing her in. Normally I'm one of the first in the office each morning, the first one up, but this morning, I find myself happy to stay in bed and wrap myself around my mate.

My lips drop to her neck, to that empty space I'm rapidly becoming obsessed with.

Soon.

I need to mark her. It's becoming an obsession.

I need everyone to know that Fallon Matthews is mine.

I need everyone to know that she's a Quill. *Ours.*

Gently I let my teeth graze over that spot, torturing myself as the sleepy noise she makes stiffens my cock against her back.

I follow it up with my tongue. Rasping it over that spot as if I can feel the teeth marks beneath that will publically brand her as *mine*.

My mate's breathing changes. Becomes a little choppier, her heart rate increasing.

I smile against her skin. "Good morning, mate."

"Good morning...," she hesitates. "Would you like me to call you alpha?"

I nuzzle her neck. "Call me whatever you feel comfortable with. I'm not especially a fan of it, but it's up to you."

I'm not so self-obsessed as to demand she refers to me by my designation. I've seen it in other relationships, and always felt uncomfortable at the blatant power imbalance.

Omegas should be cherished. Not pressured.

"Although," I whisper. "I might *ask* you to call me Alpha in bed. Occasionally."

The little hitch in her breath gives me oxygen. My mate likes that, her body heating as I carefully slide my hand beneath her pink shirt, rubbing her stomach. Petting her.

I can feel her smile. "Why do I love that so much?"

"Petting?" I murmur. "It's an omega trait. It's okay to enjoy what feels good."

And I *want* to pet her. I want to pet my mate until she's a purring, satiated bundle in my bed. Knotted and full of me.

Tone it down, Fox.

But Fallon wriggles until she's facing me. I suck in a breath when my mate's smooth leg hitches over my hip. I'm wearing gray sweatpants – much to Fallon's quiet delight when she saw me in them – but they do nothing to stop the heat of my cock from pressing into the soft swell of her stomach.

Her small, breathy noise does things to me. Like making me stiffen even more.

"I'm sorry," I murmur. I brush my lips across hers. "Occupational hazard as your mate. You are utterly irresistible. But I'll get up now. It's still early, so we can have breakfast before we leave."

But her leg tightens over my hip when I shift. And Fallon... Fallon presses herself into me. She swallows, her cheeks pinking. "What if... what if we skipped breakfast?"

My heart skips a damn beat at that. "I don't want to rush you—,"

Her hands come up to trace my bare chest. Pale skin against my olive tone. "You're not, Fox. You haven't once rushed me. And I want to... explore. But I'd like you to show me, too. About- about knotting?"

Fuck. My knot starts swelling up at her small words. So damn hungry for this omega. "You've never been knotted before?"

I don't want to bring any of her past into this space. But I need to know, to know how gently to treat her. This... this first time.

Breathe, Fox.

She doesn't look at me. "I have. But something tells me it won't be like this."

Oh, mate.

I pull Fallon into me at that, wrapping my arms around her. My fingers tangle in her silky hair. "No. I promise you that it will be *nothing* like before."

Her lips press against my chest. Then the tip of her tongue. I stay still, barely breathing as Fallon presses soft kisses against my skin until her tongue circles my nipple.

The low growl in my throat makes her jump, eyes flicking to me uncertainly. "Explore me all you like, mate. I promise that I'll enjoy *everything* you choose to do."

Even if it kills me.

My mate's exploration is eerily close to the death of a thousand cuts. Her lips are feather light as she nudges me onto my back and climbs over me, her heat brushing my cock as we both inhale.

She moves over it again, as my hand slips to her hips. Rocking against me, her plump little lips parted.

In Wilder's pink shirt, her hair everywhere...

"Heaven," I say before I can rethink it. Carefully I reach up, gently cupping her breasts as she sways toward me. "You feel like heaven, Fallon."

She blushes. "Flattery will get you everywhere."

"I mean every word."

She runs her hands over my chest, plays with the dark sprinkle of hair that covers my pecs. And her lips follow everywhere she touches, as if she needs to try both ways.

She reaches my face, and a soft laugh slips out as she mimics a bite into my neck.

My hands threaten to crush the railing of my bed, my eyes glazing. "Just to warn you, that is absolutely a fast-track to a knot. I like your teeth on me a little too much."

She's smiling as her fingers trace the other side of my neck. Teddy's small bite is embedded in my skin as permanently as my own bite sits in his. "I'm looking forward to biting you properly, Fox Quill."

I'm going to lose my mind. But this time – our *first* time – my mate can explore as much as she pleases. And then all bets are off.

Her fingers graze over my sweatpants, and my cock jumps.

She curls her fingers into the top and tugs them down, my cock springing free as I lift my hips to help her.

Fallon stops, her lips parting.

I have to bite my cheek to stop my purely alpha grin at the expression on her face. Releasing the headboard, I drop my hand down and squeeze it. "It will fit."

She blinks. "In a subway tunnel, maybe."

My laugh bubbles out of me. "You were made for me, Fallon. I can't wait to watch your little pussy stretch around my knot."

My mate's perfume is my reward. It settles over me like a blanket as I run my hand up and down my cock and she watches me in fascination. Even her eyes on me threaten to make me spill all over the bedding.

I bite the inside of my cheek again as she reaches for my knot. *Hard.*

Her soft hand grazes the swollen ring at the base of my cock. It swells further beneath her touch.

I throw my arm over my face, biting into the skin there. But I can't stop my hips from bucking up.

And when the tip of her tongue touches the head of my cock, I muffle my shout.

Jesus fuck. She's killing me.

She makes a murmuring sound before she licks it again. "It tastes... good."

Mother of God, help me.

I pray to every deity in existence and a few that I'm sure I've only read about in books before she pulls away. Gingerly, I lower my arm.

My mate licks her lips. "I think I'd like your knot now."

Slow, slow—

She yelps as I dive for her. Fallon's back lands against the mattress. I'm breathing heavily, pressed against her. "You're sure?"

She nods breathlessly. "What... which way do you like it?"

Groaning, I sink my face into her neck. "Fallon. I... we'll try that another time."

But her hands tug at me. "No. I want it that way, Fox."

"On your knees?" I breathe into her skin. "Your face pressed into the mattress. Your little ass up in the air for me, your little cunt tight around my cock as I hold you down and fuck you until your legs give out. That's what you want?"

Because that's what I want. What I *need*.

Total, utter submission.

I'm not trying to scare her. But I need her to understand what she's asking for.

But she moans. "Yes. *Please.*"

I flip her so quickly her cry cuts out mid-air. My mate lands on her stomach as I push her knees up the bed, spreading her until she's wide open for me. "Look at all this pretty slick, just for me. Last chance, mate. I won't ask again."

But Fallon only pushes her ass up further into the air, dropping her upper body down.

She's perfection.

I settle behind her, drinking her in as I rub my hands over her skin. I grip her ass, squeezing it before I run my hands over her back, straightening as I move higher.

Fallon shifts as I notch the head of my weeping cock against her. "*Please.*"

"Mate," I whisper reverently. "Mine."

And I push inside, her body stretching around me as I thrust in shallow waves until I'm buried inside her snug little channel. Fallon's back arches, but I trace my finger down her back as I lean forward. My voice is firm. "Down."

She drops, panting as her fingers tangle in the bedding.

One hand braces us both against the mattress.

And the other grips the back of my mate's neck, holding her in place as I pull my cock out and thrust.

This is not sex.

This is possession. Ownership. Worship, as I pound into my mate's pussy and she takes it, screaming and clawing at the mattress as I pin her in place.

My brain almost wipes out, but I force myself to focus, to listen to any sign in her voice or body that she needs me to stop.

But she grows slicker around my cock, perfect and dripping as I hold her, giving her what she never even knew she needed. What we both needed.

Perfection.

I'm not going to last long. I need my knot to be deep inside her, to pin her in this last, final way. To fill her little cunt up until she's overflowing with me and her body stretches for me to press my knot into her, to keep me inside her, the way it damn well should be.

My grunts, her moans, they fill the room around us, our bodies slapping together. She doesn't move an inch, even as she twists and bucks under my hold. I vaguely hear a tearing sound, glance at the sheet she's torn in her desperation.

I slow as I feel my balls tighten, my knot swelling to a width I thought was fucking impossible as I nudge it against her entrance.

Fallon stretches her knees wider, shoving her face down and biting into the pillow beneath her as I push inside. She whimpers, even as her cunt stretches for me. "Shh, baby. You were made for this."

Impossible pain. Impossible pleasure. She trembles and moans under me as I move my hand from her neck to under her stomach, lifting her when her legs give out. Fallon twitches around my cock, her pussy fluttering with the aftershocks of her release as I nudge the last part of my knot inside.

She took it all. Every part of my knot is buried inside her, locking my cum inside her pussy as I lower us both down into the bed and press down over her limp body.

My teeth, my lips, my tongue – they're everywhere as I push her damp hair away from her neck and massage the place where I held her down.

Praise falls from my lips. Praise and adoration for my mate.

"So perfect," I stroke her back, shifting slightly as she shivers beneath me. She tries to move, my knot keeping her in place. "Stay, Fallon."

Her pussy squeezes me again. "You like me telling you what to do in bed? Like my hands on you, pinning you down?"

She nods into the bedding, still catching her breath.

Her back is plastered, damp and shivering against my chest as I roll us.

When she whimpers, I stroke over her stomach. "What are you doing?"

I kiss the side of her neck as I shift onto my back. Fallon is still tight on my knot, my hands skating over the front of her body before I spread her pussy lips apart. "Fox—,"

I stroke my fingers over her clit. "Breathe. Relax, baby."

I hold her open as she lays on top of me, her clit exposed to the air. Her small, gasping breaths are like music as I pet her, stroking her clit until she tightens and flutters around my knot for a second time.

I wrap my arms around her. Drag a blanket over to wrap around us. Fallon is shaking in my arms, and a hint of worry snakes in. But I can't scent anything apart from her arousal, her slick, her need.

"Fallon." I press my lips to everywhere I can reach. The top of her head. Her ear. The small space just below it that makes her shiver. "Are you alright?"

I don't stop touching her. Bringing her back down gently as she adjusts to my knot.

"It's so heavy," she whispers finally. "I feel so full."

"You are full," I nuzzle her. "Full of me."

"That was...," she falls silent, and I wait, stroking her hair. "I want to do it again?"

I bury my smile in her hair. "We will."

Many, many times. A lifetime of them.

She shifts again, but my body is nowhere ready to release my mate yet. "How long does it normally take?"

"Fifteen minutes, maybe?" I kiss her hair again, wondering at the feel of her in my arms. "But this first time... possibly longer."

Forty-five minutes, to be exact. Forty-five minutes to play with my mate, to stroke her clit to orgasm – twice – while she's caught on my knot until both of us are well and truly late and Fallon has to be carried to the bathroom for clean-up because she can't walk.

As we walk into the Ink & Quill office more than an hour later, Fallon nudges my arm. "You look very... smug."

"Me?" I wrap my arm around her shoulders and pull her closer, breathing her in.

She's fucking smothered in my scent. "Damn straight I am. You're going to smell like me all day, mate."

And I'm going to smell like her. My smile grows.

She gawks at me as I kiss her forehead, seeing her into the elevator and pressing the button for Teddy's floor before I back out. "Have a good day. I'll see you later."

I'm whistling as I stride off.

60

FALLON

Teddy is waiting for me outside of the elevator.

Snagging my wrist, he pulls me out before the doors have even fully opened. He's almost vibrating with excitement as he throws his arms around me.

"Did you – you *did*!"

I start laughing as his face buries in my neck. "God, you and Fox together smell *phenomenal*."

He backs off, a sheepish look crossing his face. "Sorry. I'm really pleased for you."

"Thank you," I say teasingly. "But I'm ready to work."

I'm not starting with the Editorial department for a few days yet, so I'm going to help Teddy while they start the search for a full-time replacement.

He gives me a pleading look. "The manuscripts, Fallon. They're *watching me*."

I stifle my laugh as I follow him to his office, stopping in the doorway. "Wow."

I forgot how many there were. And most of them have been shoved into a big pile of papers, all mixed in together.

"I'm so sorry." Teddy buries his face in his hands dramatically. "They attacked me. And I feel really bad, because each manuscript deserves to be reviewed, you know? But it just got a bit too much."

"It's okay." I start rolling up the sleeves of my blazer. I feel much more comfortable here now that I'm dressed more appropriately. My navy blazer covers a cute little blue and white-striped blouse, my cropped trousers a dark gray with functional but still pretty navy shoes. "I'll make a start here. Do you have calls to make?"

Teddy waves his hand. "I can take them in the big meeting room. Are you sure?"

"Yes." I'm already kneeling, pulling one of the smaller stacks toward me. "Go on. I'll see you soon."

"Thank you," he breathes earnestly. "You're my hero, Fallon."

I'm engrossed in a page when the phone at the desk behind me begins to ring.

"Did you order something?" I pop my head around the meeting room door. "It's on the way up."

Teddy scratches his cheek. "Honestly... very possibly, and I just forgot."

But when the elevator opens, we both stop to stare.

Two delivery workers stagger out, each of them carrying a *massive* bouquet of flowers. "Fallon and Teddy?"

We exchange glances. Teddy is grinning. "Yep. That's us."

He squeals as they leave, already darting to my desk. I follow him more slowly, my heart thumping as Teddy points to one of the bouquets. His eyes are scanning a small written card. "That one's yours. Holy *shit*, Fallon. That must have been some freaking knot."

I blush, but I'm grinning as I flip open my own card.

Mate,

Until next time.

Such a good girl for me.

Fox

God. I swallow, trying to succinctly press my legs together. But Teddy cackles, and I have to join him, my hand over my mouth as I take in what he's holding up.

He wipes at his eyes before waving the silver handcuffs at me. "The note says they're for next time we get in trouble."

I pull out my phone.

Thank you for the flowers. They're beautiful, Fox.

He's typing.

You're welcome. Not as beautiful as my mate.

"Damn," Teddy breathes, peering over my shoulder. "He's good."

He really is.

61

ZEKE

I force out a breath as I stare down at the gift I have for Fallon.

It's not especially pretty. Or new.

But I'm hoping it's the right one.

When it's finished.

When my phone rings, I answer it absently. "If you're calling to brag, I've already had a good ten messages from Teddy sending me photos of their flowers."

But Fox's voice is hard. My body turns to ice as I listen. "We'll be down now."

I can hear Fallon humming, a sweet, melodic sound as I walk up to Teddy's office. She rocks back on her heels, smiling at me. "Hey, you."

I try to smile back at her, but it feels forced. "Hey."

Fallon stiffens, picking up on my tension. A little crease appears between her eyebrows. "What is it?"

"Zeke?" Teddy appears from behind me, glancing between us.

"Something's happened," Fallon whispers. She pales. "With the Smith pack. Hasn't it?"

"Nothing you need to panic about," I force out, striding to her. She doesn't respond as I tug her to her feet and pull her into me. "Nothing bad is going to happen, sweetheart, I promise you. Fox is down there with our legal team, and Ro is down there too. But they want to speak to you."

"Who?" Fallon whispers. She grips onto my suit jacket tightly.

"The cops." I cup her cheeks, stroking her soft skin. "The Smith pack... they're accusing us of abducting you, Fallon."

***

Teddy and I exchange concerned glances as we descend in the lift.

"I'm not staying behind," he snaps at me again when I open my mouth. His face is flushed. "Not a damn chance, Zeke."

Fuck. Fox is going to lose his mind.

And Fallon... Fallon says nothing. She's gripping her own arms, hugging herself in that way that she has of retreating when it all gets too much. Her breathing is deepening by the second into panicked breaths that rip at my heart.

We can hear the shouting before the door even opens on the first floor.

"We have a meeting room here," I say quietly. "Fox took them there."

Except that's blatantly obvious, because I can hear Fox yelling from all the way down the hall. Teddy lets out a soft whine at the fury in his voice.

—not taking my fucking mate anywhere—

And Rowan. Rowan is arguing with Fox, trying to calm him down. Fuck, I hope Wilder isn't in there.

"This will be sorted out in a few minutes." I turn to Fallon.

She's staring at the meeting room door.

And then my mate takes off at a *run*.

"Shit," Teddy breathes as we both stop in shock.

But I'm already pelting after her. "Fallon!"

She bursts into the meeting room ahead of me. By the time I catch up, I'm expecting to dive into a clusterfuck of alpha rage and my mate's panic.

But that's not what I get as I skid into the doorway, ducking to push my way through.

The room is full. Against the far wall, two uniformed cops are tense, watching the scene in front of them. And another alpha male not in uniform is staring in shock at my mate.

Fox is growling, the sound rippling through the room.

But it's not the only sound.

Because standing in front of him, with her teeth bared, is my mate...

And she's growling louder than Fox.

62

FALLON

I snap at the male in front of me with my teeth when he takes a step.

"Stay away from them."

The room is silent, Fox's fury the only noise behind me. His hand brushes my back.

I don't know what this is. I've never felt this before – this surge that feels like electricity in my veins, lighting me up from the inside. Like a dormant volcano, suddenly come to life and crushing every submissive instinct under a wall of flowing lava.

Because I'm so angry that I take another step toward the far more dominant alpha, and I growl. My scent twists in the air, the nutmeg suddenly overwhelming. Spice and anger and heat as I spread my arms out. "Leave them alone. They didn't do anything."

And even my voice is deeper. More guttural.

Behind me, there's a frantic flurry of whispering. Rowan's voice comes from beside me, aimed at the men trying to hurt my pack. "You need more damn proof? Here she is. Safe and well. And *scent-matched.*"

They're here for them. For my mates. For Rowan. For Teddy.

I growl again, snapping my teeth.

I don't move. But I allow Zeke to come up behind me, to press his chest to my back, to stroke down my arm. "Fallon."

I can hear the anger in his voice. But there's fear, too. "Nobody is in danger, love. They're just checking to make sure you're alright."

To make sure the Quill pack hasn't kidnapped me.

I can't back down. Can't lower my arms. My whole body is nearly vibrating with the frenzy that tears through me. "*You're not touching my pack.*"

A rumble of approval through the room.

Someone edges in front of me, and I snarl. Hands land on my face. Gentle. Familiar.

Wilder's jaw is tight. His eyes are edged with gold. "We're not going anywhere, mate. Everyone is safe. None of us are in trouble. You understand?"

He throws his next words over his shoulder, his tone icy-cold. "*Tell her.*"

The male behind him sighs, and I tense. "Damn pack politics. Miss... Matthews. Fallon, is it? We're just doing a welfare check, as requested by the Smith pack. Your... mate, is right. Nobody is in trouble. We can see that you're here by choice."

A welfare check.

And it's Teddy who laughs, but it's edged with rage. "Where was your damn welfare check when Fallon was with *them*?"

The violence in my body recedes slightly. I shift, lowering my hands an inch.

"That's it," Zeke murmurs in my ear. "It's alright, Fallon. Nobody's going anywhere. Nobody's in trouble."

It recedes further, until I can think clearly. I press back into Zeke, leaning on him as the strength drains out of my body.

But the anger is still there. Still seething.

"Teddy is right." My voice is hoarse. "Where was your welfare check when they stole my *life*?"

The males around me growl, even Rowan.

Wilder shifts enough for me to see the male. He looks older. Mid-fifties, maybe, with graying hair and a stern expression that flickers with surprise. "I'm sorry. I don't understand."

I take a breath. "When the Smith pack took over. When my parents died. Where was my check then? When they took my identification and closed down my bank account? When they locked me in a house and punished me if I stepped out of line?"

I'm shaking. A tear trickles out of my eye. "Where was your damn welfare check when Ellis Smith put me in a cold shower and used his bark to keep me there?"

The atmosphere drops. Behind me, Zeke goes rigid. "Fallon."

But I can't stop. Can't stop the words. "Or when I lost a dollar – *one dollar* - from the grocery shop change, and they cut up every piece of clothing I owned and threw my things away? Where the hell were you then?"

The male looks stunned. "I – well—,"

"But you come here," I snarl. "When I am finally *happy*, and you try to take me away from this pack? *My* pack?"

"Fallon," Teddy whispers. And he's crying, his eyes dark and his cheeks damp.

"You tell them this," I say hoarsely. "You tell the Smith pack that if they *ever* come near my pack again, I will come after them for every penny of what they took from me. And I will tell everyone I can that the Smith pack took an omega into their care and abused her for seven damn years. You tell them that, in the results from your *welfare check*."

I can't do anymore. I spin, folding myself into Zeke. His hand is shaking as he rubs my back, but his voice is tight with anger. "What can we do? Detective?"

The male – the detective – stays silent for a minute. "We can take a statement. Put it on the record. And we can investigate any abuse claims."

"But only five per cent of domestic abuse claims result in conviction in this country." Ice drips from every word as Wilder slips in front of me, keeping me tucked between him and Zeke. "Isn't that right, detective?"

A sigh. "Unfortunately. But we can still pursue it."

"I'll make a statement," I whisper.

To protect myself. To protect my pack. "What if they do it to someone else?"

Wilder's hand slips into mine. "We're staying. All of us. Unless Fallon wants some space."

I shake my head. I can't think of anything worse than facing this alone. But with them beside me... "Can we do it now?"

63

FALLON

Wilder finds me first.

I scent him before I see him. His rich, myrrh scent, little hints of toffee and vanilla that I soak in as I sit, curled up on the floor of his closet.

I stare up at him miserably. My voice is a whisper. "Hi."

"Little mate," he whispers back. I'm bundled in enough blankets that I look more like a little mountain than an omega. "How are you feeling?"

I can't cry anymore. I've cried for most of the day, curled up in Fox's arms. Zeke's. Rowan's. Teddy's. "I don't want to cry anymore, Wilder."

"Easier said than done." He settles next to me, catching another tear that threatens to drip from my chin.

"Rowan is looking into the power of attorney with the legal team," he says quietly. But there's anger there, in the flash of his eyes. "They don't think it's a legitimate document, Fallon. Otherwise they would have tried it with us, and nothing has been registered officially. Unless it's notarized by someone independent, it's not valid."

I nod. "So just something else they tried to keep me in line, then."

Figures.

"I hate that they did that to you." I can hear the agony in my mate's voice. "I hate that you felt so alone, and we were here and clueless."

I sniff, trying to go to him. But my mountain of blankets nearly topples me to the ground, my arms pinned down, and Wilder scoops me up, settling me across his lap. "You found me."

He sighs heavily. "Not soon enough."

I push my nose into his throat, seeking comfort. He gives it so easily, his cheek rubbing against my hair. "I thought we might have seen the Wild Side today."

There's a teasing note in my voice as I try to push away the dark thoughts. Wilder huffs above me. "He tried. But it was a bit easier to push him away, for once. It felt like... like he understood that it wouldn't help. It's never been like that with us before. Fox thinks that the scent-matching might calm things down, make me... less volatile."

I frown. "I kind of like your feral side, though."

Wilder boops my nose. "And he very much likes you too, but not anybody else, unfortunately. Although he'll tolerate the pack, mostly. Besides, there was only room for *one* feral pack member in there."

My cheeks flush. "I honestly have never behaved like that in my life."

"It was adorable." He laughs softly when I pretend to growl at him again. "You wanted to protect *us*, Fallon. I didn't know whether to be furious or proud."

I hum. "I would prefer proud."

It's the truth. I want my mates to be proud of me. To be proud that I'm their omega.

Wilder shifts, his fingers clasping my chin. "I am *very* proud to be your alpha, Fallon Matthews."

My heart swells, but he presses his lips to mine. Once. Twice.

And then he pulls away, smiling as I follow his lips with my own. "We have time. No rush."

What?

I press a kiss to his neck instead. "You know... Fox knotted me this morning."

Wilder swallows as I lick a line up his throat. "All the more reason to not bombard you. You had a tough day—,"

"I did." I gently sink my teeth into his neck, drinking in the growl. "And now I would like my mate to help me have a better one. Please."

His low groan makes me smile. "You're far too fucking tempting. Especially when you say please. It's like a superpower."

Pushing the blankets off me, I kneel in front of him and bite my lip. "Please."

"Fallon," he nearly snarls.

I shrug my blazer off. "*Please*, Wilder. You want me to beg?"

A flash of gold in his gaze, and he grits his teeth. "You're making things awfully hard—,"

"Oh, I hope so." And I have no idea where the purring words come from as I peel off my blouse, but I don't care, because they finally tip Wilder over the edge.

He pushes me down into the nest of clothes, his mouth sealing over mine before he sinks his teeth into my lower lip and tugs. "Naughty, naughty mate."

Gasping, I rub my aching nipples against his shirt. "For my mate, absolutely."

"Say it again." He runs his tongue down my neck. "Tell me you're mine, Fallon."

"I'm—,"

I gasp as his hot mouth wraps around my nipples and sucks, hard. "I'm yours. Your mate, Wilder."

His approving whine vibrates around my nipple as I lay back and he kisses down my stomach. My trousers are tugged off and thrown somewhere in the closet, and he stares down at me, his nostrils flaring. "I could live on your scent for the rest of my life and die happy."

There's clearly something wrong with me. Because I slide my fingers down, watching Wilder's face as I slip my fingers into my underwear and rub them over my clit, gliding them through my slick.

His jaw clenches as I pull them back out and offer them to him shyly. "Taste?"

Wilder's eyes are a deep, deep blue as he grabs my fingers and sucks them into his mouth. He closes his eyes as he swirls his tongue around, chasing every drop. "Ambrosia."

We both wrestle with his jeans, each of us losing patience with the game. "I want you inside me. Now."

I don't want to wait anymore. I want to feel Wilder's weight on top of me, the comfort that comes from being covered in my alpha's scent, held by him.

I'm pretty sure his jeans are still hanging off one ankle when he rips my underwear off and slides his fingers through my pussy, testing me for himself.

"I'm fine." It's a whimper as I rock my hips. "*Please.*"

He knows what I need. Wilder covers me like a blanket as his thick, hard cock flexes into me slowly. He sinks in inch by inch as he presses my hands above my head and holds them there, my thighs spread wide by his hips as he starts to thrust.

His teeth graze my neck, and I moan. "More. Harder."

It will never be enough. I will never get enough of them. I want every part of them. His knot teases my entrance, and my whine soaks into the air with a burst of orange blossoms.

"Not yet." He cups my throat, gentle but possessive as his other hand keeps my wrists pinned. "If you want my knot, little mate, I want you to beg for it."

His brief kiss tells me it's a game. And his words heat me from the inside out as I tip my head back, giving him my neck and begging for all I'm worth. "Please, Wilder. Please."

He nips at my mouth as his hips thrust into me and he swivels them, making me see stars. "More."

"I need it," I almost sob as he picks up the pace. Even the sound of him pushing into me, his body over mine sends shockwaves down my spine as I push against him. "Please give it to me."

"You beg so prettily." He nips at my shoulder next. "But I want to hear my mate say dirty things, too."

His eyes gleam as I search around in my suddenly empty head. "I want you to... to....,"

He slides a hand under my back, his other arm gripping the back of my neck as he bucks, pinning me against the floor. "God, you're perfect."

I nearly bite through my lip before the scream tears free. "I want you to fill up my pussy. My... my cunt. With your cum. And your knot. Please."

"Goddamn," He hisses the words into my throat. "What my little mate wants, she gets."

My back bows with the force of my orgasm, a tsunami tearing through me as Wilder roars. He fills me, heat and wet that flows out of me, even as he pushes impossibly deeper. "Breathe, baby. My knot is thick."

It's not just thick. It's mammoth. My mouth opens in a silent scream, and Wilder swallows it, kissing my lips as he coaxes my body into stretching wider for him. "You were made for us, Fallon. Made to be trapped by this fucking knot. I want to look at it stretching out that glorious little cunt."

Another burst of slick, and he's inside. My choking breaths fill the air as he keeps thrusting in tiny little movements that nudge him deeper still. "Good girl. My perfect little omega mate. You're clamping down on me so tightly, baby, keeping all that cum like the dirty girl you are."

My pussy flutters again, tightening. He doesn't stop moving.

"I can't," I breathe finally. "It's too much, Wilder."

His thumb grazes my lips. "Yes, you can. You're going to come again around my knot, Fallon. I want to feel that pussy clenching."

He rolls us to the side, gripping me tightly as his hand slips down my back. He rubs against the place where his knot is locked in, and I keep my dazed eyes on his face. He doesn't look away from me as I feel his finger nudging at me, and *how the hell is that only one finger*?

"There," he whispers when my eyes open wide, my lips parting. "Relax for me, baby."

I can't have anything else inside me. I'm too full. But Wilder nudges his way inside my ass, sliding in slowly.

He crooks his finger, and I gasp into his throat. "You like that, baby? Because you're squeezing me like you do."

My nod is rapid, and he laughs softly. "Good girl."

I tense as he adds another finger, but he slides them in and out, working them against me. And he was right – my pussy starts to flutter and clench around his knot again. "Fuck, you look good with my fingers deep in your ass."

He curls them, and my back arches as sensation rips through me. He rocks me through it before gently sliding his fingers free. I slump against him, still pinned by his knot as he strokes me. "Sleep now, little mate. Or I'll end up taking you again."

And my mate begins to purr against me, a soft vibration that rocks me to sleep - even with his knot still deep inside me.

"Much better now," I murmur sleepily. And then I pat my mate's arm. "Good job."

64

TEDDY

"It's Saturday," I announce as I breeze into Fallon's room the next morning. "Rise and shine, fuckers."

Literally.

Clearly, she and Wilder graduated here sometime after he rocked her world. Several times.

Soundproofing is becoming a priority.

Not because I care. Because I'm a jealous little shit, and I want some Fallon time.

I bounce on top of them, and Wilder groans, throwing his arm over Fallon to shield her. "It's ridiculously early, Teddy bear."

"Wrong, knothead," I sing. I flick his ear smugly. "It's after lunch, and you haven't fed your omega."

The speed at which he shoots upright is hilarious. "What?"

I immediately dive into his vacated spot, snuggling up to Fallon and mentally praying that they moved here *after* making all the wet spots. She pats my arm. "Morning, Teddy bear."

God, her voice is all throaty and husky in the morning.

"Rowan and Fox have abandoned us," I whine. "And Zeke has gone again—,"

This time, Wilder flicks my ear.

Shit.

Fallon's eyes open fully. "He has?"

"Mmmm," I murmur non-committal. "He had an appointment. But it means I get you all to myself."

Wilder puts his hands on his hips, looking offended. "What am I, scotch mist?"

"Naked scotch mist." I start snickering as his cheeks turn red – both sets – and he grabs a pillow to shield his bits. "But you also have an appointment. It's on the calendar."

"Damn." He frowns. "I forgot about that. It's only the garage. I can reschedule."

"No," I say primly. "I am stealing my Fallon back, and we're going to watch movies and sink enough junk food that we have cavities before the end of the day. It's an omega necessity. Pampering included."

Fallon's head pops up at that. "Pampering?"

I smirk at Wilder. "Yep. All the pampering."

***

This was such a bad idea.

Beneath me, Fallon moans as I run my thumbs down either side of her spine. She wriggles slightly, and my eyes cross. "God, that feels so good."

Down. Bad boy.

"How do you feel?" I ask her, pushing back up again and pouring a little more oil into my hands. She sighs as I move up to her shoulders, rubbing them.

"Like I've been *alpha'd*," she mutters. "But in the best way."

"Huh." I shift down, moving onto her bare legs and running my hands over them.

Why the fuck did you think this was a good idea—

I had good intentions, I swear. But now Fallon is half naked and wriggling and *oiled*, her skin is gleaming, and my cock feels so fucking hard that I'm scared it might actually snap off.

It would be a real shame to lose the eighth wonder of the world like that.

"Teddy?"

My cheeks flash scarlet. "Uh. Sorry."

But she's propping herself up, glancing over her shoulder. I swallow when she pulls herself up to sit properly, grabbing a blanket and wrapping it around her. "What's the matter? You can tell me."

I choke. "I'm fine, I swear."

She frowns. "No, you're not."

"I am!" I almost yelp it, scrabbling backwards as she reaches for me like she'll give me a damn *cuddle*. A half-naked, oiled-up cuddle. "I just – uh—,"

Her eyes drop.

So do mine.

And fuck me, it's about to poke her in the eye.

Fallon bites her lip. Her cheeks flush a beautiful shade of rose, but she lifts her eyes to mine. "Is that... for me? Or just a random thing?"

I swallow. "I wanted to pamper you. Genuinely. It wasn't a – an excuse or anything. I'm not a creep, I promise."

I'm desperate to give her everything those fuckers never did. "But – you smell really good, Fallon, and you were making those little noises—,"

Fallon's lips press over mine, and I still.

I've never kissed an omega before.

Fox's lips are strong. Dominant, even in the feel of his lips on mine. Unyielding.

And Rowan is a little softer.

But Fallon.... I sink into her lush mouth, tasting orange blossoms and the strawberry sweets we ate earlier, and I'm lost.

We both pull away, both of us breathing heavily, and stare at each other.

"Fallon," I try not to let my voice shake, but I'm pretty sure I fail miserably. "You don't have to – I mean, I'm not one of your scent-matches."

"Neither is Rowan," she says almost shyly. "But we're all Pack, aren't we?"

"We are," I breathe. "Can I... can I kiss you, then?"

When she nods, I almost dive on her. Our noses bump together, and she's laughing as my lips collide with hers almost clumsily.

You have way more game than this, Teddy-bear.

I cup her cheek, slowing down and really *tasting* her, this omega who walked into our pack and flipped our lives upside down in the best fucking way possible. The soft sounds she makes as my tongue brushes hers in gentle question has me nudging her down onto the blankets we spread out across the living room floor.

I'm wearing a shirt, but all I can feel under my hands is soft, smooth skin as I touch her, my fingertips lightly skating down her collarbone as she shivers.

When I brush against her breast, we both inhale.

"God, Fallon." My voice is ragged. "You are...,"

She smiles at me, amber eyes shining. "Can I take off your top?"

I nearly swallow my tongue as she pulls me down, her fingers undoing my buttons until she slides off my shirt.

I press myself against her, and it feels like I can breathe as I dip my mouth to hers, my hand cupping her breast and massaging the skin there before I move lower.

"I want to kiss you here." I brush her nipple with my finger.

"Here." Lower, across her stomach.

She sucks in a breath when I brush the shorts she's wearing. "And here."

Fallon doesn't say anything, but she hooks her fingers in her shorts and tugs them down. I catch a glimpse of dewy, dark curls, my throat tightening as I lean in and suck her nipple into my mouth, laving it with my tongue.

I'm an omega. I like to think I've learned something about sex in the years I've spent having a damn lot of it. And I flip that knowledge, use it shamelessly in my touch, my hands, my lips, until Fallon is gasping beneath me as I nudge her hips wide and inhale.

Fresh fucking nectar. I start with her clit, rubbing it before I carefully fix my lips around it and suck in short pulses. Her gasps turn to moans, Fallon's hands tangling in my hair as I take my time, learning what she likes.

And what she fucking loves.

And my girl *loves* me licking her wet little cunt.

Her thighs are shaking around my shoulders after only a few long licks. I sink my tongue inside, thrusting as I chase every drop of her and play with her swollen clit, tracing my fingers around it and down her sensitive, puffy pussy lips.

She pulls me back up far too soon. "I want to play too."

My eyes widen as Fallon shifts down my body, her hair trailing over my scent. Our scents hang around us in glorious, heavy sheets, chocolate and orange and nutmeg and it's so fucking spicy that all I want to do is inhale it.

Fallon takes her time inspecting my cock, and it jumps under her finger. "It won't bite you."

She grins. "It's just... different. Like, softer? But it still feels like steel underneath."

"Yeah," I say roughly. "And just to warn you, I make a *lot* of slick. Like... a lot of it."

Especially when I'm overly-excited. And that doesn't feel like enough to describe how I feel as Fallon hovers over my cock, holding it gently as she lowers herself and I feel the first brush of her wet heat.

Two matching, needy whines filter into the air.

"Oh my god."

Both of us twist, panting, to face the door.

Rowan stares at us both. Fox appears over his shoulder, his eyes darkening as he takes us both in. "I can't leave you two alone for a moment, can I?"

"Please," I beg. I'm not sure who I'm begging, but Fallon is definitely included at the top of the short list. "*Please*, Fallon."

Fox steps into the room. His hands brush Fallon where she kneels, frozen. "We'll watch this time. Rowan?"

Rowan is scarlet as he follows Fox over to the sofa. Fallon and I stare, almost hypnotized as Fox sprawls, dragging Rowan down onto his lap and dragging his teeth over his neck. "Carry on."

Fallon looks back at me. I stare at her.

And she slowly, painfully, fucking gloriously lowers herself onto my aching cock.

"Oh my god." Her words are a mixture, half-whine, half-moan. "Teddy. You're so *warm*."

I can't speak. All I can do is watch as Fallon rocks against me, steadying herself on my chest as she raises herself up and then grinds herself down on my dick.

It's so fucking wet. Both of us are soaking already, and my slick is already flowing as Fallon rides me. I grip her hips, massaging them as our moans ring out and she finds a rhythm.

I'm fucking lost for her. It's not enough – I want to press myself against her, to feel every inch of her, so I roll us over until I can fuck myself into her slick, heavenly heat.

My hips undulate and her hot pussy clamps down on me. My head presses against her shoulder. "I'm going to—,"

"*Stop.*"

Both of us stop at the bark that ripples from our alpha, wide-eyed. My fucking orgasm ebbs away as I twist to face Fox. "*Seriously?*"

He grins at my whine, offers a smaller, more intimate smile to Fallon when she turns her face to his, lips parting. "A little edging is good for the soul."

Oh my fucking god.

"Start again," he murmurs, and I pick up the pace, Fallon frantic beneath me as we both chase the orgasm just within—

"Stop."

Fallon moans, her head tipping back as she pants. "Fox. *Please.*"

"You're trying to kill us."

But fuck me, if our releases aren't going to be fireworks.

He keeps us hanging for only a few seconds. "Start."

This time, Fallon is gripping my ass, her ankles hooked around my back as I wrap my hands around her upper back and fuck like my life depends on it.

Her pussy ripples around me before Fox can stop it, and my own orgasm hits so fucking hard that I nearly black out. My cock floods her hot little channel with slick until we're soaked, the blankets underneath us full of... *us.*

I collapse onto my side, heaving for air as I tug her down with me. Fallon crawls onto my chest, panting.

Note to self – plan a shower for every time I have sex with Fallon. Or a bath. With candles.

"I'm dead," I croak. "That was the best damn experience of my life."

Fallon laughs, her lips brushing my cheek.

And Rowan – Rowan's groan has us all turning. He pales, his hands slamming down over his jeans.

"Did you just...,"

He buries his face in his hands, still sitting on Fox's lap. And my alpha is grinning. "Best damn experience of my life, too."

My laugh comes out as a snorting, muffled choke. "This is amazing. You came in your—,"

"*Teddy!*"

65

FALLON

I haven't been in their garden before.

Your garden now, too.

I shake my head at myself, smiling. Even my thoughts have been *Teddy-fied*, my pack inching their way into every piece of my heart.

I can't *stop* smiling.

Carefully, I grip the coffee in my hands. Greenery sprawls out in front of me across the large space, and I follow the winding path until I reach the converted shed Wilder told me about.

Zeke's workshop.

"Zeke?" My voice is quiet. Too quiet, so I call a little louder. "Zeke?"

I start chewing on the inside of my cheek.

He's my alpha. My scent-matched mate.

So why do I feel so... *nervous*?

At the crash that comes from inside, I step back, startled. Zeke appears at the door, out of breath. "Fallon!"

Suddenly shy, I thrust the coffee at him. "I made you this. I'll go now."

I'm turning when a hand gently snags my arm.

Zeke studies my face, his eyes softening. "Hey, sweetheart. What's the matter?"

My lip starts to wobble.

Grow up, Fallon. Stop being so damn needy.

"Fallon." Zeke looks more alarmed now. He slides his hand down to tangle in mine, tugging me through the door of the shed and setting the coffee I made him down on a sideboard before he turns to me. "Please. What is it?"

I swallow. "Are you... disappointed? In me?"

It would be unusual, but it does happen. Scent-matches are fairly rare, and all the more revered for it, but it wouldn't be the first time an alpha rejected their mate.

And that would be fine.

I have Fox, and Wilder. Teddy and Rowan.

I burst into tears.

Zeke doesn't pause. He sweeps me up easily, cradling me like he did that day when he ran with me before he strides over to a chair and settles us both in it. His lips are pressed together, and I duck my head.

I shouldn't have asked.

But his large hand nudges up my face. And he looks so upset at that moment that my stomach bottoms out. "Zeke—,"

He slams his lips against mine. Hard, fast possession, his hand reaching up to grip the back of my neck as my toes curl.

And beneath me...

He pulls away. "Does that feel like I'm *disappointed* in you, sweetheart?"

Mute, I shake my head.

In fact, it's a little frightening. It feels as though I'm sitting on a tree trunk.

But he's not finished. "Fallon... I'm so sorry if I've given you any impression that I'm disappointed in you. I feel incredibly lucky to be your scent-match."

I'm flushing now, because I'm an idiot. "It's just – you've been leaving early a lot. And coming back late. And I thought—,"

His brows crease. And he sighs. "I knew I'd make a mess of this."

Carefully, I slide my fingers over his cheek, feeling the scraping of his beard. "You're not making a mess of this."

"I am." He turns and presses a kiss to the palm of my hand. "I... I've been making you something. That's why I haven't been around so much. I was trying to get it finished, so you could have it as soon as possible."

My heart leaps inside my chest. "You have?"

He nods. He kisses my lips again before he shifts me on his lap. "Knees either side, so I can keep my hands free."

It places his cock directly between my thighs as I face him. My scent trickles out, and Zeke's ears turn an interesting shade of scarlet as he reaches for a drawer in his desk, pulling it open. "Close your eyes, baby."

I hear what almost sounds like a whispered prayer before he places something in my hands. "You got me a book?"

"Open your eyes and see." His words are gruff.

Slowly, I open them, and look down.

"It was the only thing you wanted to bring with you," he says softly. "I've never rebound a book before, so I had to learn quickly. It took longer than I thought it would."

The paper cuts on his hands.

The disappearances.

And—

I can barely breathe as I stroke my finger over the cover. The familiar, slightly cracked cover of *The Light in Us* gleams back at me. "You *fixed* it. For me?"

My voice is a whisper.

Zeke clears his throat. "I tried. A few pages are slightly shorter from the tearing. But they were all there, thanks to you."

I carefully crack the cover open.

My dad's words are still there, still on the title page in his familiar handwriting. My eyes begin to burn.

Ellis ripped it apart. And Zeke... Zeke put it back together.

A little like me. The Smith pack ripped me apart.

But this pack... the Quill pack is piecing me back together.

"I know it's not a typical mating gift." Zeke rubs the back of his neck awkwardly. "I'm not... I've never been very good at guessing. And I thought you'd rather have this. But I'll learn what you like, and you can have anything—,"

His words cut off as I throw my arms around his neck, making sure I keep hold of the book. My tears soak into his neck. "Thank you. *Thank you*."

He runs a gentle hand over my back. "You never need to thank me. Especially not for this."

I don't say anything. I just hold onto him, gripping him tightly with one hand and my other clutching the book he learned how to fix, just for me.

When I've stopped crying, he wipes at my eyes. "I promise I haven't been avoiding you. That's the last thing I want you to believe."

My laugh is choked. "I do. I'm sorry."

He smiles as I carefully set *The Light in Us* on the desk behind me. "And thank you for the coffee."

I grin back at him. "Your present beats mine by a landslide."

Zeke brushes his finger against my lips. And his eyes are almost wondering. "Not to me."

My heart clenches for my mate. For this huge alpha with a bigger heart. "You could ruin me, you know, Zeke Quill."

His brows knot. "I'd never do that to you."

I believe him. He inhales when I lean in and press my lips to his.

This time, his lips are more... uncertain. He grows bolder as I trace the line of his mouth with my tongue, his hands sliding down to grip my hips as he presses into me.

Testing, I rub myself over the behemoth between my legs, and Zeke freezes. "What are you doing, mate?"

I flick my eyes up from under my lashes, feigning innocence. "Nothing."

When I rub again, his eyes narrow. "Really?"

"Mmhmm." I swivel my hips, and he hisses between his teeth.

"Fallon, I... I haven't...done this before."

We haven't been together like that. Smiling, I aim for the area of throat on display above his black tee, sucking on it as he shudders. "I know. This is our first time."

I hope.

"No." He's blushing now, his cheeks a deep red. "I mean...I've never done *this* before. Any of it. I was waiting. For... for you."

My movement stops. All of it.

"Oh," I whisper. "*Zeke.*"

He shakes his head. "I know it's stupid. I'm twenty-eight. But I never... I never met anyone I could imagine wanting to do that with, when I was hoping my mate was out there somewhere."

I drop my gaze. "I...,"

But his hands are firm. "I don't care. Not in the slightest, Fallon."

He runs a reverent finger down my neck, and I shiver. "I just wanted you to know. In case I mess it up."

"Impossible," I murmur, leaning in to kiss him again.

I mean it. Our lips dance together, the soft music playing in the background the only sound as I slide my hands beneath Zeke's tee. He's breathing heavily when I peel it over his head and toss it. Slowly, I raise my hands up.

His hands span my ribcage as he pushes my soft sweater up and over my head.

"I don't like bras," I whisper. He swallows, shaking his head.

"Perfect."

His hand swallows my breasts, covering them entirely and half of my ribs on top. He's completely focused on me as he massages them, and I brace myself on his knees as I lean back against the desk.

He leans forward. He doesn't suck on my nipple. He kisses it, so fucking gently I want to cry. "You're exquisite, Fallon."

I feel it, as he touches me. I shift to my feet for a moment to tug off my jeans and watch him do the same. His cock—

"Fuck," I breathe. Even the tip of Zeke's nose turns scarlet.

He shifts uncertainly. "Maybe we should go to the floor?"

I shake my head and take my mate's hand.

I'm going to show him exactly what he's been missing.

He follows my lead as I press him back into his chair, but his breathing stops as I drop to my knees and wrap my hands around his cock.

Zeke's scent pours out, woodsy and herb-like. Comforting, like an embrace as I lean down and suck his head into my mouth.

He almost roars my name, his hips bucking. "Fallon!"

And I smile around him as I take him deeper. Inch by inch, my cheeks hollowing out as I take as much of Zeke's cock as I can manage, covering the base with my hands and pumping in time with my head.

I hear a crack, glance up to see Zeke releasing the arm of his chair.

"Come here," he says hoarsely. "Please, baby. I want you on top of me."

And I want my mate inside me. So much so that when I stand, Zeke's eyes zero in on the slick coating my inner thighs. He shudders. "Let me see you. Please."

My breathing stutters as I slowly lower my hands, and spread myself, so he can see my pussy. Cool air brushes over my clit, making me shiver, and I whimper when Zeke's hand shoots forward to cover me.

"My mate will never be cold." He growls the words as his palm massages against me and I grind my clit against *him*.

I have the feeling that once we've practiced a few times, Zeke will well and truly take control of our time together.

But for this time, for the first time, I drink in the uncertainty, this gift that he's giving me as I climb over him and bear down.

Slowly.

There's a deep v between his eyebrows, his teeth sinking into his lip and a muscle ticking in his jaw as I slowly rock into him, finding a rhythm.

Our chests are pressed together, his arms a band around me as I gently rock. "You're so big, Zeke."

His knot is going to be... a whole new experience.

He pushes my hair back so he can see my face better. "We don't have to do the knot today."

I kiss the tip of his nose. "Cute. But I'm definitely taking your knot today."

I breathe in the noises he makes, the grunt and moans. And he does the same, avidly watching every shift, eyes flickering at every moan.

I gasp when he presses down on my hips. "Softly, baby. But my knot... it's ready for you."

My whine rolls out of me as I feel it. Heavy and solid, but with enough flex that I can slowly rock myself over it, feeling it push inside me until it finally seals.

My sweat-soaked forehead drops to Zeke's chest as he groans beneath me. A low, almost quiet sound, but his heat bursts between my legs, inside my pussy, filling me until I can feel him dripping around the seal he's created in my body. "Come for me, Fallon. I want to feel you."

My pussy is already twitching, his words the last thing I need to drag me over the edge as I clamp down with a cry. My teeth sink into Zeke's shoulder, marking him as his hips shift up.

I slump against him. "I think... I mean. Was that good for you?"

His laugh is almost shy. "I can't wait to do it again. My knot... it feels so heavy inside you."

"Because it's holding all of you inside me." I kiss him gently. "I could use a nap. All that tree-climbing."

We grin at each other, both of us suddenly absurdly happy.

"How old is everyone else?" I ask drowsily a little while later. I'm propped against his bare chest, listening to his heartbeat. "I realized I haven't even asked."

Zeke kisses the top of my hair. "Fox is twenty-nine. I'm a few months behind him, but twenty-eight. Wilder is the same. And Ro and Teddy have the same birthday. Twenty-six."

I stretch lazily. "What date?"

"April fifth."

My mouth falls open. Zeke's eyebrows fly up. "No way."

"Oh, Teddy is going to love this. A *triple* birthday celebration?"

I can't wait.

66

— · —

FALLON

Rowan glances at me. We're huddled together, staring at his screen.

"Wow," I breathe. "Rowan, this is...,"

He shrugs. "It wasn't too hard to find. The accounts information was harder, obviously. More finding patterns of behavior than contact information. But this is the number for the lawyer."

I take the card he gives me, curling it in my hand before I press my lips to his. "Thank you. I mean it."

My stomach flips. My dad's lawyer. The man who handled his will.

The man who can explain exactly what happened to all his money. To his *legacy*.

Although Rowan has pieced together a huge amount. Including some interesting information about Ellis, Shaun and Rory.

"Fallon," Rowan says softly. My gaze jerks to him "It's your decision. Nobody else's."

Slowly, I nod, and he jerks his head toward the door with an understanding smile. "Go on. You have a big day ahead. And have fun."

My smile grows. "I intend to."

I blow him a kiss before I grab my laptop and dash from the room. Nobody is walking with me today, although Fox wanted to. Everyone wanted to.

I scan my employee ID at the entrance to the elevator and walk in, nodding to someone else who gets in with me.

My excitement only grows as the floors rise.

I step out alone, taking a moment to look around. To breathe it all in.

I don't intend to waste a minute of my time on this floor. Not a single minute.

My new boss's door is closed. Heart in my mouth, I tug the collar of my shirt into place and knock on the door.

I *feel* like an editor, in my crisp white shirt and fitted brown trousers. My hair is pulled up into a sleek ponytail, a few strands left free and my face neutral. Laptop under my arm. My bag is filled with books and pens and notepads.

I feel like one. And Ed Burrows is the man who's going to make sure I become a damn good one.

Emotion tightens my throat as the door swings open and he grins at me, holding out his hand. "Fallon Matthews. I'm so pleased you're joining us."

My handshake is firm.

"Not nearly as glad as I am."

"Come on in." Ed steps back, revealing a meeting table with a handful of others. "We'll introduce you, get you set up. Busy day, I'm afraid."

My smile feels as though my face is too small to hold it. "I don't mind that at all."

Ed gives me a considering look as he waves me to a seat and points to the coffee pot. "For once, I actually believe it. Want to introduce yourself, or should I?"

"I'll do it." I turn to my new colleagues.

"Hi," I wave awkwardly, my heart feeling fit to burst. "My name is Fallon Matthews, and... and I'm the new Acquisitions intern."

67

Fox

My mate is glowing, bouncing from her first day in her new job. She giggles. "*Fox*. Where are we going?"

"Just wait." I wrap my arm around her as we duck past a large group.

We stop in front of a building, and I watch Fallon's eyes widen as she takes in the stacks in the window.

"This is the biggest bookstore in the state," I tell her. "And when we started Ink & Quill, I took everyone here separately for their own rite of passage. And today is your turn. For your new job."

Fuck, I love the stunned expression on her face almost as much as I hate it.

"Come on."

I feel almost as excited as my mate looks as I lead her directly into the middle of the store, pausing on top of the vast golden compass painted directly into the floor. She grins, spinning around. "What do I do?"

I pull out a stopwatch. "You have fifteen minutes to choose as many books as you want and bring them back here. And they'll all go on your new bookshelves at home. Shockingly enough, Teddy holds the record for the most books collected."

"What new bookshelves?" She eyes me suspiciously, and I wince.

"The ones we're going to make space for. Are you ready?"

She squeals. "Maybe?"

I hit the button. "Go!"

I follow her. I can't help it. My arms are folded and I'm grinning like an idiot as I watch my mate dash around. She actually takes her time, looking at blurbs and touching covers.

It's the same thing I do when I come here. Wilder did my challenge, and he couldn't believe how few books I picked.

I'm waiting when she rushes up, just a handful of books in her hands. "Oh, fuck."

Her eyes fly to mine. "What is it?"

I wave a hand. "I forgot to start the timer. So we'll start again."

Reaching forward, I snag the four books she picked. "We'll still keep these ones, though. Off you go."

She narrows her eyes at me. But then she laughs, darting off again.

We stroll home with a grand total of eight books. I'm frowning, and Fallon is grinning like someone just bought her the whole damn library. "That was incredible."

"Teddy managed to get seventy-two books," I grumble. "You picked *eight*."

"Eight books that I can't wait to read." She nudges me. "Thank you."

"What did I say about thanking me?"

I pull out my phone to check as we get closer to home. There's a thumbs-up from Wild, and I slip my phone back into my pockets with a whistle.

We hear the shouting as we walk through the door. Fallon twists to look upstairs. "Is that – is that Teddy?"

I bite my cheek to hide my smile. "Sounds like it."

But she's already running. I follow her, feeling a little guilty as she races up to the attic space, following the sound of Teddy's bellowing.

He cuts off mid-scream when he spots her, and beams. "There you are!"

We both watch Fallon blink rapidly. "What... what was that?"

"Oh," Teddy exclaims. "We have a surprise for you."

He gestures to the door of the room beside his own nest. "Go on. You'll have to excuse the alphas. They're not nest trained yet."

Fallon hesitates.

I brush my hand over her hair. "You don't have to use it. We won't be offended, Fallon. But you need a nest space, mate."

"Just look," Teddy pleads. "If you don't like it, we'll change it, I promise. It's more than just a nest."

I can see the indecision on her face. "I'm sorry. I'm really grate-ful—,"

"Stop," I say softly. "Go in and see."

Neither Teddy or I are breathing as Fallon pushes the door open.

She stops in the doorway.

The ground layer is an office space. Cozy patchwork rugs and a huge, old wooden desk take up most of the room, a floor lamp and wide reading seat in the corner for her to curl up in. The main wall that runs up all three levels is filled with empty bookshelves, a rolling ladder in place to help reach them.

To our right, a set of wooden stairs lead up to a just-visible sec-ond level. Much more enclosed. Jeweled sheets hang from the ceiling, sending colored light dancing into the confined space below.

Small. Cozy. And a replica of the nest she had before.

The nest she *lost*.

"If it's not right, we can change it. Or we can make it bigger, as you get more comfortable." Teddy's voice is soft. "I know it's not the same, sweetheart. But I wanted to give you something you would *want* to use. And what better than one you designed yourself?"

Wilder, Zeke and Rowan aren't breathing either. They're covered in paint and dust and various other things from their day as I watched over Fallon at work.

Fallon covers her face with her hands, her shoulders shaking. "It's beautiful. You... you got it so right, Teddy. How did you even remember?"

He's pulling Fallon's hands from her face as he tugs her into a hug. "You described it so well. And you mentioned it again last week. The rest was a little bit of imagination."

She steps a little further inside, staring at the empty shelves. "Now I know why Fox was so annoyed I picked eight books."

We're going back next week. She can have an hour.

Teddy's mouth drops open in horror

"You only picked eight books?"

68

FALLON

Teddy comes to stand beside me. My eyes nearly pop out of my head. "Wow."

He studies us both in the mirror with pride clear on his face. "I'm a freaking genius."

My head just bobs in agreement. Because he *is*.

I spin, unable to help myself. The sleek, midnight blue gown spins with me, glittering in the light. Matching sleek netting connects from my waist to the edges of my white gloves. And my hair is a shiny, silky sheet that falls down my back.

"They're going to lose their shit," Teddy is watching me with a small smile. "I want to tumble you back into that bed and fuck you in that dress."

I shiver. "Later. *After* my first gala."

Teddy grins, checking his phone. "They're waiting for us. *Not* so patiently, I might add. I get to go first, so I can see their faces when you walk down."

He tugs at the sleeve of his tuxedo. "It's warm in here, isn't it?"

Frowning, I glance around the hotel room. "It is?"

He shrugs, offering me his arm. "It's this tuxedo, I swear. Looking this pretty takes sweat. May I escort you, my lady?"

Giggling, I slide my arm through his. "You may."

We stroll out of the room that connects us to the others on the floor. Fox went a little overboard and booked us a full hotel floor for the night when Teddy insisted on attending this event.

More than enough space for Teddy to claim an area as our personal dressing room.

And as we walk down the stairs, the look on my pack's faces tells me his efforts were *definitely* worth it.

Fox smoothly sidesteps the others, strolling to the bottom of the stairs. His purple eyes glitter, and I nearly lose my breath.

They're all in perfectly matching black tuxedos, hair swept back. My scent begins to prickle, and Fox's nose flares. "Mate. You look and smell *delicious*."

He brushes a kiss against my lips, careful not to smudge the lips Teddy spent a good fifteen minutes on, before he does the same to Teddy. "Luckiest pack in the city."

"In the country," Wilder interjects. Fox takes Rowan and Teddy, and I slip in between a speechless Zeke and Wilder as we head toward the ballroom where the gala is being held. People are entering in groups, chatting and clutching glasses of champagne as a string quartet plays in the corner.

Zeke clears his throat. "You look beautiful, Fallon."

I feel beautiful, surrounded by my mates. They're noticed as we walk in. "People are watching you."

"Are they?" Wilder murmurs. "Or are they watching you?"

I nudge him in the ribs. "*Definitely* from a book."

His blue eyes sparkle with amusement, and something hotter as he scans me slowly. His smile is a glint of the feral side of him. "Maybe. But I mean it all the same."

I smile down at my feet. Wilder hands me a glass of champagne, and I sip on it as I scan the room. Spotting Ed in the corner, I wave. "Can we go over?"

"Sure." We start weaving in that direction, and somebody moves in front of me.

I glance up with an apology on my lips that fades, my body stiffening.

My mates both still. Wilder's arm tightens beneath my grip, almost vibrating.

"Fallon." Ellis smiles at me. But there's no warmth there as he holds up a champagne glass in silent salute. "Fancy seeing you here. Not dead after all."

Zeke lets out a rumbling growl. "Walk away, Smith. Before I make you."

Ellis tuts. "That's not very nice. What else were we to think? Our omega gone, our home almost destroyed?"

I find my voice. "*My* home, I think you'll find. With my money. And I'm not your omega, Ellis. I never was."

Irritation flickers in his face. "I'm not sure Rory would agree with that. Would you?"

He grabs the shoulder of the male next to him.

It's clear that Rory is drunk. His cheeks are already flushed, his eyes glazed. They clear as he stares at me. "Fallon?"

I take a step back. Wilder's arm wraps around my waist. "Don't you fucking talk to her. You don't deserve to breathe the same fucking *air* as her. How the hell did you even get in? We checked the guest list. Your names were *not* on it."

I glance up at him. Watching his eyes flicker. Blue, to gold, to blue. *Not here.*

But Rory is frowning. "Fallon, come here. It's time to come home."

I almost choke at the demand in his words. "Absolutely fucking not."

"Come here. *Now*."

It's not a request.

It's a *bark*.

My feet move forward before I can stop them, a chill settling into my bones as Zeke yanks me back. He pulls me behind him and shifts forward. "I'm going to tear your fucking head off and I don't care who's here."

But someone else pushes in front of Zeke.

"What the *fuck* did you just say to my mate?"

Teddy and Rowan flank my back. Teddy lets out a quiet whimper, and I tangle our fingers together as we shrink back.

Rory doesn't back down. He shoves himself up against Fox. "She's *my* fucking omega. Not yours."

Fox doesn't move. I don't see him shift.

But Rory is suddenly choking, his face darkening as Fox grips his neck.

Ellis jumps forward, but Wilder is there. "I don't need any more fucking reasons to put you on the ground, Ellis. *Believe me*."

"Fox," I whisper. My hand brushes his back. "They're not worth it."

"They're not worth anything," Fox says quietly. "Because Wordsmith collapsed today. Many authors – *good* authors, who didn't deserve it – have lost their livelihoods overnight. Rumor has it the Smith pack is facing federal fraud charges. Maybe you could confirm, Rory?"

He only chokes, struggling against Fox's grip. I suck in a breath.

Fox drags him closer. "You are not worth a single damn thing to me. But my mate is worth everything. And not only did you put her through hell, you dared to *use your fucking bark* on her. You are a worthless excuse for an alpha and putting you down would be a fucking mercy to humanity."

He drops Rory. "Get on your damn knees. *Now*."

I've never heard Fox sound like that. Both Teddy and I drop, whines at the back of our throats, but Zeke and Rowan keep us upright.

The dominance.

And Rory – Rory collapses to his knees, staring as if he can't work out quite how he got there.

As do several other people around us.

I stare at Fox's back.

He's *that* strong.

He just chooses not to abuse it.

Someone else pushes through the gathering crowd.

Shaun.

He doesn't say anything. Doesn't intervene. He just watches Rory on the ground, then Ellis, backing away from an enraged Wilder.

But not feral. Not yet, at least.

Rory starts to get up, his face flushes with humiliation. But Fox isn't done yet. "*Stay.*"

Only we hear his words as he leans in. "If you so much as *look* at my pack again, I will have you tear off your own cock and eat it. Nod if you understand me."

Through gritted teeth, Rory nods. "*Let me up.*"

"No." Fox turns. "Wilder. Zeke. Can you take out the trash? I believe the police will be along shortly to arrest them."

I glance around for Rowan. He's on his phone, but he offers me a wink. And a choice.

Thumbs up. He mouths. *Yes?*

Thumbs down. *Or no?*

Fraud charges, Fox said. Fraud that *Rowan* found.

And now he's making them pay for it. But he won't, if I ask him not to.

Ellis rips himself away from Wilder with a snarl. "I'm going."

This asshole stole my family's money. Stole *everything* I had left of my parents.

My lips curl. And I give Rowan a double thumbs up.

He grins, nodding as he begins to speak rapidly into the phone.

Turning his back on Rory, Fox turns to me, his eyes immediately softening as they shift between Teddy and I, clinging to each other.

Teddy is shaking, the movement almost violent.

"It's okay," I whisper, trying to soothe him. "They're going."

My brows knot when it doesn't ease. "Teddy?"

Fox is beside me. He reaches for Teddy's face. "You're burning up."

Teddy is gritting his teeth. "*Heat.*"

I don't know who turns more pale. Me, or Fox. He's already barking instructions to a member of waiting staff nearby.

We're in a hotel. More than an hour away from home. From Teddy's nest.

And Teddy.... he's holding on so tightly, trying not to let it out in front of everyone.

I don't even know how he's doing it.

Fox lifts him into his arms. If people weren't watching before, they definitely are now.

I'm almost shoving people out of the way to make space through the crowd. Rowan appears, nudging me back as he takes over, his height making it easier to cut through. "It'll be okay. Stay with Teddy and Fox, okay?"

I do as he says, racing with Fox back up the stairs as Rowan disappears. "What do we do?"

"Rowan will clear the hotel."

Fox kicks open the door to a bedroom, carrying Teddy inside. Teddy moans and twists, and Fox cups his cheek, forcing Teddy to focus on him. "Let it out. *Now*."

I stagger back against the wall as Teddy's perfume *erupts*. A powerful, crashing wave of chocolate and melted marshmallow that punches straight into my abdomen, *squeezing* it so hard I have to wrap my hands around my middle.

Fox keeps his hands on Teddy's cheek. He's almost vibrating with tension, his jawline so tight it could cut glass. "You are safe. We're going to make this right, Teddy."

"Fox," Teddy moans. He twists again, and Fox sways. "It hurts."

"I know, love." Fox's eyes are glazed when he turns to me.

"It's okay," I breathe. I run to him, stroking his face, his chest. "Stay with him. He needs you."

Fox's growl rumbles through the room as his head flashes between the two of us. "I—,"

But Teddy cries out again, his hips bucking.

And Fox's eyes darken. Actually *darken*, the purple almost turning black as his pupils expand.

When I turn, he snatches my wrist, pushing me down beside Teddy. "*Stay*."

My whole body loosens, something unfurling at the sound of my alpha's bark. My skin flushes all over as I go limp on the bed.

And then a matching wave of my own perfume pulses into the air.

My whine is torn from my throat as sweat prickles on my chest. My dress is suddenly too tight, too constricting.

A second wave of perfume. This one is stronger.

Almost as strong as the agony that tears through my body. All of it focused on the intense need that consumes my abdomen, my pussy clenching around air.

Fox roars. It's full of panic and rage as he staggers back

I lock eyes with Fox just as the first wave of my own heat drags me under.

His eyes are the last thing I remember.

And they turn *red*.

69

— · —

WILDER

My knuckles are bleeding as we stroll back to the hotel, my eyes finally bleeding back to blue. Zeke has his arm around my shoulders. "Shit, you're heavy."

"Sorry." I push myself upright, but I have no regret in my chest for the beating we just delivered to Rory and Ellis. Even if my memory of it isn't the strongest. "God, that felt fucking good."

As we turn the corner to the hotel, we both see it.

Zeke straightens. "What the hell happened?"

We both take off toward the crowd, pushing through and searching for any sign of the pack.

When we reach the main doors, the security guard pushes us back. "Emergency closure. An omega went into heat."

Both Zeke and I still.

It takes us a second to burst past the guard and into the foyer. It's empty, champagne half-drunk on every side and the instruments from the musicians abandoned.

Rowan is talking frantically to an older woman, running his hands through his hair. He exhales when he sees us. "It's Teddy. We've locked down."

Fuck.

In the middle of the fucking hotel.

We all take off for the stairs at the same time. Rowan is with us, talking frantically. "They'll bring supplies to the top of the stairs for us to grab. Blankets, pillows. Whatever they can find."

But none of it will be Teddy's things. His *nest.* "Can we get him home?"

Rowan shakes his head. "Not without it causing him a *lot* of anxiety. We're better off making do here. At least it's private."

As we reach the top of the stairs, Zeke and I crash to a stop. Rowan spins back, gaping at us. "What are you doing? Fallon will—,"

"Heat," Zeke rasps. I'm still wrapping my head around that impossible scent, my vision wavering at the edges. "*Both* of them."

Rowan's face turns slack. "They – what?"

My cock punches to life inside my tuxedo. And it's screaming for my omega, my *mate.*

She's *hurting.*

I can sense it, her pain enough to have me tearing down the hall, following the cloying, heated scent of her and Teddy's slickness.

Fox spins with a growl as we barge in. His eyes flicker.

"Is he... oh god," Rowan breathes. We're all staring at Fox's red eyes. A line of scarlet, similar to blood, swallows the purple whole, leaving us with a pack alpha in full blown fucking rut.

He's buried deep inside Fallon, her hands clawing at the bedding as he thrusts into her. And beside him, Teddy is whining, his ass up in the air and Fox's fingers buried in his ass.

No. It's his *fist*, the closest he can get to a knot without splitting himself in half.

What a clusterfuck.

Rowan is pushing the door shut. "I'll get this place up and running. *Go.*"

Fox rips himself free of Fallon with an almost pained grunt. She arches her back, glazed eyes sweeping us hazily. "Knot."

I can feel her heat dragging me under. I'm going to lose myself, either to the heat haze or the fucking Wild Side, desperately pushing to get through.

We strip off as quickly as we can. Fox is desperately fucking Teddy, one hand around his neck as he holds him up and the other pumping Teddy's cock. Slick already covers the bed, Teddy, Fallon – fucking everywhere.

Zeke palms his monster cock as he climbs up onto the bed. "Where—,"

"Her mouth." A starting point. Fallon's happy moan as she swallows Zeke's dick has me thrusting into her and thanking fuck for the slick that eases my path. She bucks and trembles beneath me as I grip her hips and pound into her, her throaty cries hitting me harder with every push into her clenching, weeping pussy.

A bonding mark.

This is it.

But we haven't talked about it. Didn't *prepare* for it.

I mean, we assumed, but—

Shit.

"Fox," I say desperately, craning my head. Teddy's head is lolling, Fox's knot in his ass and his movements slowing as he lowers Teddy to the bed.

But he doesn't *stop.*

He won't stop. Not until he comes out of the rut.

I lock eyes with Zeke. "Bonding marks. Bites. What are we doing?"

Zeke doesn't hesitate. "She's ours. *Bite.*"

I can feel my knot pulsing, preparing to push into her, to fill her up. And I want my mark on her skin.

I tilt Fallon's neck to the right. Her left side is for Fox, for the pack alpha, but as my knot pushes into her weeping pussy, I sink my teeth into my mate's neck with a bellow as I spurt into her pussy, my release *endless*.

That's about the time I lose my damn mind.

***

Fox's back is up against mine, both of us rocking our omegas when Rowan rushes back in. His eyes start to glaze over as he drops another pile of blankets.

There are... a lot of blankets on the floor. Piles pushed up against the wall, out of the way.

I blink. And... drinks on the side. Lots of drinks. Many of them are empty. "How long have I been out?"

Rowan's look is dry. "Around six hours. This is day three. The Wild Side was having a *phenomenal* time while you were unavailable. Handy guy to have around during a heat."

My head collapses back. "Fucks' *sake*."

I feel drunk. Drunk on Fallon. Zeke is passed out, but Fallon is sucking on his cock with happy little noises that would be adorable if she wasn't on the verge of sucking every bit of moisture from our bodies.

I lean over her, pressing my lips against her bonding mark. It pulses, a flicker inside my chest connecting me to my mate.

I can feel her contentment. Her desperation. Her neediness.

Everything I need to take care of her is right here inside my chest.

It's fucking *incredible*.

I pull my knot out as Zeke jerks awake. Without either of us, Fallon jerks upright, whining as she launches herself at Zeke.

She's sinking down onto his cock within three seconds, and he pushes her down into the bedding, his hips flexing as he thrusts into her overflowing cunt. He's pretty much smothering her, but we've worked out she prefers it that way.

Rowan tosses me a bottle of water. "Electrolytes."

Thank fuck. My mate is the omega equivalent of the Sahara freaking desert.

I twist to watch Fox. He pins me with a glare, his arm curving over Teddy before he turns his head to Fallon.

"He doesn't know what to do," Rowan whispers in realization. He crosses to Fox, tugging off his shirt. "He's desperate to be with Fallon, but he needs Teddy to be safe too. Fox, it's okay. I'll look after Teddy for a little while."

I don't know where the hell Ro got the massive knotting vibrator in his hand, but I'm impressed. "I can take a turn if he needs it."

It wouldn't be the first time I've cared for Teddy during his heat. But it's care, affection for a packmate rather than the deep, tearing need I feel for Fallon.

Fox snaps his teeth at me. I hold up my hands. Honestly, I'm fairly sure my knot might have packed up and run away to the circus anyway. "Fine. Have it your way, Vader."

"Not funny." Rowan curls up beside Teddy. His eyes are half-open, our omega barely conscious from the knotting as Rowan starts wiping him down. "You should do Fallon."

"I will." I knew that. But shit, is it easy to lose track of time during heats. I'm carrying back a wash flannel from the adjoining bathroom when I feel the pleasure in my chest.

My mate is upright. Her head is buried in Zeke's shoulder as his teeth sink down a few inches above mine, holding her steady.

Her second bonding mark, tying her to us.

Zeke settles her against him as I press the flannel to the back of her neck. She sighs and shifts, arching against the cool as I carefully wipe her down and give her a little bit of water.

Fallon starts to snore softly against Zeke's chest. "That's a good sign, right?"

"Yeah." I stroke over her hair. "She can rest through the urges. Means they're weakening."

A low rumble from behind me.

Fox is staring at Fallon. Rowan is pushing himself into a moaning Teddy, the vibrant purple vibrator linked to his cock disappearing inside his ass, ring by ring as Rowan coaxes him to take it deeper.

But Fox... he climbs over, shoving past me. Intention in every movement.

"Fox." Even Zeke's eyes flicker with wariness. "She's still knotted. You'll hurt her."

A deep snarl, as if our pack leader rejects the very idea of hurting his mate. Fox buries his face in Fallon's shoulder and breathes her in, licking over her skin in long, caressing strokes.

Over her new bonding marks.

A faint echo of pleasure flickers through my own chest. My brows fly up.

Unexpected.

But he doesn't push. Fox waits like a coiled animal, red eyes gleaming in the darkness. Rowan has some lamps going, but I'd say it's the early hours of the morning.

"Teddy's heat has broken," Rowan murmurs behind me. "Three days. That's a record."

"Probably because of Fallon's being so strong. It dragged his out for longer." I turn to check on him, but he's out like a light. I jump up and grab a fresh blanket, dragging it over him and Rowan.

But I'm waiting.

So is Zeke, both of us more than aware of our pack leader as Zeke's knot deflates and he... swoops.

Something primal beats in my chest.

Fox is our pack leader.

Fallon is our mate.

And now we're going to watch as he claims her.

Fallon's throaty moan has Fox pausing as he lays her carefully over fresh bedding. He strokes her, pets her until our mate is mewling beneath his hands for more.

He yanks up her knees, pushing them wide and giving us both a perfect view of Fallon's dripping, swollen, heat-fucked pussy. Her slick trickles from her, slick and cum and all of our fucking bodily fluids, but her pussy still flutters, her ass pushing back when Fox impales her on his rigid cock.

Fallon bounces with the force of his thrusts. Enough awareness trickles in that she weakly grasps the bedding before Fox pounces, gripping her wrists and pinning them down as he slams into her, with no sign that he's spent the last few days in a goddamned *rut*.

He gives her what she wants. Her alpha, claiming her. More primal than I've ever seen as he pins her in place, her body locked underneath him as he keeps up that savage movement. His hand twists into her hair, and he slows enough to gently tilt her head to the side.

To the empty space on her neck.

He growls then. Nuzzles at Fallon until her eyes flutter open.

She moans. "Fox."

And our pack alpha slams his teeth down into her neck, as the full bond fills my chest and snaps into place.

Fuck me. I can feel all of them.

Fallon. Zeke. Fox. Teddy. Even Ro, a calm, steady presence, cool air on a hot day.

Now this is a pack bond.

70

FALLON

Zeke grips my hand in his as I stare at the lawyer. "I thought it was all gone."

The beta male shakes his head, opening a file in front of him. "As part of his will, your father had ordered that in the event of your parent's death, the proceeds from his work would be placed into a trust account. The age for access is thirty, so you're a while off yet. But it's an extremely healthy account, Fallon. It's been building for years, and it's frequently topped up. Your father's books are still popular."

He smiles as he slides a note across the desk.

My mind blanks as I stare down at the number of zeroes. "But... I don't understand. I thought the Smith pack took it all."

The lawyers' lips press together. "Terrible business. I'm so sorry. But as this is a trust account, they weren't able to access it."

He picks up something else and hands it to me. "The last time they were here, one of them asked me to place this with your family documents, and to give it to you when you came."

It's a letter. My heart leaps for a moment, but then I recognise the writing.

I wait until we're back in the truck to open it. I curl up against Zeke, his arm around my shoulders. He kisses my head. "Take your time."

Slowly, I slide my finger beneath the flap and pull the handwritten sheet out. A key falls into my hand.

Fallon,

Sometimes we make decisions that we can't take back.

If you're reading this, then I hope you got out. Maybe I even helped you.

I hope I did. But I doubt it.

On the day we met, I suggested you were only in college because of your father. I know that's not true. And I'm sorry, again. I didn't mean it then, not really. But I do now.

I made a choice that I regret, a choice out of anger, and fear. A choice that I'm stuck with. My story is the same as many others. I won't bore you with it. An unhappy childhood with not enough to eat and a house that was never warm enough.

I know I'm hard on you, and it's not right. The groceries are just one example. I need to know that we have enough, that we're not going to run out of food. It keeps me awake at night. But I doubt I've ever explained that to you, and I probably won't.

I hate this life. I hate that we forced it on you when you didn't deserve it. I would leave if I could, but I made a decision, and now I have to live with it. And leaving you with Ellis and Rory is not something I'm comfortable with. I'm scared they'll take things too far.

We've already taken things too far. We had a plan to befriend an omega, but it snowballed into something much darker.

This isn't some sort of redemption letter. I have no good reason or rationale for what we took from you.

But I'm sorry. All the same. And I'll do what I can to make sure that if you decide to walk out the door, you don't have any connections to us to drag you down.

And if you ask me for help, I hope that I give it to you.

There is more money, the lawyer said. Ellis drained most of what he could access through your accounts, but he can't touch that. And I want you to know that I only ever spent money out of what I earned. The grocery money, all of it. I tried to keep it as low as possible because it was your money.

The power of attorney is false. Ellis forged your signature.

As you know, the house was sold. But I had everything in it put into storage. The address is on the back of this letter, with the password for entry, and the key is included.

If you're reading this, I hope you're free.

I hope you're happy.

Shaun

Inhaling, I lift my head and hold out the letter. "You can read it."

"Asshole," Zeke snarls as he finishes. "What the hell is this?"

I shrug, still a little stunned. "It doesn't... it doesn't change anything, Zeke."

Maybe he was scared. But he was weak. And fear isn't an excuse for the fear he caused *me*.

But I do remember how focused Shaun was on my heat cycle. On making sure I took heat blockers.

Because if I didn't have a heat, I couldn't have a bite mark.

And no matter how much Rory suggested otherwise, he always made sure I had them.

No, it doesn't change anything. Not really. But it gives me a little more understanding into that part of my life than I had before. Into the grocery runs that became a thing I was scared of.

And my family's things. My photographs. Everything is in storage.

Maybe he was truly sorry. Or maybe this was another form of gaslighting, in case he ever needed to use it.

I'm not going to know. And I need to make my peace with that.

That part of my life is over.

Zeke waits for me to wipe my eyes.

"Let's go."

71

FALLON

Leaning against the tree, I lift my face up, letting the breeze caress it.

Pulling my battered, precious copy of *The Light in Us* closer, I hug it to me as I speak to my mate. I don't normally take it out of the house anymore, but I wanted it with me today.

"Fox," I say patiently. "I'm fine. I'll be home soon."

I can *feel* his stress levels ramping up. I glance around me before I murmur into the phone, checking for anyone close by. "I'll let you use the handcuffs again. Tonight. With Rowan and Teddy."

His frustrated growl turns into more of a purr. "*Fallon.*"

"*Fox,*" I tease. My eyes scan over the sea of people crowding around the steps on the other side of the road. "I promise, I'm okay. I'm not going near it."

He sighs. "I wish you'd let me come with you."

"I know." I bask in it, in the concern and love of my mate. Fox's bonding mark tingles on my neck, as if my body can sense him. "But I needed to do this on my own."

"I love you," he says quietly. "Very much."

My heart squeezes. "I know. And I love you too."

"I'm making fettuccine tonight."

Because he knows it's my favorite. I start smiling. "I won't be long."

I duck into the coffee shop behind me and order a vanilla latte to take out. It still feels a little strange to hand my card over without panicking.

When I step back out, a car is pulling up across the road. The crowd surges toward it, cameras flashing and people asking questions as they get out.

I wait for the panic. For the fear to set in, to tighten my throat.

But I don't feel anything as Shaun gets out, his mouth set in a thin line as he pushes a camera out of his face.

He made his choices.

Rory follows him. He looks tired, his blonde hair shorter now than it used to be as he jogs after Shaun.

Ellis gets out last. He stands for a moment, holding up an arm as if blinded by the flashes.

But then he turns.

Across the road, I pause. His eyes sweep over me, ignoring me.

And then they come back.

We stare at each other for a moment.

He chose his path a long time ago. And today, he's going to face the consequences.

Just as I told him, on my last night in that house.

One day soon, I'm going to watch you learn your own lesson. Because actions do have consequences, and when you face yours, I'm going to be watching.

And here I am.

Smiling, I hold up my coffee in a silent salute.

They may have extinguished my light. But I found it again. And now, I have a pack that adores me. A job that excites me. A life that makes me happy.

I have everything I ever wanted.

Ellis's face tightens. And then he's gone, swallowed up by the people around him as he goes inside to be sentenced.

I heard it could be up to twenty years, for the level of fraud they carried out.

"Damn, that looked satisfying."

My smile grows as I turn. "I *knew* you couldn't leave it be."

Teddy bounces on his feet. He shrugs, his smile curling up his mouth. "Nice coat."

"Thanks." I preen, stroking my hand down it.

I might have many, many coats of my own now. But my favorite will always be the one Teddy gave to me on the first day we met.

I turn back to the courthouse as he strolls up next to me and slips his arm into mine.

"Where are the others?" I ask drily. "Don't tell me they're not here."

I can see him biting his lip. "Wilder and Zeke are in the car over there."

My laugh catches in my throat. "Fox?"

"At home," he says gleefully. "Technically, he was the only one who actually promised *not* to come. He's furious about it too, so he's cooking enough pasta for the next week."

"And Ro?"

Laughter shakes his chest. "In the... bush. Behind you."

A low, stifled curse.

I can't hide my laughter anymore. "Come on. I've seen everything I needed to."

"Does it change anything?" he asks, searching my face. "Seeing them again?"

I shake my head and lean in, brushing my lips against his. "I have everything I ever wanted, Teddy. This was just... closure."

Rowan jogs up beside us. Twigs stick out of his hair as he offers me a mildly apologetic look and slips his hand into mine, squeezing it.

I smile at them both.

"Let's go home."

— . —

STALK ME

— · —

PLAYLIST

Made in United States
Troutdale, OR
10/25/2024

24126334R10224